CHAPTER ONE

FRIDAY, NOVEMBER 24

Charlotte. Tenth Floor.

Mallory Newell's stomach did flip-flops when she saw Charlotte's name on caller ID.

Could it be?

Was today the big day?

Was she the one?

Was it the moment she'd worked so hard for?

Her hands shook as she picked up the receiver.

"Muh-Mallory Newell."

Geesh, girl. Get a grip and stop that stammering.

"Mallory, it's Charlotte. Mr. Key wants to confirm your availability for an out-of-town trip."

She gulped and hoped Charlotte couldn't hear it. "Yes. Of course."

"Don't you at least want to know when it will be?"

"Uh...no... I mean... Whenever is fine."

"You'll leave sometime next week and be away until Christmas."

Oh, my gosh! It's happening! It's happening! I'm being assigned to work with Dawn Darby Endicott! In Bora Bora!

Calm down.

"Please tell Mr. Key that I'll be ready."

"I'll tell him. And Mallory, please keep this confidential until a formal announcement is made."

It took a few seconds for Mallory to get her breathing under control. If Hogan were there, he would tell her to calm down. *Act like you've gotten a big job before,* he would say.

But she hadn't. At least nothing like this one.

Personal editor to Dawn Darby Endicott.

Working with her at her home in Bora Bora.

She had to tell Hogan!

She grabbed her phone.

Voicemail.

Leave a message? She would rather tell him in person, but who knew when he might be available? She was about to bust, so voicemail it was.

"Hogan…it's me… I just got the best news…"

Shhh. Keep it down, stupid. The walls are as thin as paper. The last thing you want is for someone at the firm to find out before it's announced.

She lowered her voice to a whisper. "You know what I'm talking about. I can't wait to tell you everything. Love you. Bye."

On a dreary block of dilapidated storefronts, Flip's Barbershop shone like a beacon. From several doors away, Jake Springer spotted several people seated inside. He would know all of them. And they would know him and pick at him mercilessly from the moment he walked in.

He picked up his pace as a frigid wind cut through his jacket. On one side of the street, a storefront church displayed a large sign in the window.

A Kansas City Christmas Romance

Robin Paul

Lakewood Ranch, Florida

Everyone Welcome!

The growling pit bull glaring through that same window said otherwise.

It was an area of the city that didn't attract the usual shopping crowd. Several storefronts were empty or boarded up. Those open for business included a wig shop, a tax office, and a pawnshop with a window full of outdated stereo equipment. Customers were few, and if history was any indication, some would be long gone by spring.

Jake jogged past Maggie's Place, formerly Skizzer's Bar. Formerly Hanratty's, Pop's Place, and the Brass Lantern. The name changed, but the clientele remained the same. Old men and a few younger ones lured by cheap beer, watered-down drinks, and a smack-talking waitress named Debbie McKinstry.

Just as the wind and cold started to numb him from the inside out, Jake reached Flip's Barbershop. He pushed open the door and entered a world that would seem completely foreign to his suburban friends. His was, as always, the only white face. The others would kid him about his whiteness. And about his clothes. And about any of a hundred other things. And he would dish it right back at them.

"Hello, gentlemen," he said as he rubbed his hands together to get the circulation going.

Flip Murray, the owner and lone barber, wasted no time ripping into him.

"Boy, are you stupid? It's thirty degrees, and you're wearing a skinny little jacket."

"It was sixty-three when I left home this morning, Flip."

Kurtis, a mechanic at one of the repair shops on Truman Road, chirped up. "Ain't you got the Weather Channel, boy?"

There was no need to defend himself, so Jake smiled, took a seat, and let them have their fun. In addition to Flip and

Kurtis, there was Thomas, a route driver for Roma Bakery, and Dewayne, a part-time security guard.

When they were finished, Jake turned things right back at them.

"It's four in the afternoon. Don't any of you fellas work anymore?"

That got things started all over again.

They called him white boy.

They called him dumb.

They called him ugly.

They called him things that were politically incorrect. Things that would get them fired from their jobs or kicked out of their churches.

But that was okay. They were his friends.

Dwayne and Kurtis had been pallbearers at Grandpa Springer's funeral. Flip had driven to Magnolia, Arkansas to bail Jake's father out of county lockup after he was picked up for possession of hallucinogenic mushrooms. Outsiders might not understand how friends could say such cutting things to one another, but Jake knew it was their way of showing love. And since neither of them had anything better to do, they allowed Jake to jump ahead in line. He made himself comfortable in the decades-old barber chair while Flip covered him with a blue pinstriped cape.

"You're a couple weeks early for a cut, aren't you, Jake?"

"Yeah, Flip, but I have someplace I need to be, so…"

Jake knew his vagueness would invite questions. And more questions would lead to more good-natured harassment.

"Someplace to be?" Dwayne asked. "Is there a game tonight?"

"No game."

Thomas said, "So if you don't have a game to go to, then it must be a woman."

Yep. It was.

A date. From one of those dating apps Jake's buddies had been encouraging him to try.

But there was no way he was going to let the guys in Flip's know that. So, he changed the subject to one topic they liked discussing more than women. Sports. And since Jake worked in sports, they enjoyed picking his brain.

"You on the road this weekend?" Flip asked as he clipped away. "Mizzou's at Tennessee, right?"

"They are, but I'm headed to New York."

Their mouths gaped open. Their eyes grew wide. Jake knew they would be impressed. New York meant he was covering the Chiefs-Giants game. He usually didn't travel to away games. The website budget was tiny compared to the local newspaper and TV stations, but there were playoff implications, so he would make it work.

Flip's regulars were not into blogs or sports websites, but they knew Jake got to hang around the players, and that was good enough for them. It didn't matter that most of them were probably making more money than he was. They spent the next few minutes analyzing the Chiefs' defense. It was four-thirty and getting dark outside when Flip pulled the barber's cape off with a flourish.

"Be sure to tell those New York boys where you get your hair cut."

Jake checked himself in the mirror. "If anybody asks. I'll tell them that Flip Murray not only cuts my hair, but he's my biological daddy."

Flip smacked him a good one on the back of the head while the others laughed. Jake paid up, said his goodbyes, and headed out.

Mallory set aside her phone and tiptoed to her office door. It was open just a smidge, but that was enough to allow anything that was said inside to escape, including her over-the-top voicemail to Hogan. She listened for a few moments to be sure the coast was clear, then pulled open the door and came face-to-face with Luis Delarossa. Their offices shared a wall, and Luis was one of several editors in the running to be Dawn Darby Endicott's new editor.

Luis was smiling. Luis always smiled. But his eyes weren't smiling. They were curious. And maybe a little worried.

"Hey, Mallory."

"Oh, hi Luis. What's up?"

Please don't say you heard. Please don't say you heard. Please don't say you heard.

"Nothing. I just finished editing a speech Mr. Key is giving at the Bookseller's Association meeting. I'm thinking about leaving a little early."

Phew. He hadn't heard.

"I heard you saying something about getting great news."

Ouch.

Time to get creative.

"What? Oh, yes, I was talking to Hogan. I don't believe you've met him."

"Maybe once. Did he come to Maria's going away party at Van Dyke's?"

"No, that was before. Hogan and I have been dating for seven months. He's an accountant. Really successful. He works for a firm over on..."

Mallory blabbed on about Hogan and his job and his apartment, but she could see that Luis was listening only out of consideration for her feelings. As soon as she paused to breathe, he would circle back to what he really wanted to know. Who could blame him? She would have done the same thing. So would six other editors with offices on the third floor. They all wanted to work with Dawn Darby Endicott. In the editing world, she was among the biggest of the big fish.

So she had to come up with something to throw him off the trail.

"Anyway, enough about Hogan. You came over with a question, right?"

"Yes, you said you'd gotten some great news."

"Oh, yes. My Aunt Vi invited us for Christmas dinner! Isn't that the best news ever?"

Sell it, Mallory!

"It's...definitely good news. I just thought that maybe you'd heard something from the tenth floor."

"Tenth floor?"

"Yeah." He moved closer and whispered in her ear, "Jeff Lansing heard that an editor would be selected this month to go to Dawn Darby Endicott's estate in Bora Bora."

Mallory blew air through her lips. "Jeff Lansing is never right. Remember last year when he heard the company wasn't giving Christmas bonuses?"

He was wrong about that, but this time he might be on to something!

Luis smiled. "Oh, yeah. That was Jeff, wasn't it? Still, can you imagine spending December in Bora Bora? And getting to work with Dawn Darby Endicott?"

"Well, as a matter of fact..."

That was the moment she nearly spilled the beans. And broke the trust of Charlotte, Mr. Key, and the other Stratford and Key partners. Luis was focused on her with wide-eyed curiosity. What was she about to say?

"As a matter of fact...Hogan has been to Bora Bora."

No, he hasn't.

"He said that maybe we would go there next year."

No, he didn't.

Luis nodded, and something changed. He appeared less concerned. Probably relieved to discover that he was still in the running to be Dawn Darby Endicott's editor.

"Like I said, I'm sneaking out early." He motioned toward the elevators. "Want to sneak out with me?"

"Actually…yes. Let me grab my stuff."

Five minutes later, they were in the lobby of the headquarters for Stratford and Key Media. It was a prominent Manhattan address for one of the industry's biggest publishers. And Mallory was euphoric that she would now be sitting at the top of the editorial heap.

"I'm going to grab a beer," Luis said. "Want to join me? We can daydream together about what it would be like to spend December in Bora Bora."

"Thanks, Luis, but I have some shopping to do."

You can daydream about Bora Bora while I pick up a couple of new bikinis for the trip.

Winter's gloom had settled over Kansas City. The Christmas decorations so abundant at Crown Center and the Country Club Plaza hadn't found their way to Jake's part of town. Other than a few hastily hung strings of light, there was little to remind pedestrians that Christmas was a month away.

Jake's grandfather had moved to Kansas City in the early fifties when the neighborhood was middle class and lily-white. Things started to change in the sixties, but by then Grandpa Springer was divorced and figured he was as well off taking his chances on Kenwood Avenue as he would be selling the place and following his neighbors out to Blue Springs. What was good enough for Grandpa was good enough for his family, and until his death and the departure of Jake's parents for the Alabama beach, three generations had lived under one roof. The neighborhood transitioned from mostly white to black and brown. More recently, something called gentrification had found its way to Kansas City. Younger people, mostly upwardly mobile couples with kids, were buying the homes their grandparents had sold a half-century before. Downtown was changing again. Some of it was good, some not so good. Still, to Jake, it was home. It would always be home.

He stopped a couple doors from Flip's to button his jacket and check his messages. There were two missed calls. The first was from his neighbor, Chris. That could wait. The second was from the 646 area code Jake recognized as New York City. He expected it had something to do with that weekend's game. Many of the officials who worked with the media still treated website guys like second-rate citizens of the press box.

But when he played the message, it wasn't that at all.

Mr. Springer, my name is Marcus Key. I'm a partner with Stratford and Key Media. Can you please return my call at your earliest convenience?

Stratford and Key? Did he know anyone there? Nope, he decided. And especially no one named Marcus Key. The guy sounded every inch a New Yorker. Could it be a job opportunity? He had said Stratford and Key *Media*. Jake was building a pretty good reputation in Kansas City, but no one from New York would have heard of him.

Would they?

It was the epicenter of the sports world, though. And while it probably wasn't ESPN or Fox Sports, maybe it was some niche media outlet that had an opening for someone willing to hustle for a story. If so, Jake was their man. Hustle was all he knew. All he'd ever known. Grandpa had noticed it early on. Brains and work ethic skipped a generation in our family, he'd confided once when it was just the two of them.

It was a verbal slap at Jake's father. Deserved, but a slap, nonetheless.

But New York? Did that interest him? He had never contemplated life away from Kansas City, and for other than the two years he'd spent completing a journalism degree at the University of Missouri, the family home at 3737 Kenwood Avenue had been the center of his world. His career trajectory had included a short stay at the *Kansas City Star* before throwing his lot in with two like-minded sports buffs he'd met at a trivia contest in a Westport bar. Together they had formed Total Sports KC, nearly starving in the process. Could he pull up stakes now? After the hardest of it was behind him?

It certainly wouldn't hurt to talk to the guy, would it? He nearly hit the return call button on his phone, but passing traffic was making a terrible racket. Couldn't risk a huge career opportunity because a passing dump truck made it hard to hear. Stratford and Key could wait a few minutes. He picked up the pace and was home within ten minutes. He unlocked the back door, stepped into the kitchen, and was immediately hit by a frontal attack from seventy pounds of golden retriever.

Mallory allowed Luis a few moments head start so she wouldn't run the risk of running into him again outside. Certain the coast was clear, she hustled out onto the sidewalk and nearly stumbled over a homeless guy and his dog making their bed for the evening.

"Watch it!" he barked. The man, not the dog.

"Sorry." Mallory reached into her purse, pulled out the first bill she could find and thrust it toward him, then pulled it back when she saw it was a twenty.

"You run me over, then don't even have the decency to leave a little something?" the guy yelled as Mallory scrambled past. She turned left at the end of the block then pulled out her cellphone to try Hogan again.

"Hello, Mallory." His tone said that he was in the middle of something work related. Screw that. She had big news.

"Guess who was told to get ready for an out-of-town trip?" She sounded like an excited ten-year-old but couldn't care less. She had discussed the possibility with Hogan. He knew she might be gone for a while but also realized what it could mean for her career. She heard him excuse himself from whatever kind of meeting certified public accountants held at their offices. A door opened and closed in the background, followed by the sound of footsteps on tile. A moment passed before he spoke again. He sounded more like his usual self.

"Don't tell me! Bora Bora?"

"It sounds like it," Mallory gushed. "I was told to prepare to be away until Christmas. Where else could it be?"

"Great point. That's a long time for us to be apart, though. You know what that means?"

Aw, he's going to say how much he'll miss me. Sweet, sweet Hogan.

"Tell me, darling. What does that mean? Are you thinking we should plan a special date night before I go?"

He chuckled. "Well, that too. Mainly, I was thinking about setting a couple meet-ups with some of the guys from work. You know? Dinner and drinks at a good steak place. Talk about guy stuff. Do guy things."

"That sounds wonderful, but what about us? Is there anything you want to do before I leave?"

Mallory appreciated how he thought on it for a few moments.

"Well...three weeks is a long time without...you know?

How about I come to your place after work. We have dinner and…" he lowered his voice to a whisper, "turn in early, if you know what I mean."

"Will you pick up dinner on the way? Chinese from that little carryout place we love?"

"Your wish is my command! See you in a couple hours."

"Corabelle! Down!"

Corabelle didn't listen. She never did. She lunged, attempting to kiss and lick his face. Jake reached out to flip on the kitchen light and watched as hair flew in every direction. Some of it was his, left on his shirt from his haircut. Most belonged to Corabelle, who shed with feverish intensity.

They played for a bit. Corabelle grabbed one of her toys and trembled with anticipation as she waited for Jake to throw it. And throw it. And throw it.

There would never be another Corabelle. There would never be another dog. Not in Jake's life. Corabelle was one extra headache he had to deal with whenever he went out of town. She was old for a goldie, nearly thirteen. But she looked and acted much as she had as a pup. She was high maintenance, ate like a horse, and occasionally dropped a load between Jake's bed and the bathroom. But she was a big part of Jake's world that he couldn't imagine being without.

And she had belonged to Grandpa Springer.

Grandpa got Corabelle in a trade with a carpenter friend. The carpenter had five pups but was short one extension ladder. Grandpa had an extra ladder, but no puppy. He wanted a male, but Blair said that would require a ladder and a laser level. Grandpa was quite attached to his, so he settled for the runt of the litter. Corabelle wasn't a runt anymore.

She was a seventy-pound force of nature who loved pinning him to the floor. They tussled a bit longer before Jake sent her into the backyard while he pulled leftover chili from the fridge and popped it into the microwave. With the house quiet, he returned the call to New York. It was after six there, but he could at least leave a message.

"Marcus Key."

"Mr. Key, it's Jake Springer from Kansas City."

"Jake, a pleasure. Your grandmother spoke highly of you."

Uh-oh. Grandma Springer. That meant one thing.

Key wasn't with ESPN. Or Fox Sports. He wasn't with the *New York Times* or the *Post*.

Stratford and Key Media Partners used to be Stratford and Key Publishing.

They published his late grandmother's novels. All of them. At least a dozen. Romances. Real snooze fests, from what Jake had seen.

Somebody had to like them, though, because when Grandma passed away last spring, Jake's parents inherited enough to pay off their massive debts and buy a place in Gulf Shores. They were probably broke again, but the condo was bought and paid for, thanks to Grandma's books.

But why was Marcus Key calling him?

"Are you sure you got the right Springer, Mr. Key? I can give you my father's number."

"You're the Springer I need to speak with. It is regarding some unfinished business related to your grandmother's passing. Wonderful woman, by the way. She's missed by everyone here."

Jake rolled his eyes. "I doubt that, Mr. Key, but it's nice of you to say. What can I do for you?"

Key didn't try to convince him otherwise. Jake had always gotten along well enough with Grandma Springer. He had been the only member of the family she was still speaking to when she died. Grandpa had referred to her as the pen-wielding witch despite being divorced for thirty years. Jake's father and mother hadn't visited her New York apartment since she'd criticized their lack of gainful employment. She had even threatened to make Jake the beneficiary of her will, but never quite got around to it. Dad inherited everything. Mom was along for the ride.

"It would be best if we meet in person, Jake. And the sooner the better. I can catch a flight to Kansas City this weekend if that works for you."

Why in the world would a bigwig like Key feel the need to fly to KC? Did Jake want to find out?

"Are you sure we can't just handle things by phone, Mr. Key? I'm pretty busy with the website, and with Christmas coming up, it's just not a—"

"It's not a conversation to have over the phone, Jake. I promise not to take much of your time. Two, maybe three hours at the most." Key paused. "If you prefer to come to New York, the firm will pay your expenses."

Wait a minute.

Did he just offer to pay for a trip to New York?

Jake did the mental math of how much that could save the website. Two nights at a fleabag motel were five hundred. Meals would be Pop Tarts in his room and whatever free grub they served in the stadium press box.

"Mr. Key, I'll come to you, but our meeting will have to be first thing Monday morning. I need to be back here that evening."

"Perfect! I'll transfer you to Charlotte, my assistant. Let her know when you want to arrive and depart. She'll take care of the rest. Let's plan on meeting Monday morning at nine."

❄

Mallory was wearing one of her new swimsuits when Hogan arrived a little after seven. If it was love he wanted it was love he would get. She'd chosen the skimpier of the two, and if his tongue lolling out of his mouth was any indication, he liked it very much. And wanted to see more. More of her. Less of the bikini.

The only problem was, he arrived empty-handed.

"I thought you were bringing Chinese."

His blank look said it all. He'd forgotten. Hogan could be like that. Work consumed him, and it wasn't uncommon for him to completely forget a conversation they'd had just a few hours earlier.

But damn it, she was really looking forward to Chinese.

"I'm sorry," he said as he came closer and snaked his arms around her bare waist. "How about we have some fun, then I'll run back out for Chinese?"

She started to object but knew she'd already set the wheels in motion by modeling the swimsuit.

And besides, it never took Hogan long to have his fun.

As he showered and dressed for his date, Jake's thoughts circled back to the call from New York. He'd done a quick internet search and learned that Marcus Key was a pretty big deal. Partner in the fourth largest publishing house in North America. Estimated worth somewhere north of fourteen million. His firm had represented Grandma Springer for years, but she was a mid-lister at best. Someone who sold enough books to make the firm a nice little profit, but miniscule compared to their A-listers.

It must have something to do with Grandma Springer's books. His parents had gone to great lengths to make sure he never saw her will, but there had been enough to buy a beach cottage and a couple luxury cars. Hey, it got them out of the house on Kenwood Avenue, so he didn't ask questions. It wasn't as if they were there a lot, anyway, given their propensity for dropping everything to chase some crazy scheme. For as long as he could remember, Jake had felt as if he was the grown up in the dynamic that was the relationship with his parents.

But Grandma Springer's estate, whatever that consisted of, had gone to them. Just like Grandpa's. How could two so completely clueless people be so fortunate?

Jake searched through his closet until he found an outfit that would work. He'd only worn the blue quarter-zip pullover a couple times. The khakis, maybe once. He debated digging out the steam iron to press out the wrinkles, but decided to hang them in the bathroom and turn the shower on hot. While he waited for the wrinkles to fall out, he returned to the dating app and pulled up his date's profile.

Olivia Jane Rasmussen, Age 30

Actuarial Analyst for Sedaris and Britt Insurance Company.

Jake had looked it up and still wasn't sure what an actuarial analyst really did.

Bachelor's Degree in Statistics from the University of Illinois.

Enjoys concerts, music, and movies.

It was her profile picture that kept pulling him back, though. Olivia Jane Rasmussen was drop dead gorgeous. Auburn shoulder-length hair, emerald green eyes, a shy smile. She was the entire package. Jake wanted to make a good first impression, and what could be better for a concert lover like Olivia Jane Rasmussen than old-school favorites Janet Jackson and Ludacris? Best of all, he'd scored the tickets at a big discount. They were still a hundred and sixty each, but if the lovely Olivia Jane was as awesome in real life as she was in the dating app, it would be an remarkable evening.

❄

It was turning out to be a miserable evening.

Oh sure, Hogan got what he wanted, but then the skies opened. It was a rare winter downpour in New York City. Hogan reneged on the Chinese, promising they could try again the next day. Mallory baked a frozen pizza, and they settled in for some TV.

Hogan was fast asleep by eight-thirty. He still had a slice of cold half-eaten pizza in his hand. Very unsexy. When it tipped and fell onto his favorite sweatshirt, Mallory pretended she didn't see it.

It served him right for forgetting the Chinese.

How had he mistaken Olivia Jane Rasmussen's smile as shy?

That wasn't a shy smile. It was a dumb smile.

World-class dumb.

It took about three minutes to figure out. The first hint was when she came to the lobby of her apartment building in bedroom slippers. Pink fluffy bedroom slippers.

Oh, sure, something like that can happen to anyone. Jake had certainly had his share of brain farts. It's embarrassing, but you laugh and go on.

Not Olivia.

She giggled, then asked where he was parked. When he told her he was at the end of the street, she requested he pull his car up to the door and she would meet him there. He assumed that while he was retrieving the car, she would change into shoes.

Nope.

She went to the concert in the fuzzy slippers.

In the flipping slippers!

Perhaps she thought it was cute. Or chic. Perhaps she was trying to make a statement.

No, no, and no. She didn't seem to have given the matter any thought at all.

Jake caught the amused looks of other concert goers. And why not? It was twenty-five outside and the girl was in slippers?

Things went steadily downhill from there.

She didn't care for Janet Jackson.

And had never heard of Ludacris.

She complained that they had to stand to see the stage for much of the show. "I thought these were supposed to be great seats," she'd said at least sixteen hundred and fifty times.

Then she got frisky on the drive back to her apartment. And even after one hellaciously bad evening, it was hard for Jake not to get...stimulated by a cute woman kissing his earlobe. He dropped her off where he'd picked her up, so her fluffy pink slippers wouldn't get wet, then went in search of a parking spot.

"I'll be right back," he said.

She kissed him deeply on the lips. A real world-class kiss.

"I'll be waiting," she murmured.

When he returned five minutes later, Olivia Jane Rasmussen was gone.

CHAPTER TWO

MONDAY, NOVEMBER 27

Dawn Darby Endicott was in New York City!

That exciting tidbit might have made Mallory pee her pants, but since it was three in the morning when she saw Dawn Darby's Facebook post, and she was in bed with Hogan, she wasn't wearing any pants. But still!

Today was the day!

It was a scenario Mallory had witnessed before with other bestselling authors. She knew how it would likely play out. Dawn Darby—she always went by Dawn Darby—would meet with the partners in the tenth floor conference room. They would enjoy a lavish breakfast while they watched the sun come into view between the skyscrapers that lined the avenue. The partners would shower her with praise for her most recent release, a gripping tale of a girl who smuggles aboard a cargo ship to avoid a life of bondage. They would predict her chances for a Pulitzer while lamenting that she would have already earned one had it not been for the committee's short-sightedness. Mallory felt it was Dawn Darby's political views that torpedoed her Pulitzer more than anything else, but who cared what she thought?

When breakfast was cleared away, they would announce it was time for Dawn Darby to meet her new editor. The author would mourn the loss of her previous editor, Hans Gilbert, to a competing publishing house, and ask once more if there was something they could do to bring Hans back. They would respond with all the enthusiasm they could muster that the new editor was not only vastly qualified, but would bring fresh eyes to Dawn Darby's work.

Then they would summon Mallory.

She glanced toward the coat closet where she had stashed her suitcase and overnight bag soon after arriving at the office at five-thirty that morning, long before anyone else might see her and ask questions. While it wasn't out of the ordinary for Stratford and Key employees to show up with luggage, her third-floor colleagues would put two and two together. They, like Mallory, followed Dawn Darby's social media accounts and knew she was in town.

Dawn Darby Endicott.

Bora Bora.

Mallory's new swimsuit was bright red and as skimpy as she dared to go. She would wear it to the beach, when she could be certain Dawn Darby wouldn't see her. Her other one, a more modest black one piece, would be reserved for the hotel pool and for those times she was invited to swim at Dawn Darby's estate. Hans had bragged that he was a regular in Dawn Darby's pool, and that swimsuits were optional. Well, they might be optional for Hans, who was a pudgy fifty-something guy, but Mallory would be the epitome of propriety and decorum. Modest black swimsuit in Dawn Darby's pool. Skimpy red number for the beach.

She checked her watch for the millionth time. Nine o'clock. They were probably just getting started on the tenth floor. It would be at least an hour before they needed her.

Now if she could only calm down enough to get some work done.

Workers were hanging Christmas decorations in the Stratford and Key lobby when Jake entered. He looked around uncertainly and was about to consult a directory on the wall when he saw someone coming his way. The guy wore gray slacks and a matching vest over a shirt and tie. Jake had planned on pressing and wearing the same blue slacks and red sweater he'd worn at the previous afternoon's game, but nacho cheese wouldn't wash out in a hotel sink, so he was left with jeans and a black hoodie. He regretted not packing an extra set of dress clothes.

"Mr. Springer?" The guy was about Jake's age and didn't seem the least bit put off by his attire. He said his name was Bruce, and that he would take Jake up to Mr. Key's office.

"Have you enjoyed your stay in New York?" he asked in the elevator. "Your Chiefs put a beating on our Giants yesterday."

Jake acknowledged the beating but didn't mention he had been at the game as a member of the media. The elevator opened to a quiet lobby where two desks were arranged in front of a wall displaying the publishing firm's name and logo. Everything seemed perfectly suited for a place that made books. It even smelled like them. Bruce showed Jake to a waiting area, offered coffee and pastries, and after bringing them back, said it would be just a couple minutes before Mr. Key was available. Jake was three bites into his Danish when Bruce reappeared escorting a petite blonde in a too-short skirt. While he had been exceedingly kind to Jake, the attention Bruce lavished on the blonde made Jake wonder if she was visiting royalty. He guessed her age at anywhere between fifty and seventy-five. She was tan and fit with killer legs. Jake had never been attracted to older women, but if he was going to start, she would be a great choice.

"Hallie will be with you in just a moment," Bruce said in a tone that sounded as if he was fearful of her. "We are so sorry she wasn't here to meet you when you arrived."

"Don't worry about a thing, darling," she cooed. When she turned and spotted Jake, she allowed her gaze to linger for several moments before saying, "If I must be kept waiting, at least I have something pleasant to look at." She winked. Jake blushed. She passed by five empty chairs to take the one next to him. She pulled at the hem of her skirt, but it only rose further up her thighs. Then she turned and smiled.

"What's your name, love?"

"Jake." He offered his hand, but she didn't accept. Nor did her eyes leave his.

"Do I detect a midwestern inflection in your speech, Jake? Omaha, perhaps?"

Jake chuckled. "Close. Kansas City. I'm impressed."

She nodded, obviously pleased with herself. "I study people, Jake. I watch them, listen to them." Her eyes drifted from his face to the rest of him. "And my observation is that you are quite well put together. Married?"

"No, but I'm open to offers."

Her laugh was melodic and real. It was easy to see she was a woman used to getting what she wanted. She was undoubtedly someone important or famous, but also not so full of herself that she couldn't be bothered with people like him. She patted his knee and was about to say something when a stocky woman with the look of a spinster librarian appeared.

"Dawn Darby!" She came toward them, arms open for a hug. The blonde squeezed Jake's knee again then rose with the grace of an aristocrat.

"Hallie, darling, so good to see you." Her tone wasn't as

enthused, and Jake was impressed by the way she side-stepped the librarian's open arms as she moved past. "My time is limited," she said. "Let's make the most of it."

Then, just before disappearing around the corner, she turned back. "Jake, darling, leave your contact information with the nice boy who brought me up here." She winked. "Who knows? Maybe I'll find myself in Omaha and need a strong young man to show me around."

Before Jake could correct her, she was gone. The librarian lady watched her walk away, then turned to Jake. "Delivery?" she asked.

"Uh, no, ma'am. I'm here to see Mr. Key."

She looked at him curiously, then high-tailed it after the blonde. Jake finished his pastry, wiped his fingers on a napkin, and was about to pull out his phone when Bruce reappeared.

"You must have made quite the impression on Dawn Darby. I'm supposed to get your phone number. Of course, we already have it in your file. Is it okay to give it to her?"

File? Why would these people have a file on him?

"Sure. Give it to her, Bruce. Who is she, anyway?"

Bruce's mouth fell open. "What? You don't know who… that was…is…Dawn Darby Endicott."

Jake nodded slowly. "Okay."

Bruce seemed shocked, but what could Jake do? Dawn Derby What's-her-name wasn't in his Twitter feed or on any of the shows he streamed. He didn't remember her from any movies. Then it came to him.

How could he be so stupid?

Stratford and Key published books.

Dawn Debbie must be an author. And judging by the way people were fawning over her, a pretty good one.

"Ahh," he finally said. "I didn't recognize her at first."

He didn't recognize her at all.

Bruce seemed to perceive that, but he didn't mention it. He motioned for Jake to follow him.

Marcus Key was waiting.

The office was spacious with city views along two walls. The man was smaller than Jake expected. Not jockey-small, but probably no more than five-five and one-forty. His suit was impeccable. His grip, firm. His smile, sincere. Jake felt underdressed and unprepared. What was so important that this man would spring for a suite at the Ritz Carlton? And room service. And cabs, including the ones he'd taken out to New Jersey for the game.

They took their seats. Key behind a desk with a gleaming finish and almost nothing on it. Jake in a maroon leather chair that made his butt feel rich just by touching it. Jake expected small talk, but Key caught him completely off guard.

"Did you enjoy the game yesterday?"

Jake opened his mouth to reply, but nothing came out. He tried again, but could only grunt. Key watched him for a moment before picking up a remote and pushing a button. A large-screen TV over a fireplace came on with a moment in the previous day's game frozen on the screen. Key pushed another button, and they watched as the Chiefs' quarterback threw a deep pass that was picked off by a Giants' safety. The network replayed it twice, then zeroed in on a poor sucker in the press box just as he jumped to his feet and spilled nachos down the front of his shirt.

Jake recognized that poor sucker as himself.

Key stopped the action on the screen at the point where Jake first realized what had happened, his mouth forming a perfect circle. Key threw back his head and roared with laughter. Jake started to plead his case, but was cut off.

"You don't owe me an explanation, Jake. I know you were in town to cover the game. And if Stratford and Key could help save you some money, all the better." He pointed to the screen and started laughing again. "But…that is about the funniest thing I've ever seen. Had I not done my research, I would have never known it was you."

Funny thing about Key. Though he was laughing, Jake didn't get the feeling that he was laughing *at* him. It wasn't about making fun of someone. The man was just enjoying a funny moment, and that was okay with Jake. It was pretty funny.

"I heard you charmed our Dawn Darby Endicott," he said as he turned off the TV.

"Truth is, Mr. Key, I've never heard of her."

"She writes literary fiction. I'm guessing you don't read her kind of stuff." He glanced toward the door, as if to make sure it was closed. "Me neither, really. I prefer a good whodunit any day. Dawn Darby takes seven pages to describe the petals on a flower, but her books are the rage. And she's in town to talk to a movie producer that's interested in her latest. If they adapt it to the big screen, it will be her fourth."

"Maybe I should get to know her." Jake was joking. Sort of. Key waved him off.

"She certainly loves younger men but just uses them and moves on. But enough about Dawn Darby. We're here to talk about you."

"Me?"

"Yes, Jake, well, you and your late grandmother. Did I mention how much she's missed around here?"

"You did, and I find it hard to believe. Most people who knew my grandmother found her difficult at best. Impossible otherwise."

Just as during their initial conversation, Key didn't take the bait regarding his personal feelings for Georgia Springer. "Georgia had signed a contract for one final book, Jake. It was to be the last installment in her Stella Duvall series. I'm sure you're familiar with those."

Jake blinked several times. How terrible would it sound that he'd read none of his grandmother's books?

Probably no worse than dumping a plate of nachos all over himself on national television.

"Not familiar at all, unfortunately. Her books were around our house when I was a kid, but she wrote romance and I was more into sports."

"Of course," Key said without a hint of disappointment. "Everyone has their favorites. That's what keeps us in business. But like I was saying, she had a contract for a final book. She was about a third the way finished when she passed."

"That's unfortunate. But I'm sure her readers will understand. I mean, it's not like she just up and quit."

Key nodded. "It's not quite that simple, Jake. We can't leave the series unfinished. Georgia's readers are expecting to have everything tied together. In her last book, Stella, the protagonist through fifteen books, had just met a young man. Her first beau."

Beau?

Did anyone say that anymore?

"Within hours of announcing Georgia's death, we were receiving emails from readers wanting to know when her final Stella Duvall book would be released." Key took a deep breath. "We have too much invested to just forget about it."

"Have someone else finish it," Jake said with a shrug. "How about Dawn Darlene? She's obviously a talented writer."

"Dawn Darby gets a seven-figure advance for her books," Key said with a chuckle. "And while Georgia was certainly popular, she wasn't in that league." He cleared his throat.

"And there is the matter of the advance. One hundred and fifty thousand dollars."

Jake sat up straighter. "Grandma made that much?"

"That's just up front. It doesn't count royalties. But the issue is that the advance was already paid."

Okay. Now Jake saw what was going on. Grandma had cashed her royalty check. Key wanted to know what happened to the money. That was easy enough.

"Mr. Key, I suspect that money is long gone."

Key sighed. "That's what I was afraid of."

"Well, not really gone. It's now a beach house in Alabama."

Key nodded and sighed again. "Your parents?"

"Yes, sir."

"That explains why they won't return my calls." Key pursed his lips, wiping at a spot on the sleeve of his jacket. "Jake, I don't want to sue your parents, but if we can't figure this out, I may have to."

"It wouldn't be the first time they've been sued."

Geesh, if Key only knew. Jake's earliest memory of his parents' inability to manage money was second grade. They had invested in an ice cream truck that would make them rich. Being the kid whose parents owned an ice cream truck was pretty cool for about seven months. But Jake also remembered looking out his bedroom window one night as it was being loaded onto a tow truck. That was the first time he remembered hearing words like default and bankruptcy. They became more familiar over the years.

"Mr. Key, with all due respect, if you think you can get the money from me, you're wrong. I've barely got two pennies to rub together most of the time."

Key smiled and shook his head. "That was never the plan. From what I can tell, you're doing fine. Your website is growing. A friend of mine who works in sports journalism says you're getting some traction in terms of readership."

Jake was impressed that Key had done his research. But still, he couldn't figure why they had brought him to New York. Why had they dropped a couple grand on a midwestern guy who was part owner of a fledgling sports website?

Unless they were thinking...

"Jake, we think you can finish Georgia's book."

"There's no way," Jake said, getting to his feet. He studied Key to see if he was joking. The man's face was stoic. "I don't know the first thing about writing books, Mr. Key. I don't even read them."

He cast a sideways glance Key's way. He seemed resistant to Jake's argument. "And in case you're forgetting, my grandmother wrote romance novels. I'm the last guy you want trying to write that stuff. I spend my time writing about stick and ball sports."

Key waved him off. "Don't sell yourself short, Jake. I'm not one of those self-absorbed athletes you have to cozy up to for soundbites. Don't think for a moment that I'm buying into that dumb jock image. You have a degree from one of the best journalism schools in America. And you're Georgia Springer's grandson, and I know from negotiating with her over the years that she was one of the sharpest people around. It's only one book, and not an entire book, really. Just two-thirds. And besides, we have people who can help you along the way."

"Sorry, Mr. Key, but I'm not your boy. Even if I were, I don't have the time. I spend my nights in press boxes or courtside, then I spend my days writing about what I saw. There's no time left for—"

"We'll pay you $25,000."

Wait! Time out.

Key picked up an envelope from the credenza. He held it out, but Jake didn't reach for it. Not that he couldn't use it.

There was less than $400 in his checking account. Maybe double that in savings. His truck—Grandpa's truck, actually—was nine years old and in need of tires and a tune-up. And while the website was starting to turn a profit, very little was available for personal use. $25,000 could take care of a lot of those niggling issues like property taxes, Christmas gifts, and the gym membership he'd allowed to lapse.

But he would have to write a book first. And not just any book. A romance. The kind that made women swoon. What did he know about that? It would be impossible. There was just no way.

"How long would I have?"

"We need it by Christmas."

Jake couldn't be sure he had heard correctly. But when he looked at Key, he knew he had. "It's not as bad as it sounds," Key said. "Georgia already had thirty-thousand words written. You need just 50,000 more."

Fifty-thousand words? His story about the Chiefs' victory came in at 1,100 words. He typically wrote four posts a week, 1,500 words each. That was 6,000 words. And he hardly broke a sweat.

How hard could it really be?

Then Key sweetened the pot. "We will provide you with an editor who can review your work daily. They will make recommendations and offer advice. And since your work schedule is somewhat unorthodox, we'll have that person spend the month in Kansas City, so they are available at a moment's notice."

"You would pay someone on your staff to spend time with me in Kansas City?"

Key nodded.

Jake's first thought was that he was being underpaid. If Stratford and Key had the money to send someone to Kansas City for a month, then they could afford to.

"Forty-thousand," Key said, making Jake wonder if he was reading his thoughts. "But don't even think about a penny more." Jake was surprised, but not surprised, when Key again pushed the envelope toward him. He had fully expected Jake would want to negotiate.

But when he reached for the envelope, Key pulled it back. "There's a contract to be signed. It stipulates that you finish the book by January 1 or repay the money plus interest."

"Get me that contract, Mr. Key."

It was 10:27 when Mallory's desk phone rang.

Charlotte. Tenth Floor.

She grabbed the receiver so fast that the phone fell to the floor. She lunged for it and banged her elbow on the edge of her desk.

"Ouch! Flock of geese!"

"Mallory? Are you okay?"

"Yes. Just a moment, please." She returned the phone to the desk and sat down. There was a cut on her elbow that was starting to bleed. She tried to snag a tissue from the box next to her laptop, but pulled out six. She wadded them up and placed them against the cut.

"Yes, this is Mallory."

"I know who you are. Did you just say, *flock of geese*?"

She had an image of Charlotte at her tidy tenth-floor desk. Straight-laced, sixty-something Charlotte in her clunky shoes and Hillary Clinton pantsuit, wondering why a seasoned editor like Mallory would utter something so stupid.

"Yes, ma'am. You see, I dropped the phone. And when I reached for it, I struck my arm on the desk. It's bleeding and —"

"And you substituted flock of geese for an expletive?"

Mallory's face burned. She wished they could back up and start over. Fortunately, Charlotte saved the day, saying, "I often use sharks as my expletive substitute."

The thought of Charlotte uttering anything stronger than *my goodness* made Mallory giggle. If the call was going off the rails, it might as well go all the way.

When she spoke again, Charlotte was back to business as usual. "As soon as you stanch the bleeding, come up, but don't take long."

Key stuck Jake in a conference room while he went off in search of someone to notarize the contract. The place had everything. Snacks, soft drinks and hard liquor, and even a selection of books published under the Stratford and Key imprint. What was lacking was phone service. At least service for Jake's budget cellphone company. So he grabbed a Dr. Pepper, then stuffed another in the pocket of his hoodie, helped himself to bags of Cheez-Its, pretzels, and salted peanuts, and returned to the waiting area where service was better. He was deep into a call with his business partner, Adrian, when the elevator opened and another beautiful blonde emerged, this one younger and prettier than the one before. She scanned the waiting area, then her eyes fell on him. When Jake nodded, she gave him one of those looks reserved for street corner panhandlers and door-to-door salesmen, then took a seat as far away as she could. Jake went back to his call.

"Look, Adrian, I'm waiting on some paperwork, then I'll be on my way back."

"What did the book people want?"

The last thing Jake needed was for Adrian to know he was

coming into some cash. Nor did he want his partner to know he would be moonlighting over the next few weeks.

"Just some unfinished paperwork. They couldn't get a response from Dad, so they called me."

Jake put the phone back in his pocket and noticed the Cheez-It crumbs on the front of his hoodie. No wonder the woman across the waiting room was giving him the stink eye. He flicked the crumbs away and checked her out while she stared at her phone.

Then she looked up and caught him.

Seriously?

As if there weren't enough creeps on the streets, now they were hanging out in the building? The guy had on jeans and a thrift-store hoodie. Why hadn't Bruce or one of the other assistants had him removed? And why was he was leering at her like a perv? She'd had plenty of experience with weirdos. The best thing to do was address it head-on.

"May I help you?"

His eyes grew wide. Probably not used to being called out for his boorish behavior.

"I'm good." He held up a can of Dr. Pepper and a nearly empty bag of Cheez-Its. "Just having a snack."

New York had been Mallory's home her entire life, save for the four years she'd spent in New Hampshire getting her English degree at Dartmouth. She knew the best pizza places, where to find a true gourmet hot dog, and the Italian restaurants that hadn't been discovered by tourists yet. She also had a handle on the city's darker side. It was a wonderful place, an exciting place. But if a girl didn't watch herself, also a dangerous place. And as much as she wanted to let the guy in the hoodie know what she thought of him, she kept it to herself and turned her attention back to her phone.

That lasted two minutes. Two minutes of listening to him crunch his Cheez-Its, slurp his Dr. Pepper, and stifle a belch. Then he spoke again.

"You're bleeding." He held up his left arm and pointed to his elbow. What the hell?

Then she remembered.

She was bleeding through the Sponge Bob bandage she'd hurriedly slapped on.

"Oh, shit." She looked around for a box of tissues, but there were none. The guy stood up and came toward her, holding out a napkin.

"Here."

She took it, mumbled thanks, and held it against the cut.

"Paper cut?" he asked.

"Excuse me?"

"Paper cut? You look like you work from a desk. I figured you got a paper cut."

Why was he so damned chatty? New Yorkers didn't strike up conversations in waiting rooms. Mallory shook her head, then pulled away the napkin. The bleeding had stopped. Fortunately, she had thought to bring along another bandage. This one was Scooby Doo. She replaced Sponge Bob with Scooby, then tossed the napkin and old bandage in a trash can.

"Thanks," she said again as she returned her attention to her phone.

"You're welcome. Want some Cheez-Its?"

"No."

"Pretzels?"

Mallory looked up and made a face that she hoped conveyed her irritation. "What?"

He pulled a bag of pretzels from his hoodie. "Pretzels. I have peanuts, too. Salted. You're welcome to them."

She waved him off.

"I have an extra Dr. Pepper if you—"

Mallory extended her right arm as her eyes bored into him. "Look, I appreciate the napkin, but I'm really busy here and would prefer to be left alone."

He shrugged, opened the pretzels, and shoved one into his mouth. Then after taking one more long look at her, he stood, stretched, and headed off.

Jake had been back in the conference room for just a few moments when Marcus Key returned with the notarized contract and apologies for taking so long. Jake had a good feeling about Marcus. They were on a first-name basis now, at the older man's insistence. Jake appreciated that he was so straightforward.

"We have a car standing by to take you to LaGuardia, but I first want you to meet the editor we've assigned to work with you in Kansas City." He reached for the phone in the middle of the conference table. "Charlotte, is she here?"

Jake suspected that he might have already met the *'she'* Marcus was referring to. And if he had? Oh, boy. This was going to get interesting.

Mallory heard Bruce before she saw him. Bruce was Charlotte's counterpart, but they were total opposites. Male, under forty, and black, Bruce was dedicated to the firm, but also maintaining a busy life away from the office. While Charlotte remained squirreled away at her desk in the partners' inner sanctum, Bruce's was often the first face seen by VIPs and others fortunate enough to make it to the tenth floor.

"Dawn Darby, it's always a pleasure," Mallory heard him say. "They've called her, and she should be here any minute. Are you sure you don't want to wait in the conference room?"

"I'll be fine out front," she replied. "Thank you, Bruce."

Mallory stood up and smoothed her skirt. Things usually weren't done this way at Stratford and Key, but Dawn Darby Endicott wasn't just some mid-list author. Perhaps she wanted to meet her new editor without the partners looking over her shoulder. One thing was certain. What Dawn Darby wanted, Dawn Darby got.

She came around the corner to where Mallory was seated. She was smaller than expected. The author photographs always made her appear taller. Up close, she was a sliver of a woman. Mallory felt momentarily in awe of her, but quickly recovered because it was essential for their professional relationship. They preached that at the firm. Respect, but don't kowtow to authors. Don't do their bidding. Do your job and do it well, but don't get lost in their shadow. Mallory had spent years working toward this moment. Being assigned to an A-lister was a statement to the publishing world that she had arrived as an editor. And by gosh, she was ready to grab the opportunity and run with it.

"Dawn Darby, I'm Mallory Newell."

A frown crossed Dawn Darby's face, but disappeared quickly. "Hello, dear, a pleasure. Are you ready?"

"I certainly am. And may I say I'm looking forward to working with you."

So far, so good.

"Well, that's nice, dear. Where are we going first?"

Uh-oh. Nobody said anything about what happened next.

"Perhaps we should see what time you're scheduled to—"

"Excuse me? Mallory?"

Bruce had reappeared. He seemed concerned about something.

"Yes, Bruce. Dawn Darby and I were just planning—"

"Mallory, Mr. Key needs to see you immediately." He approached and extended his arm to Dawn Darby. "And I'll make sure our favorite author gets squared away."

What the hell was going on?

Had she jumped the gun? Charlotte had told her to come up. Perhaps it was Dawn Darby who was at fault. Maybe she misunderstood and assumed they would meet alone. Mr. Key would know. She scurried down the hallway to the last door on the right. It was open. His office was empty.

"Mallory?" It was Mr. Key, calling to her from the conference room across the hall. "We're in here."

We're?

She took a deep breath, threw back her shoulders, and stepped into the conference room.

What in the flock of geese was going on?

Mr. Key was seated at the conference table with Cheez-It guy. They stood as she entered.

"Mallory Newell, meet Jake Springer."

Mallory looked from Mr. Key to Cheez-It guy and hoped it was a bad dream. He still had crumbs on his cheap hoodie. He grinned as he came around the conference table. "Miss Newell, a pleasure to meet you."

Mallory thrust out her hand. His was warm, and a little crumby.

Mr. Key invited her to sit down. "You're familiar with Georgia Springer's work, aren't you, Mallory?"

"Of course, sir."

Was she ever? Brenda, a third-floor colleague, had edited one of Georgia Springer's previous books. Stilted, sappy drivel. Written by a cantankerous old woman for other cantankerous old women.

"Jake is Georgia's grandson."

"I see," Mallory nodded and flashed a smile she didn't feel. This was looking like a money grab. Cheez-It guy was probably left out of the old biddie's will. Now he shows up here looking for a handout. It had happened before. Some authors were eccentric and had eccentric families. Others were just batshit crazy.

Mr. Key explained that Jake was from some place in Kansas and had come to New York for a football game. Why he felt the need to share this with her when Dawn Darby was waiting was…

Wait a minute!

What was that on the table in front of Grandson Cheez-It?

Was it.. *no!* It wasn't a check, was it?

Without being too obvious, Mallory reached for a pitcher of water in the center of the table. The move allowed her to steal a glimpse of the check without being too obvious. It was a check all right. The Stratford and Key logo was embossed in the corner. And the amount was…?

Five figures? She angled for another look as she returned the pitcher, but Grandson Cheez-It slipped his cheesy hand over it. When Mallory glanced up at him, the smarmy slob winked at her.

Mr. Key was oblivious. And still talking. "Sadly, since Georgia passed before finishing her final book, Jake has graciously offered to step in and put the finishing touches on it. Isn't that great, Mallory?"

Wait. What?

Grandson Cheez-It was a writer?

A romance writer?

"That's…great, sir."

❄

She had no idea what was going on.

And she had no idea that Scooby Doo was dangling from her elbow. It had been that way since she reached for the water pitcher. Served her right for trying to see how much he was being paid. It was a pretty smooth move, actually. Marcus didn't catch it, but then Marcus probably went to some Ivy League school where students didn't need to cheat. Jake spent two years at community college, and knew all the tricks students used to get a look at other students' test papers. He might have even used a few of them.

For all Mallory Newell knew, he was some low-life farm boy. Probably in town to see if he could rattle loose some spare change from the company that published his grandmother's books.

And if that was what she thought, he was good with it. He had survived by beating expectations. And if Mallory Newell was his next hurdle, so be it.

He had to admit, though, she was a very attractive hurdle. Straight blonde hair pulled back in a ponytail. Sky blue eyes. No, not sky blue. They were… What was that color?

Azure!

Thank goodness for that art history elective back at Mizzou. And for a professor who was a stickler for identifying colors by their correct shade. Sky blue? Not exact enough. Mallory Newell's eyes were…azure. Stunningly azure.

She needed to smile more, though. Even when Marcus had invited her in, she wore a look of uncertainty. She nodded when introduced, but no smile. A smile would raise her from beautiful to incredibly awesomely beautiful.

And when Marcus said that Jake would finish Grandma Springer's last book, any vestiges of good humor drained from her face. Her eyes darted from Marcus to Jake. She nodded slowly, probably wondering if he even knew how to string together a sentence.

"So, you're a writer, Mr. Springer?" Those lovely eyes bore into his, and Jake decided that azure was definitely a better descriptor than sky blue. Sky blue was pleasant and sunny. Azure sounded less certain. Like a storm brewing on the horizon. Jake suspected there was a storm brewing inside Mallory Newell. And that if he wasn't careful, he might be at the center of it.

"Jake works in sports journalism," Marcus interjected. "He's well respected for his accomplishments."

"Sports journalism." It was obvious from the tone of her voice that she wasn't impressed. She was treading lightly, though. Marcus was her boss. Had he not been in the room, Jake had little doubt she would have had more to say.

"Yeah," Jake said, playing up the country boy image. "I don't have much experience with writing books and stuff, but Marcus seen something in me that everybody else missed."

She winced at his mangled verbiage, then winced again when he held up the check while making sure the amount was concealed from view. "Because now I got a few weeks to write one."

"And Mallory, we've selected you to provide editorial assistance," Marcus said. "As one of our most experienced editors, we need you to help Jake meet this deadline."

She looked as if she'd been hit by a truck. "You want me to help? Like, go to Kansas?"

Marcus seemed perturbed. "Didn't Charlotte confirm your availability for an out of town assignment?"

"Yes, but I assumed she meant…uh…that I would be assisting…"

She slumped in her chair, and Jake felt a twinge of

sympathy for her. She had obviously been expecting a different assignment. Probably somebody high profile, like the brassy blonde who squeezed his knee in the waiting room. She recovered quickly, though.

"Of course, sir. I'll finish up a few things here and leave on Wednesday." She stood, pushed in her chair, and looked for a moment as if she might cry. She bit her lip, turned to Jake, and said, "I look forward to working with you, Mr. Springer. And if it isn't asking too much, perhaps you could read through your grandmother's unfinished manuscript and begin writing. Then, when we meet, I can critique your work and offer some suggestions."

Oh, I've got some suggestions, all right. How about we start with this one?

Give back the cash and go back to writing about sports.

Mallory didn't express those thoughts. Even with Mr. Key pissing all over her career, she kept her mouth shut.

That smug Cheez-It eating country bumpkin smiled and said he would begin writing as soon as he got back to whatever god-forsaken part of the dust bowl he hailed from. Mallory gathered her things and hurried from the conference room, leaving the men to discuss sports or strip clubs, or whatever men talked about when the women were out of earshot. She was mentally running through a list of publishing houses that might have openings when Bruce caught up to her near the elevator.

"Sorry about the snafu with Dawn Darby," he whispered. "She was waiting for one of the personal assistants to take her on a little shopping adventure. I never expected that you would... Sorry, Mallory."

She grabbed Bruce's arm and looked both ways to make

sure no one might overhear. "One question, Bruce, and you at least owe me an answer after embarrassing me in front of Dawn Darby."

"Ask away, dear."

"Has an editor been assigned to work with her?"

He leaned in close enough that Mallory picked up the hint of garlic on his breath. "Not yet. But soon."

Ugh. How would she be able to plead her case from some barn loft in the middle of nowhere? She considered returning to Mr. Key's office to see if she could convince him to send someone else, but knew it would do no good. To move ahead at Stratford and Key, you did what you were asked.

But nothing said you had to enjoy it.

She reached her office door without encountering anyone. She planned to duck inside, grab the suitcase containing the new bikinis and her other summer clothes, and make a dash for the back stairs before anyone knew she was gone.

But Luis was sitting on her sofa. He jumped up and excitedly came toward her.

"The place is buzzing," he exclaimed. "Word is you met with Dawn Darby and Mr. Key." He motioned to her closet. "I peeked in and saw your suitcase. I'm so excited for you!"

Mallory knew better. Luis was a great guy, but he was vying for the same advancement opportunities. Even so, it was nice of him to at least put on a show of support.

"So, tell me all about it! Bora Bora? When do you leave? How long?"

Just hearing him say it nearly caused the dam to burst. She clenched her fists to keep the tears away a bit longer, then barely above a whisper, replied.

"It's not Dawn Darby, Luis. It's some nobody trying to make bank off his dead grandmother's romance novels.

"And it's not Bora Bora. It's..."

The first tears fell despite her best effort to keep them at bay.

"...it's Kansas."

With an entire flight in front of him, Jake settled into his seat, woke up his iPad, and began reading his late grandmother's prose.

Stella stepped into Mr. Patterson's office, where he was busy studying the renderings of the new paper factory. When completed, it would bring two-hundred new jobs to Adair.

"You're the toast of the town, Mr. Patterson," she said as she straightened his desk. "I would imagine that the big TV stations will come around for interviews when word gets out about the factory."

He looked up and smiled. It was far from the way things had been just five months before, when Stella started at Patterson Paper. Mr. Patterson was notorious for chewing up secretaries, but Stella had been bound and determined that she would not be his latest victim. She had a lot at stake by remaining in Adair. Her Aunt Bess lived just a few miles away. The cozy cottage she was renting from Herb Farquhar was too adorable for words. And, of course, there was Terrence. Handsome, gallant Terrance. Might he try to kiss her after their date later that evening? They'd been dating for nearly a month, so he just might.

And if he did?

Oh, my goodness, the possibility caused her to swoon.

"What the—" Jake stopped himself before uttering something he might regret. Good thing, too, as the sweet older lady seated next to him on the flight to Kansas City was watching him curiously.

"Sorry," he mumbled.

"Must be quite a book," she said, glancing at his iPad.

"You can say that again." He turned off the tablet and stowed it in the seatback. Another chapter of Grandma's unfinished manuscript and he might need an airsick bag.

"Life Saver?" the lady asked, holding out a roll of the butter rum flavor he hadn't seen since he was a kid. He plucked one from the roll and popped it into his mouth.

"They still make these?"

She laughed. "Yes, but they're hard to find. I order them twenty packs at a time online. They're expensive, but what would a grandmother be without a roll of butter rum candy?"

Jake sat back and closed his eyes while the candy's taste and feel evoked memories of long-ago Christmases. A few pleasant, like Mom taking four-year-old Jake to sit on Santa's lap at the downtown Jones Store and, later, after it closed, to the food court at Blue Ridge Mall. Skating at Crown Center. The Plaza lights.

And other memories not so sweet. By his eighth birthday he had figured out that the magic of Christmas was a ruse. His parents started saying things about Santa cutting back on how much he loaded in his sleigh, or how the elves were overworked and needed a vacation from toy making. None of the other kids knew anything about overloaded sleighs or elf vacations. He later learned how often Grandpa Stringer had swooped in to save the day when Mom and Dad were too tapped out or spaced out to remember Christmas gifts for a little boy who desperately wanted to believe. With each passing year, it became more obvious that his family was different. His friends' parents didn't have vodka bottles stashed in the back of the bathroom cabinet. They didn't sneak behind the boxwood hedge to conceal the smell of their pot. And they never took their kids on late-night trips to some of Kansas City's most dangerous streets.

"So, what book are your reading?"

The old lady again. And she was holding out the candy roll again. Sure, why not?

"It's one that I…purchased by mistake. I wanted to at least give it a try, though."

"Aw, that's too bad. Do you think you'll make it to the end?"

It's not like I have a choice now. "I think so. Yes." It was time to change the subject. "Do you enjoy reading?" he asked.

When Jake got a look at the dog-eared paperback she'd pulled from her purse, he nearly spit out his candy.

"She's my favorite," the old woman said, holding up a copy of one of Grandma Springer's older books. "Especially the Stella Duvall books. Have you heard of them?"

Jake took the book and turned it over. The photograph on back was at least twenty years old. Grandma Springer with dark hair and a contemplative smile.

"She was originally from Kansas City," the lady said. "She writes books that people like me can appreciate. No smut or sex." She giggled. "Not that I'm a prude, mind you. I couldn't be married to my Ralphie for fifty-one years and be a prude. But even though she writes in the present day, she takes me back to a more innocent time."

"You don't find it boring?"

Her eyes had taken on a dreamy quality. "What's boring about a young woman with strong morals who wants to get ahead in the world on her own terms?" She jabbed her finger into Jake's arm for emphasis as she said, "Your generation has made things so complicated. And I understand the world needs to change, especially in how we treat some parts of society. But Stella Duvall? She treats everyone with love and dignity."

Jake could hardly believe they were having this conversation. But he also had to admit she had a point. Stella might come across as submissive or weak, but even in what little he had read, she used those traits to her advantage. Stella Duvall was living her dream. And if that dream was to serve as secretary to some old guy who took all the glory, who was Jake to say it was wrong?

But what if she chose different dreams? Many people did. They started down one career path only to find it wasn't what they expected. They were faced with a choice. Continue living a life that was boring or unfulfilling, or try something different.

What if Stella wanted more?

Then Jake could help her find it. Together they could chase Stella's dreams in any direction he thought they should lead.

And as the plane touched down in Kansas City, Jake knew it had fallen to him to help Stella take the next step in her life.

And he had 50,000 words to get it done.

CHAPTER THREE

WEDNESDAY, NOVEMBER 29

Mallory crawled into the first cab she found outside the airport.

"Happy holidays," exclaimed the driver, a middle-aged guy in a ball cap.

"Fountain Monarch Hotel," she replied.

"Downtown or Plaza?"

Mallory double-checked the instructions in Charlotte's email. "It doesn't say. Which one is in Kansas?"

The cabbie laughed. "Not from here, are you?"

"Can you get me there or not?" Mallory snapped.

"I can, but neither of the Fountain Monarchs is in Kansas. Both are in Missouri."

Had the travel department sent her to the wrong place? "This is Kansas City, right?"

"Yes, ma'am."

"But neither of the Fountain Monarchs is here?"

"They're both here."

This wasn't going well. She placed a quick call to Rachel in travel, but it went to voicemail. Of course it did. It was just past five back in New York. Rachel was gone for the day.

The cabbie was watching her in the mirror. "Ma'am. Perhaps I can help you."

"Apparently you can't. I need to get to the Fountain Monarch Hotel in Kansas, and you seem to be unaware that it exists. Are you new at your job?"

"Nope. Been driving since the steel plant shut down twenty years ago. There's two Kansas Cities. Or just one, depending on how you look at it. The state line runs through the middle of town, and both Fountain Monarchs are on the Missouri side." He paused and turned to face her. "How about I run you by the downtown Monarch first, since it's on the way? If that's not where you're staying, we'll head to the Plaza."

It sounded logical, but also like a way to squeeze her for more money. It happened all the time to unsuspecting tourists in New York. Unscrupulous cab drivers would take them out of their way. Locals knew the routes and were harder to fool.

"I'll try to find the number. Give me a minute."

"Suit yourself." The driver put his head back and relaxed while Mallory searched for the number. After a couple minutes he pulled out his phone, and made a call.

"Hey, this is Tommy Shapiro with Speedy Cab. Is Latoya there?"

He turned and spoke over his shoulder. "They're getting Latoya."

Was this for real?

"Happy holidays, good-looking! Hey, I got a fare who isn't sure which of your properties she's staying at." He paused and turned in his seat. "What's your name, ma'am?"

"I'm not giving you my name," Mallory snapped.

"She doesn't want to give me her name, Latoya. I'll put you on speaker." He pushed a button and said, "You can tell Latoya your name. She works in the hotel business office."

"Hello. If you give me your name, I can tell you where you're registered."

"I just said I'm not giving my name." She glared at the cabbie. "How do I know this guy isn't an axe murderer and you're his accomplice?"

The person on the line, allegedly Latoya, giggled. "Tommy an axe murderer? That's funny. But I'll tell you what. If you have your confirmation number, I can use it to trace your reservation."

Mallory read the confirmation number, and Latoya directed her to the downtown location. If Tommy was insulted by being called an axe murderer, he recovered quickly. "Can't you at least get her an upgrade, Latoya? After everything she's been through?"

"Maybe. Let's see." The sound of keystrokes echoed through the phone, then Latoya said, "Good news, Miss Newell, I mean, ma'am. Sorry about that. I've moved you into one of our two-room suites on the concierge floor."

"Concierge floor," the cabbie exclaimed. "That means free snacks and stuff. Nice work, Latoya!"

He disconnected and pulled out of the airport. Obviously proud of his hometown, the cabbie kept up a steady stream of chatter about famous landmarks and people of Kansas City. Mallory's worries of him being an axe-wielding madman became guilt pangs for the way she'd spoken to him. He probably deserved an apology, but then, he had brought much of it upon himself by being too darn friendly. The guy wouldn't last a week driving a hack in New York.

The scenery changed as they crossed a bridge into downtown. Industrial complexes and railroad tracks gave way to high-rises as several freeways converged, then just as quickly went their own ways. A brightly lit casino promised loose slots and plenty of fun. The cabbie eased off the highway onto a narrow block similar to New York. Loft apartments offered a free month's rent with a two-year lease. Tall buildings cast shade over the streets as commuters jockeyed for position during the afternoon rush. Within minutes, they pulled up in front of a newer-looking brick and block building with a large fountain flowing freely despite temperatures near freezing.

"Here you go, Miss Newell," the cabbie said as they came to a stop. He hit the button on the meter and told her the cost, then quickly processed her Stratford and Key Amex card. Mallory thanked him and reached for the door handle. Nothing happened.

"That old thing," the cabbie said as he opened his door. "It's been sticking since September, but what can you do?"

As he struggled to get out, it became apparent that Tommy the cabbie dealt with physical challenges. The car rocked a bit as he used the door as leverage to get to his feet. Even the short distance he had to cover to come around the car appeared daunting. Mallory guessed he had an artificial leg, and when she got a look at the left side of his face, she saw the kinds of scars that burns leave behind. Still, he smiled as he pulled open her door.

"Enjoy your stay in Kansas City. I hope we cross paths again."

Those guilt pangs returned with a vengeance. Mallory wasn't sure if she wanted to shake his hand or throw her arms around him and give him a hug. She wouldn't have to make that decision, though, as a bellman hustled out of the hotel and grabbed her bag.

"Checking in?" Then, "Hey, Tommy!"

"Hiya, Patrick. This is Miss Newell. Latoya got her a room on the concierge floor. Take care of her, okay?"

"You betcha, Tommy. Follow me, ma'am and we'll get you registered."

Mallory glanced over her shoulder and waved at Tommy.

He was leaning against the cab, struggling to catch his breath, but still smiling. She waited until they were inside before asking the bellman what had happened to him.

"Desert Storm happened to him," he replied. "Sad, too, because Tommy's a helluva guy."

The hotel was nice, though certainly not on a level with the Four Seasons or New York's other luxury hotels where Stratford and Key clients stayed. But then Mallory was just an editor, dispatched to the wilderness to prop up some wannabe writer. What a waste of her talents.

Screw the partners. She would show them that she was capable of much more. She'd spent the previous day applying for positions at publishing houses around the city. Her work spoke for itself, and as long as the people doing the hiring didn't learn that she had been relegated to Stratford and Key's editor exile program, she would have a good chance at landing a new gig. With a little luck, maybe even by Christmas. Hah! That would show Mr. Key. She smiled at the idea of informing him about her great new job. She would do it right after lunch on Christmas Eve. That was the day that Key and the other partners made a big show of going from office to office, handing out bonus checks.

"Here's your bonus, Mallory. Thanks so much for—"

"Screw you, Mr. Key. I start work at another firm–a better firm–in January. You're going to regret the day you sent me to Kansas! I mean, Missouri!"

Of course, she would only make such a sassy proclamation *after* she had her bonus check in hand. No need to be frivolous when there were bills to pay.

The suite's living room had a sofa, two chairs, and a desk where Mallory plugged in her laptop and checked email. Buried amidst the usual Stratford and Key announcements and reminders was one from the aspiring writer and grifter Jake Springer.

Let me know what you think. Thanks, J.

Who signed emails with their initial anymore? That was so 1990s. Who signed their emails at all? This was going to be harder than she'd imagined. She double-checked to see if any of Stratford and Key's competitors had replied to her applications. They hadn't, so she opened the attachment to Jake Springer's email and started reading.

Her name was Gwyneth, and she'd been dispatched to Jake's dingy and mostly unused second-floor office by the University of Kansas to address his negative coverage of their athletic department. Their assertions were true. Jake had been firing off volleys of social media posts about his lack of access to coaches and players of the university's big money programs. It was his way of shaming them for what he saw as second-class treatment. The fact that KU sent a twenty-two-year-old who had been out of school for less than six months showed how lightly they took the matter.

But that wasn't Gwyneth's fault. She was delightful. Funny, witty, and, off the record, sympathetic to Jake's claims. She was also brutally honest. Decisions about who got access to student athletes and coaches were way above her pay grade. Then, in a startling turn of events, she said that if Jake wanted to take her to dinner, perhaps they could come up with a plan that might make both sides happy. The thought of having dinner with the lovely and personable Gwyneth already had Jake smiling.

By the time they had finished a Minsky's Prime Cut pizza and a couple of beers each, they were quite chummy. Particularly Gwyneth, who had scooted her chair closer so their knees were touching. The issue of access to athletes seemed less important with Gwyneth's knee against his. It was forgotten completely ten minutes later when her hand brushed against his thigh.

"It's such a long drive back to my place," she said. "And it's pretty late."

It was an opening wide enough to drive a truck through.

"You can come to my house," Jake suggested, hoping he didn't sound as smarmy to Gwyneth as he did to himself. He quickly added, "I've got a spare bedroom."

You're such a knucklehead. Do you think that's what she's angling for? No wonder you're still single at twenty-eight.

Smarmy or not, it worked. Gwyneth got in her car and followed him to Kenwood Avenue. He'd already learned over dinner she was a small-town girl from Baxter Springs, Kansas who one day hoped to be the Athletic Director of a major university. There was a boyfriend back home, but that didn't seem to be an issue. The evening was looking better and better.

When Jake pulled into his driveway, he noticed a soft glow through the living room window. Either Chris, his next-door neighbor, or another of the folks who lived along the street and knew where he hid his key, had probably stopped by to let Corabelle out. It happened occasionally, and he was grateful, especially when it was Mrs. Sampson, the widow who lived across the street. She not only gave Corabelle a bathroom break, but usually left a little something in the refrigerator for dinner or a late snack. As it was getting close to Christmas, he hoped it might be one of her mouthwatering applesauce cakes.

He walked Gwyneth to the door and pulled out his key. "Get ready. My dog goes crazy when she meets someone new. She's harmless, though."

"How about you, Jake?" Gwyneth said, grabbing his butt. "Are you harmless?"

The move caught him by surprise. He yelped, then giggled. And sounded like a schoolgirl.

He put the key into the lock and turned it. They were met with silence. And that was concerning.

"I hope everything is okay," he murmured as he opened the door. Corabelle's age was always a concern. But when he looked into the living room, he saw her stretched out on the couch, watching his arrival with little interest. Jake sighed with relief, then his breath caught when he spotted the editor from New York seated at the opposite end of the sofa.

"Hello, Mr. Springer."

"Uh…hey."

Gwyneth pushed past and stepped inside, her eyes coming to rest on Corabelle. Then the editor. Then on Jake. "Friend of yours, Jake?"

"She's… How did you get in here?"

"I knocked, but you didn't answer. The nice lady across the street said you would be home soon and asked if I wanted to wait inside."

"Well…" Jake was at a loss. "I've got a work meeting that I need to—"

Gwyneth said, "It's okay, Jake. Really. I need to be at the university early in the morning. I'll just head back."

"No, Gwyneth. Please stay. I'll…" It was hopeless. Her mind was made up. And the editor was hanging on every word he said, probably enjoying watching his plans go up in flames. She rose from the couch. The traitor Corabelle did too, obviously taking sides with her. "We have work to do, Mr. Springer. Time is wasting. I didn't come from New York to hang out with you and your girlfriend."

Jake knew he was whipped. "Gwyneth, I'm sorry for the change in plans. Maybe another time?"

She said all the right things, but Jake could tell by the tone of her voice that he'd seen the last of Gwyneth. As he walked her to the door, he spoke to the editor over his shoulder.

"At least give me a couple minutes to walk her out."

When he glanced back, she was smiling. "No problem, Mr. Springer. I'll set up my laptop on your kitchen table. We can work there."

Jake Springer was not a happy camper when he came into the kitchen.

"Was that necessary?"

"The bigger question should be, why are you chasing a teenager? Is that legal out here?"

"Not that it's any of your business, but she works for the University of Kansas. And I wasn't chasing her. We had a business matter to discuss and—"

"Yeah, business. You can keep telling yourself that, Mr. Springer, but I heard you giggling like a girl scout while you were trying to unlock the door. And I saw the look on your face when you came in. That wasn't work I saw. That was a guy hoping to get busy with a cute coed."

Jake took a deep breath. She was so New York. Rude, abrupt. Certain she was right about everything. He wanted to tell her as much, but dang it, he couldn't remember her name.

Megan? Madeline? That sounded right.

"Look, Madeline, the least you could have done was call and let me know you were in town."

"You never gave me your number. And it's Mallory."

"You had my email. And my address."

"And that's why I'm here." She glanced toward the living room, smirked, then added. "And now that your evening is open, let's get to work."

Spotlights swept back and forth as Terrence led the way onto the dance floor. His ripped Levi's were new. And Stella noticed they weren't the only thing that was ripped. Where had those biceps come from?

"Have you been spending time at the gym?" she asked as they began moving to the beat of the latest Christina Aguilera hit. Her question made Terrence smile.

"You noticed, huh? Yeah, they give us a free gym membership at work. I decided to put it to use." He flexed his left arm, and she felt herself gasp. Was it Terrence's new physique? Or the fact that she had just been shoved from behind by a guy in a white Hollister shirt. The impact was enough to send her new iPhone 14 skittering across the dance floor.

"Hey!" she said, turning to see who was behind her.

Hearing their words read aloud could be an eye-opening experience for new writers. Mallory had used the tactic many times, usually when she was representing the agency at writers' conventions. Aspiring authors would make their pitch, then she would ask them to read a page or two of their work. Some handled it without a problem. Others would get a few paragraphs in before realizing how unprepared they were.

Jake Springer fit into the former category. He was handling his lack of writing skill quite well. In fact, he was smiling.

Smiling.

Had he appeared deflated, she might have gone easy on him. But nope. He seemed perfectly satisfied with the passage she had just read. Not a care in the world. Happy to half-ass his way to a big payday, while ruining his late grandmother's reputation.

There was no way she was letting him get away with it. Working at the kitchen table was a smart first move, much better than the couch where he had likely made out with dozens of busty, brainless, immature girls. He was seated to her left, phone in hand, probably sneaking a peek at the sports scores while she assessed his writing skill.

His *lack* of writing skill.

"Where to begin?" she said, carefully enunciating each word while she shook her head.

"There's plenty more," he said, leaning forward to view the screen. "Did it all come through?"

"Oh, it came through. I don't need to read anymore, though."

"But I finished the chapter."

"True, but if the first few paragraphs are indicative of what follows, you have a lot of work to do."

That wiped the smile from his face. Mission accomplished. Now, if she could get him to see how ridiculous it was to believe he could suddenly morph into a romance writer, she might be back in New York by the weekend.

"I don't understand," he stammered.

That much was obvious.

"Let me try to put this to you as delicately as possible, Mr. Springer."

"Jake."

"Okay…Jake. I'll go through this passage sentence by sentence."

He leaned in and placed his elbows on the table.

"Take notes, Jake. There's no way you'll remember everything I'm about to tell you. And I prefer not to repeat myself."

He held up his phone. "I can do it on here."

She slid him a legal pad she kept in her briefcase. "Write it out. It will help you remember."

"Got a pen?"

Mallory sighed. He certainly wasn't the most intuitive guy around. She pulled out a pen and handed it to him. His fingers touched hers. By design? If so, he was barking up the wrong tree. He wasn't dealing with that little Kansas coed.

Mallory read from the screen. "'Spotlights swept back and forth as Terrence led the way onto the dance floor.'" She looked up at Jake. "What do you envision when I read that?"

He shrugged. "A dance club? Lots of bodies swaying to the music."

"Why isn't any of that included here?"

He appeared annoyed by her question. *Good!*

"There are spotlights. And it's obviously crowded. He's leading her to a spot where they can dance."

Rather than debate the matter, Mallory moved on. "'His ripped Levi's were new. And Stella noticed they weren't the only thing that was ripped. Where had those biceps come from?'" She shook her head. "Really? Do you have any idea how long it takes to build biceps?"

Jake sneaked a glance at his arms. "I spend some time in the gym. I know what I'm talking about."

"She sees him every day, Jake. Wouldn't she know if he had been working out? She would have noticed his improving physique or, more likely, he would have mentioned it a few hundred times."

Jake opened his mouth to respond, but nothing came out, so she continued. "'Have you been going to the gym?' she asked as they began moving to the beat of the latest Christina Aguilera hit.' Jake, do you have any idea how long it's been since Christina Aguilera was relevant?"

"I just listened to her yesterday in my truck. That's why I used her name."

"If you must name a performer, select one who is newer to the scene. It helps your writing stay relevant for a longer period."

"Do you think Grandma's readers would know the difference? They're musical tastes peaked at Barry Manilow. It's not like they're on the cutting edge of pop culture."

Rather than responding, she looked back at the screen. "'He flexed his left arm, and she felt herself gasp.' Jake, have you ever felt yourself gasp?"

He seemed reluctant to answer, so she answered for him. "No, you haven't. You have probably gasped, but you never *felt* yourself gasp. And to think that a man's bicep would be enough to make Stella gasp gives the impression that she's a very shallow woman."

"Stella's boring, for crying out loud. I was trying to add a little excitement to her life."

It was the first sensible thing he'd said. Stella Duvall was everything a contemporary woman wasn't. At least he had that much figured out.

But still.

"Perhaps a more experienced writer could enhance the character, but that's not your job. Your grandmother spent years developing Stella Duvall. Stratford and Key put a lot of money into marketing the series. This is the last book. Go with what works, Jake."

He pointed to the laptop. "You think this works?"

What to say? The truth? That she considered Stella Duvall mind-numbing and the storylines shallow and unimaginative? He would probably call Mr. Key to let him know that his editor was disparaging Georgia Springer's work. And even though Mallory had feelers out for other jobs, she couldn't risk her boss's ire. One negative word to prospective employers from the publishing giant could kill her career.

"I understand what you're saying about Stella, but you

need to focus on improving your writing and finishing this book." She nodded at the screen. "And frankly, your writing needs lots of work."

"Like what?"

"Start with emotion. What did Stella feel when Terrence pulled her onto the dance floor? And keep it real. Women today don't swoon. I'm sure you've been on plenty of dates. Did any of them swoon?"

He grinned. "Gwyneth kind of swooned, but you killed any chance of that going someplace."

His unguarded comment made her laugh. "I'm sure you will have more opportunities with Miss Kansas, but in the meantime, you need to take another run at this chapter."

"I'll start tonight."

"Excellent. We'll meet again tomorrow evening."

"Okay, but there's one thing. I work tomorrow night... Hey, do you like basketball?"

Mallory rolled her eyes. "Not in the least."

"Not even the Knicks?" Jake asked, leaning forward in his chair. "You at least like the Knicks, don't you?"

"I've heard of them, but couldn't tell you anything about them."

"How about you meet me tomorrow night at Municipal Auditorium? Mizzou is coming to town to play UMKC. We can talk about my writing during halftime."

"It sounds dreadful. I don't even know what a miss-you is."

Jake laughed. "Mizzou is the University of Missouri. They are playing our local college team, the Kangaroos."

"Kangaroos are interesting, but...I'll pass. How about the next day?"

"I'll be in Oklahoma for a few days, so it's tomorrow night or Sunday when I get back."

"That won't work. We're under a deadline." Mallory

checked the calendar on her phone, even though she knew it was clear. "I guess I'll meet you at the game."

"Great! I'll send you my updated chapter by noon. I could pick you up, but you would be stuck waiting courtside while I chase interviews."

"I'll find my way there. Just send me the time and place."

CHAPTER FOUR

THURSDAY, NOVEMBER 30

How could there not be a single available Uber at 7 p.m.? Was Kansas City's nightlife that nonexistent? Did everyone spend their evenings at home watching professional wrestling and listening to hillbilly music?

After repeatedly entering her destination and getting no response, Mallory went to the Fountain Monarch's front desk to request a cab. Patrick, the bellman who helped her the day before, grinned when she told him she was trying to get to Municipal Auditorium.

"It's three blocks that way," he said, pointing to his left. "Big white building at Thirteenth and Central. All decorated up for the holidays. You can't miss it."

The evening air was fresh and crisp. There was a chance of snow overnight, but the walk was brisk and invigorating after a day spent catching up on work and touching base with friends at other publishing houses. One possibility that intrigued her was with a start-up aimed at up-and-coming indie writers. A college friend, Talia, knew the people involved and promised she could get Mallory's resume in front of them.

Kansas City's wide sidewalks were light with pedestrian traffic. A few blocks behind her, past the hotel, she could see bright lights and marquees. Earlier, in the hotel restaurant, she'd overheard two men mention a nearby shopping and restaurant area. Perhaps, when she got over being sorry for herself, she might check it out.

Municipal Auditorium's art déco façade soon came into view. The area was a sea of people decked out in gold and black sweatshirts proclaiming their allegiance to the University of Missouri Tigers. Mallory overheard several refer to it as *Mizzou,* just as Jake had. She made a mental note to find out where that nickname came from. Mixed in were a few blue and gold shirts emblazoned with Kangaroos. Kangaroos were cuter and cuddlier than tigers, and if she had to pick a team to cheer for, it would be them. She moved past the main entrance to a side door manned by a lone security guard.

"I'm here to meet Jake Springer."

"Who?" the guy asked, not bothering to check his clipboard.

"Jake Springer. He said to come here, and I would be allowed in."

"Sorry, lady. I've never heard of the guy. You need to buy a ticket like everybody else."

Before Mallory could step away, the guard turned on a megawatt smile. "Just kidding. Jake said to expect you. You're Mallory, right?"

Mallory smiled back at him and decided to have a little fun of her own. "What if I'm not? What if I just said that to get in for free?"

Suddenly the guard was all business as pointed toward the main entrance. "Buy yourself a ticket."

"I really am Mallory."

"I don't believe you. Go away."

They were at a standoff for a few seconds before his easy-going smile returned. He opened the door and motioned her past. "Five doors down on the left."

The interior was lovely in a stately way, like the lobby of Radio City Music Hall, with rounded corners and ornate wall coverings. Mallory wandered the corridor and admired the architecture until she reached the fifth door on the left. She pulled it open, stepped through a curtain, and found herself amid a group of tall sweaty men in white jerseys throwing basketballs at her.

"Watch out, lady!" one of them called out as a ball zipped past. Before she could step back, another came her way that didn't miss. It smacked against her forehead and bounced off. Laughter rippled among the spectators in the seats above her as a security guard swept in and yanked her back.

"What the hell are you doing?" he shouted. "Stay off the court!"

Mallory was seeing stars as she croaked, "Fifth door..."

"You turned too early! Don't you know anything?"

Before she could find her voice to let him know that she knew plenty, Jake approached and took her by the arm.

"I got this, Avery," he said to the guard, spiriting her away from danger.

"Make sure she stays off the court, Jake!" the guard snapped as he headed off.

They stepped behind the curtain, out of sight of spectators and the tall men throwing balls. Mallory put her fingers to her forehead and winced.

"Let me see," Jake said.

She didn't move her hand. "I should never have come here."

"Coming wasn't a mistake. You just took a wrong turn. Let me see where the ball struck you."

She lifted her hand, and he leaned in to inspect the damage. He smelled nice up close. Clean, with a hint of cologne. She would have expected sweat or some discount store aftershave.

"Wilson," he said, touching the spot on her forehead.

"Who?"

"Wilson. The ball that hit you is a Wilson."

"How do you know that?"

He gently ran his finger across her forehead. "It says so right here. It left an imprint."

She pulled his hand away. "Oh, my gosh! Really?"

"No," he chuckled. "It's just a little pink. It will be gone by tipoff. Come with me. I'll take you to your seat."

She stepped back. "No way. I'm not going back out there."

Jake motioned for her to follow him. "Travis should have given you better directions."

"Who's Travis?"

"The security guard out front."

"Oh." Mallory glanced over her shoulder. "Well…he might have, but I got a little sidetracked, so…"

They returned to the corridor with Jake in front, then made another quick turn. When they entered the arena, they were on the side of the court rather than the middle. People seated nearby pointed at Mallory, and she expected more laughter.

"Hey lady," a beefy guy in a Mizzou sweatshirt called out. "You okay?"

"That was a hard hit," the woman seated next to him said. "Need anything, hon?"

"No, I'm okay." She looked at Jake. "That was certainly nice of them."

"Welcome to Kansas City. Not everyone is like that, but most of us are."

"I slipped on an icy sidewalk in Manhattan last month

and everyone laughed and made TikToks. Eight thousand people viewed them."

"Only eight thousand? That's nothing. Did Marcus Key show you the nacho video?"

"What nacho video?"

Jake grinned. "It can wait. The game is about to start."

Mallory Newell actually had a soft side. Who would have guessed?

All it took was getting smacked upside the head with a basketball to bring it out. The only question that remained was whether she owned any clothes that weren't business attire. Who wore a skirt and blazer to a basketball game?

Jake led her down press row to their seats near mid-court. Several more fans and a couple of journalists asked Mallory if she was okay. Their kindness reminded Jake of yet another thing besides barbeque that he loved about his hometown. They were getting seated when the scorer blew the horn alerting the teams it was time for tipoff. The sound startled Mallory. She was very much out of her element and obviously knew nothing about basketball. Perhaps he could fix that. He leaned in closer and identified the two teams.

"Yes. I saw them outside."

"You saw the teams outside?"

"No. The people who came to support them."

Jake smiled. "Their fans?"

She nodded. "There are a lot more supporters of the Tigers."

"They're the big state university. UMKC is more of a local school."

"I'm choosing them. The Kangaroos."

He laughed. "You'll probably lose, but that's certainly your prerogative."

"Yes," she said as the refs and players moved to center court. "It certainly is."

While he paid close attention to the action on the floor, Jake occasionally checked Mallory out, too. She sat in quiet, rapt attention as the first half played out. As predicted, Mizzou pulled out to a quick lead. They were larger and more physical, but UMKC kept it from becoming a blowout. The first half ended with Mizzou up by eight.

"Well," he said, turning so he was facing her. "What did you think?"

"They certainly are in incredible physical shape. The way they keep going up and down the field like that." She picked up her purse and placed it over her shoulder, then rose from her seat. "The game didn't last as long as I thought it might. Did the Kangaroos win?"

"Oh, no. It's only halftime."

She glanced at the overhead scoreboard. "There's more?"

He motioned to her chair. "Yes, but we have a few minutes now if you want to talk."

Mallory sat back down. "Did the Kangaroos do well?"

"Not bad. They're keeping it closer than I thought they would. You really don't know basketball at all, do you?"

She shook her head.

"Didn't you go to your high school games?"

"I was homeschooled."

"Did you father watch sports?"

"Perhaps. I don't remember, really. Our family likes to read. I guess that's why I work in publishing. What do your parents like to do?"

"Get high, get drunk, and lose money in casinos."

Mallory appeared stunned by his revelation. She started

to speak, but was cut off by a kid seated a few rows behind them.

"Excuse me?" the kid called out as he came closer. "Can I have your autograph?"

Jake wasn't sure who the kid was speaking to. He was looking toward both of them. He stood up and moved toward the kid, but he shook his head and pointed to Mallory. "Not you. Her."

Mallory's hand went to her chest. "You want my autograph?"

"Yeah… Yes, please, ma'am. It's for my father." The kid pointed over his shoulder at a guy in a Kangaroos t-shirt.

"Well…sure. Does your father like books?"

The kid handed down a game program and pen. "He likes them okay, I guess."

Mallory looked at Jake, shrugged, and signed the program. The kid glanced at her signature, said thanks and returned to his seat.

"That ever happen before?" Jake asked.

"Never. And if it were to happen I would never expect it here."

"What does that mean? You think Kansas Citians don't read?"

"I'm sure they read, but who would know an editor? I get recognized sometimes, but mainly among the New York literary set. And they would never ask for an autograph."

"Well, you might be more famous than you know. Now, tell me what you thought about my writing, Miss Famous New York Editor."

She blushed. It was adorable. As she pulled several printed pages from her bag, the kid returned. "Excuse me, but my dad wants to know who you really are."

"I thought he knew," Mallory said.

"He thought you were that lady from ESPN."

The look on her face was more than Jake could handle. The laughter came hard and fast.

"What?" A look of irritation clouded her face and made Jake laugh harder.

"He…the kid's dad thought… Oh, heck, that's great. He thought you were a TV reporter." He got it under control before adding. "You do kind of look like you could work on TV. Especially dressed like you are. Except for the purple bruise on your forehead."

When her hand went to the spot, he smiled. "I'm kidding. You can't even see it."

Mallory stared at him for a few moments, then pointed to the printout in front of her. "If you want something to laugh about, start with this."

She hadn't meant to sound so harsh. Back and forth banter had never been Mallory's strong suit. But before she could apologize, Jake was already staring at the red markings covering the pages. The more he read, the more discouraged he looked. Like a child who just had his favorite toy snatched away by the town bully.

Except this time Mallory was the bully.

His face crumpled as he tried to make sense of her corrections.

Vague descriptions.

Shifting points of view.

Passive tense.

But the worst was on the last of the five printed pages, and as the teams returned for the second half, she wished she hadn't been so damned blunt. If only the game would hurry and start before he reached that page. It didn't, though.

He placed an index finger under her closing comment as he read through it, almost like a small child learning to read.

This is boring. It goes no place. Your writing makes me not care about Stella or Terrence. It's more like a travelogue than a story. Make it a story.

The look in his eyes made her heart hurt. Sure, part of her job was to be a gatekeeper for the craft of writing. Keep out those whose talent didn't measure up. But she was starting to worry she had crushed Jake's soul.

Then he smiled and she knew she hadn't.

"You're exactly right," he said with more gratitude than she deserved. "How do I correct that?"

She reached out and touched his chest above his heart. "Good writing comes from here."

He looked down at her hand, then into her eyes. "My left nipple?"

That made them both laugh.

"I'm leaving town in the morning, but I'll keep working on it." He picked up the pages and ripped them up. "How about a fresh start?"

She smiled. "That's a good idea. Try to think of the emotion you felt the first time you met Miss Kansas Coed."

He rolled his eyes. "It was a work meeting."

"Then think of how you felt on another first date."

He gave it some thought before saying, "Thanks for your support." He turned back to the game. "And I'll be sure to put more of my left nipple into it next time."

CHAPTER FIVE

FRIDAY, DECEMBER 1

Michael Harper stood courtside and scanned the sea of faces as they arrived and found seats in the bleachers. Nearly all were regulars. Parents of the home team sat on one end, students on the other. A handful of fans for the visiting team clustered in the smaller bleachers on the far side of the gym. Michael's primary concern was students. As principal of Adair High School, their behavior was his responsibility, and he wouldn't hesitate to throw out any who got out of line. They appeared to be settling in, though, and the game would likely be a rout, as Adair's boys' team wasn't very good. He surveyed the late arrivals as the teams prepared for tipoff, then moved to his usual spot against the wall near the exit door where he could watch the comings and goings.

What promised to be a boring night of basketball in the boring little hamlet of Adair became a bit more interesting when a lovely blonde stranger walked in. She scanned the crowd and didn't see the errant basketball coming toward her. Michael jumped forward and batted it out of the way.

❄

Wait a minute.

Mallory looked up from her laptop just as the taxi arrived at the airport. With Jake on the road to Oklahoma and nothing better to do in Kansas City, she had booked a last-minute flight home. She would check in at the office, then surprise Hogan when he returned from work. With time to kill, she opened the updated manuscript Jake emailed earlier that day.

What was he up to? His writing had taken a sudden change in direction, introducing a new character, Michael Harper, in a scene that mirrored reality. She considered emailing Jake to find out why, but decided it could wait until she made it to New York. Her flight took off in forty minutes, and there was still security to contend with. Still, as she exited the taxi and rushed into the airport, she couldn't get the sudden change out of her mind.

It made her want to keep reading.

It happened at what seemed like triple speed. Or maybe even super quadruple speed.

Stella turned just as an orange blob was rocketing toward her face. She flinched and prepared for contact. And probably a broken nose. But at the last moment, a hand came out of nowhere and smacked the blob away.

That hand was attached to a wrist. The wrist to an arm. The arm to a man. The rest of him was there, too. A very handsome man. Wearing a sports coat and tie. And jeans. The combination was all wrong, but somehow he made it work.

"That was a close call," he said with a grin.

"Thanks for saving me. I was looking for someone instead of watching what was happening right in front of me."

"Are you with the visiting team?"

"No. I'm here to meet a man."

He chuckled. "Well, you're in luck. I'm a man. Michael Harper."

Stella's face became hot. "No...I'm not here to actually meet *a man. I already have one. He's here someplace."*

He looked disappointed. "Perhaps I can help you. What's his name?"

"Terrence Firestone. He grew up here. Perhaps you've heard of him. His family operates Firestone Realty. It's the largest realtor in Adair."

"I know Terrence. We went to school together. He's not here, though. In fact, I can't recall ever seeing Terrence at a game."

"His nephew is on the team." Stella scanned the sea of faces. "Are you sure he's not here? Perhaps you missed him."

"I never miss a familiar face. It's part of my job."

She looked up at him. "Your job? Are you a police officer or something?"

"Sort of. I'm high school principal."

A heavily tatted redhead strutted past. She batted her eyes as she said, "Hi Michael, honey." The principal groaned just loud enough for Stella to hear.

"Good evening, Renee. Hey, have you seen Terrence?"

"Why would I see that sumbitch?" Then, after glancing at Stella. "Are you the new girl at the paper plant?"

"You mean Patterson Paper? Yes, but I've been there for five months."

Tat girl rolled her eyes. "Yeah, I've heard about you, sweetie. We all have." She kept her eyes on Stella as she answered the principal's question. "I imagine you'll find Terrence at the Thompson place."

Michael looked at her curiously. "Are Tony and Anne thinking about selling? They've lived there since I was a kid."

Again with the eye rolling. "Tony and Anne are in Weber City for the evening. It's just Kayla at home tonight." Her eyes bored into Stella's as she added, "And Terrence."

Tat girl flounced away. The principal's carefree expression was gone. He averted his gaze. "Perhaps you should find a seat. I'm sure if Terrence said he would be here, he'll be here."

"No worry. Work keeps him late sometimes. Perhaps I should try to catch him at the Thompsons. Do you know where they live?"

He took her elbow and guided her away from the door. "That might not be a good idea... I'm sorry, but I don't think I caught your name."

"Stella." She extended her hand. "Stella Duvall."

He took her hand in his. "Good to meet you, Stella. If I were you I would wait here for Terrence. Or just go home."

"What aren't you telling me, Mr. Harper?"

The moments passed while he considered her question. "Perhaps we should go someplace where we can talk."

It was two-fifteen when Mallory's plane touched down at JFK. She wanted to make an appearance at the office. She also wanted to read more of Jake's manuscript. As much as she hated to admit it, he had her hooked. Sure, it would all have to be rewritten. It didn't come close to matching the tone or style of Georgia Springer's prose. But before they hit the delete button she wanted to find out what was going on with Terrence. Was he fooling around with Kayla Thompson? He had always been so upright and chivalrous in previous books. Jake was probably just creating conflict. After all, Stella and Terrence were destined for the wedding altar. That was the way things happened in Georgia Springer's world.

But Jake wasn't Georgia. That much was apparent. And why had he created the scene at the gym? The ball nearly smacking Stella in the face? And having Michael step in at the last moment to save the day? What was that about? Was it his way of mocking her embarrassing moment the night before, while casting himself as the hero?

She hailed a cab, gave the driver the agency's address, and settled in to find out what Terrence was doing with Kayla Thompson.

But Jake Springer had other ideas.

"It's probably nothing," Michael said as they got into his car and pulled out of the school parking lot. He rarely ditched his crowd control responsibilities, but this time he felt it necessary. "Yep, probably nothing at all."

He knew better. Everyone knew better. Terrence Firestone had always been a skirt chaser. Women fell for him because of his family's money. They had controlled the real estate market in Adair for generations, and while Terrence never worked more than a few hours a week, he took full advantage of his family name and standing in the community. Single women. Married women. He'd even stolen Addison Bracker away from Michael a few years before. A young guy living on a teacher's salary was no match for the expensive gifts and exotic vacations Terrence offered. It lasted four months before Terrence cast her aside. Addison made overtures that she was interested in rekindling things with Michael, but the stink of Terrence Firestone was more than he wanted to deal with. The man was trouble in expensive clothes and a nice manicure.

But Kayla Thompson? She graduated just last year. She was a college freshman, for goodness sake. Fifteen years younger than Terrence. Damn it all, that was over the line.

He should have just left it alone. Poor Stella needed to find out for herself what Terrence was really like. But he couldn't leave it alone. She deserved better. And he was tired of Terrible Terrence's crap.

Did anyone call him that anymore? Terrible? Probably not to his face. The family held too much sway in Adair. Crossing a Firestone, even a low-life like Terrible, could have consequences.

And besides, there was something about Stella that he found himself drawn to. He wanted to protect her. He didn't want to see her hurt. And when Terrence was involved, there would always be hurt.

"What can you tell me about Kayla Thompson?" she asked. Michael took a deep breath and was preparing to respond when Stella's phone buzzed. "I need to take this," she said. "It's my boss, Mr. Patterson."

Michael pretended not to listen as she took the call. Her part of the conversation was short and succinct. "Yes, sir. I can be there. Certainly. It's no problem."

Then, after putting her phone away, "I'm sorry to inconvenience you, Mr. Harper, but can you take me back to my car? Mr. Patterson needs my help at the office."

Michael felt a bit relieved at having to cut the conversation short. "Certainly, and please call me Michael."

It had been nearly an hour since she'd entered the cab. Traffic was gnarled at every point along the route.

"Sorry for the delay," the cabbie said. "Word is that the Vice-President is in town to speak at Madison Square Garden. Plus there's the usual out-of-town yahoos who come here every Christmas to gawk at the decorations."

Mallory checked her watch. At the pace they were moving, she would arrive at the office a little before five. A few colleagues would be gone for the weekend, but most would still be hard at it. Nine to five was a pipe dream at Stratford and Key. The reality was sixty-hour weeks with a briefcase full of homework each evening. She considered redirecting the cab to Hogan's place, but he wouldn't be home before seven, so she settled back and continued reading.

Stella pulled into the empty parking lot and took the space next to Mr. Patterson's Cadillac. He was cryptic on the phone, but she suspected it had to do with the end-of-month financial reports. Those always led to questions whose answers could only be found in the voluminous file cabinets in the storage room. The filing system proved impossible for him to decipher, but Stella had mastered it early on. Her acumen in that area was so good that he had given her the first of three raises she had received in her few short months on the job.

"It's me, Mr. Patterson," she called out as she entered the reception area. "Do you need me to pull some files for you?"

He appeared in the doorway of his office. He was dressed casually, as if ready to go out to dinner with his wife. There was nothing casual about the expression on his face, though.

"No, Stella. That's not necessary. Please come in and sit down."

"Here we are, Miss," the cabbie said as he pulled to the curb. Mallory had been so engrossed in the manuscript that she hadn't noticed they were close. It was four-thirty. Plenty of time to catch up on office gossip and clear her inbox before surprising Hogan. She entered the building and was headed for an elevator when a receptionist called out.

"Mallory?" she said. "I thought you were in South Dakota."

"Hi, Cassie. It was Missouri. Kansas City, actually. I had a free weekend, so I flew back to catch up on some things. What's new here?"

"I'm not sure, but there's definitely something going on. I saw the partners heading to the third floor. Maybe you can get up there and find out. If you do, let me know, okay?"

It took a minute for an elevator to arrive, and when the door opened to the third floor, Mallory heard cheering and applause in the hallway connecting the floor's two wings. She arrived as Mr. Key was shaking hands with a very happy-looking Luis. She nudged a co-worker who was standing at the back.

"What happened?"

"Luis is Dawn Darby Endicott's new editor! He leaves for Bora Bora in the morning. Isn't that great?"

Mr. Key held up Luis's arm, and the room erupted again. Mallory suspected that most of the emotion was fake. At least a dozen of the thirty-some people clustered about aspired to work with the famous novelist. None more so than Mallory. The difference between them and her was that she had worked her ass off to get the position. More clients, more hours. More late nights and early mornings. Damn it, Dawn Darby Endicott was her destiny. She considered sneaking off to her office, but when she checked to see if the coast was clear, she caught Mr. Key staring at her. There would be no sneaking away. She applauded like the others and put on a happy face. Mr. Key left Luis to bask in the spotlight. On his way out, he made a point to stop in front of her.

"Come to my office," he said. No greeting. No asking how things were with Jake Springer.

"I really have a lot to do, Mr. Key."

"It can wait."

Flock of geese!

She dallied in her office for a few moments, fretting about what the boss might want. Had Jake complained? And what if he had? She had been hard on him, but it was necessary if they were going to get the book finished by Christmas. That's what she would tell Mr. Key. If he didn't like it? Well, she didn't know what she would say to that.

The outer office was empty. Assistants and clerical help at Stratford and Key punched a clock and were exempt from extra hours. She walked down the hall and found Mr. Key seated in the conference room where he usually held meetings.

"Sit down, Mallory. I was going to call you, but this is better."

Mallory sat. Mr. Key jumped right in. "This conversation is long overdue. That's my mistake. I understand you're submitting your resume to other publishing houses."

Flocking Flock of geese! So much for confidentiality. Someone somewhere had seen her application and called Mr. Key.

"Well, sir… Uh, yes I might've sent it to…"

He waved her off. "I sensed your disappointment at being assigned to help Jake Springer."

"No, sir. Not disappointed. Just…"

"You expected to be named as Dawn Darby's editor."

Hell yes, I did.

"Well, sir…I have worked hard. And I felt that—"

Key cut her off. "Let me tell you why you were assigned to Jake instead of Dawn Darby."

"Please do, sir. I'm interested in knowing—"

"You're not going to like it, Mallory. But I feel you need to hear this. If you choose to move on from Stratford and Key, I'll understand, but you're going to hear me out."

Twenty minutes later, Mallory returned to her office and locked the door. Then she cried. When she was cried out, she looked for something to throw. Something that wouldn't make a terrible racket and draw attention. She settled on a pair of mittens she kept in her desk drawer, but they did nothing to relieve the anger and resentment she was feeling toward Mr. Key. How dare he say those things.

Close-minded.

Unfriendly.

More focused on things than people.

Impatient.

How could he say those terrible things to her? And after all she had done for the agency. She picked up the mittens and threw them again, then pulled open her desk drawer to find that damned stress ball they'd given out at the company health fair. She remembered Luis had borrowed it a few weeks earlier for an impromptu game of hallway dodgeball.

Luis.

She ran circles around him as an editor. Why, just the previous month she'd found a misspelling and two dangling participles in a book he had edited. Inexcusable. Dawn Darby would be sick of him by February. His approach was all wrong. He tried to be an author's friend, always smiling and saying, "nice job." A simpering, insincere ass.

Who was on his way to Bora Bora.

It was nearly six when she checked her makeup and opened her office door. Quiet. Everyone had left for the day. What was going on? Was everyone becoming soft? Was Stratford and Key going to hell in a handbasket? Then she noticed the note taped on her door. She pulled it off, unfolded it, and read.

Mallory, I didn't want to disturb you. A bunch of us are meeting for drinks at Minion's on 31st Streetst. If you can make it, I would love to see you before I leave. I've learned so much by working with you and want to buy you a drink as my way of saying thank you. Best wishes, Luis.

She wadded up the note and tossed it in the wastebasket.

On her way out she stopped at Luis's office. The door was unlocked, so she went in and searched his desk until she found her stress ball. She stuck it in her pocket and left the building. She considered walking the fifteen blocks to Hogan's apartment, but an icy wind changed her mind. She hailed a cab, crawled in, and pulled out Jake's manuscript. At least she could lose herself in Stella Duvall's world.

Mr. Patterson's desk was strangely clean. Nothing but a single manila folder and a pen. He cleared his throat, clasped his hands on the desk in front of him, and said, "Stella, you know by now that I'm not one to offer effusive praise."

"Perhaps, sir, but I've never felt slighted. I enjoy working for you very much."

He nodded. "I feel the same. You've done remarkable work over the past few months."

Mr. Patterson paused, and in that pause, Stella had a feeling that something very important was about to slip away. There was a sheen of perspiration on his forehead as he cleared his throat again. "Stella, my son is moving back to Adair."

"That's wonderful, Mr. Patterson. I know how much you've hoped for this moment. Will he be working here?"

"As a matter of fact, he will." Another pause. Another feeling that something terrible was about to happen. "He's taking my place as head of the company. Marjorie and I have decided to retire and spend our winters in Miami Beach."

"Oh, how exciting! I hear the weather is delightful."

"It certainly is." He removed his glasses and cleaned them with a tissue. His hands were shaking. "Stella, my son is bringing the secretary who has worked for him in St. Louis the past ten years. We... He won't need you in your current capacity."

Though she had steeled herself for whatever he had to say,

Stella still gasped at the news. She wanted to say something–anything–that would justify her continued employment. The place had been a mess when she arrived. Mr. Patterson had cycled through many secretaries. She was the first to gain his trust and confidence.

But she knew it would be useless to attempt to convince him otherwise.

Family would win out.

"All is not lost, Stella," he said with a smile that lapsed into a grimace. "We want to offer you a position on the factory floor. You will be on the night shift, but still have full benefits." He paused, his voice lower when he said, "The pay will be substantially less, but it will allow you to remain in Adair, so..."

"Damn you, Jake Springer, you—"

"Lady, are you okay back there?" the cabbie exclaimed.

"No, I'm not. I'm pissed at the world."

He caught her eye in the mirror. "Anything I can do?"

"You can mind your own business and get me to where I'm going. And stop looking at me."

Mallory pulled her phone out, located Jake's number, and punched it in. She wanted to punch more than the number. Why was his writing hitting so close to home? The basketball game, the job issues. It was a reflection of her own life, except skewed somehow. Like those carnival mirrors that make you look really short or fat.

The phone rang several times before going to voicemail. She considered leaving a scathing message about how he needed to stick to ball scores and leave the creative writing to people who knew what they were doing, but Mr. Key's presence loomed large in her conscience, so she stuck the phone in her pocket and fumed.

The chastened cabbie pulled up to Hogan's apartment building. Mallory mumbled an apology as she paid the fare. Something like surprise, or maybe fear, crossed the doorman's face as she entered the lobby.

"Uh…hey Miss Newell. Can I help you?"

Why was he acting so strange? She'd become a semi-fixture in the building over the past few months. She even knew his name.

"Hi Charles. I'm here to see Hogan. Like always."

He said nothing more. She caught the elevator and rode in silence to the nineteenth floor. She stepped out just as the door to Hogan's apartment opened, and a brunette scampered out and down the hall in the opposite direction.

And just like Stella Duvall, she felt something very important was about to slip away.

Hogan wanted space.

He wanted them to see other people.

And he already had his other person picked out.

And had for a month.

Any doubt as to how close they had become was put to rest when Mallory spotted a second toothbrush in the bathroom. It wasn't hers. It was green. Hers was pink. For whatever reason, she focused on that instead of the real matter at hand—the bimbo who was banging her boyfriend while she was out of town.

"Where's my toothbrush?" she practically screamed as she rifled through the bathroom closet, tossing toiletries and several pairs of Hogan's tighty-whiteys to the floor. "I need my damned toothbrush!"

He tried to calm her—but there was no calm to be had—so he pulled her toothbrush from a far corner of the cabinet and handed it over. Mallory wielded it like a knife and considered jabbing it at him but knew it wouldn't have the desired effect. And besides, there was a tiny blob of toothpaste on the tip. The best she could hope was to leave a nasty toothpaste stain on the front of his ugly-ass Christmas sweater. She tucked it into her coat pocket with the stress ball, then headed for the door. Hogan followed close behind, begging her to reconsider. She pulled out the stress ball and hurled it at him.

"Take that, you bastard!"

It was after ten when Mallory reached her apartment. The building's boiler was working overtime, and her place felt like a sauna. She threw her overnight bag on the sofa, headed to the kitchenette, and popped the cork of the first bottle she found. She grabbed a glass, reconsidered, and drank straight from the bottle.

It didn't take long for the booze to have its desired effect. Mallory was drowsy. Her nerves were less jangled. She changed into her flannel jammies and crawled into bed, dragging her laptop along.

Because, despite every shitty thing that had happened since arriving in the city, she still wanted to find out how things ended for poor Stella Duvall.

Terrence would understand.

He could help her make sense of everything.

But then Stella remembered. He was at the home of someone named Thompson. How long could it take to discuss real estate? She did a quick internet search to learn their address. She drove there on the outside chance she might catch Terrence as he was leaving. His car was still in the driveway, so she parked on the street to wait. Minutes passed with no movement. She considered heading to her cottage when someone knocked on the car window and nearly gave her a heart attack.

It was the school principal. She rolled down the window.

"Yes?"

"I checked your house first, but when I didn't find you there, I came here."

Stella tensed. "How do you know where I live?"

His smile was kind. "Adair isn't very big, and I've lived here my entire life." He paused before asking, "Would you like to go someplace for coffee?"

She shook her head. "I'll wait for Terrence. It's been a difficult evening, and I need his support. He probably won't be long."

His eyes flashed, making Stella wonder what she had said to make him angry. He looked toward the house, then back at her. Then back at the house. He blew air out through his mouth, then leaned in closer. "Do you mind if I ask you a personal question?"

"That would depend upon the question."

"Do you have a close friend in the area?"

"Not yet. There's a girl at my church that I've gone for coffee with, but I wouldn't say we're close. She has a boyfriend and we've talked about double-dating, but Terrence seems reluctant. He says he wants me all to himself."

He bristled. "Yeah, I'm sure. Look, Stella, it's none of my business, but—"

"There he is!"

All wrong.

Georgia Springer would be rolling in her grave about what her grandson was doing to her Stella Duvall finale. The

New York Times would write a review vilifying Jake and his editor for riding roughshod over an American treasure like Georgia Springer. Readers would revolt. Reviews would be terrible. No one would dare hire Mallory after it hit the shelves.

Jake's version of Stella Duvall didn't stand a chance in hell of ever seeing a bookstore shelf.

Mr. Key and the others would squash it like a bug under their shoe. They would demand that Jake return his advance. And they would make sure that Mallory never worked in the publishing world again. She would be waiting tables at some dreadful West Bronx steakhouse.

She grabbed the legal pad she kept bedside and started jotting notes.

Terrence has to be a good man.

Stella can't lose her job.

Michael Harper needs to stay away.

This is entirely too much like real life. Too interesting. Too good.

She crossed through that last line, then returned to the laptop to read more.

The poor, naïve woman. She certainly wasn't the first to fall for Terrible Terrence, but she was the only one without a support system to soften her fall when he broke her heart.

Did Michael really want to be her support system?

And if so, why? Why put himself out there? He had enough to worry about with running the school and completing his certification classes. Then there was the school board. Those self-serving snobs were always on his back for one thing or another. The only thing that saved him was that he was as much a local as they were. They might not like some of his decisions, but they knew if they called him out publicly, they would face plenty of throwback from locals who had watched little Mikey Harper mature from Pop Warner football star to prom king to teacher, coach, and for the last few years, school principal. He wasn't bulletproof, but he was close.

And if he wanted to reach out and help Stella Duvall understand how much of a snake Terrence Firestone really was, he would.

In fact, he was about to get his chance.

Terrence stepped out onto the Thompsons' front porch and squinted in their direction. Even in the dim evening light Michael saw he was disheveled. He recognized Stella's car first, and when he did, he turned to hurry back inside. Probably hoping he hadn't been spotted.

Too bad, Terrible.

Michael stepped back as Stella pushed open her door. She was unaware of her boyfriend's dalliances, and knowing Terrible, he wanted to keep it that way. Something about that struck Michael as very cruel. He would do what he could to level the playing field for poor Stella.

"Terrence!" she called out as she walked across the lawn, happy to see him. "I need to talk to you. It's been a—"

"Why are you here, Stella?"

Terrence's tone caught her off guard. She froze halfway across the lawn. "Why? I... like I said, I needed to see you. Mr. Patterson asked me to come to the office. I assumed he needed help with the files, but it was—"

"Mikey Harper? What the hell are you doing here? And why are you with my girlfriend?"

Stella turned from Terrence to Michael. "Mr. Harper and I met at the gym."

"She was looking for you, Terrence. But it appears you were... busy."

"Yeah...I had some work stuff." Then, focusing his attention on Stella. "I meant to call, but this came up at the last moment."

Michael wasn't having any of it. "Is Kayla buying a house, Terrence?"

"Don't be stupid, Mikey. It's not Kayla I'm here to see. It's her parents."

Time stood still. Stella had been listening back in the gym when Renee said the Thompsons were out of town. How she responded to Terrence's lie was her choice. Michael had gotten her that far. It was all on her.

She didn't disappoint.

"I want to meet the Thompsons, Terrence."

Terrible's eyes grew large. "This is work stuff, Stella. I can't go knocking on the door and introducing you. You know better than that."

Her voice grew quieter. "You're right, Terrence. I apologize for asking."

Was she letting him off the hook that easily? Maybe, but Michael wasn't. Terrence had twice called him by his childhood name, just another one of his ways to look down his nose at the kid from across the tracks.

Why not have a little fun?

"Tell you what," Michael said as he stalked past Stella and onto the front porch, "I'll introduce you. They're old friends of mine."

Terrence reached out and grabbed his arm. They stood there for a moment, an impasse that Terrence had no chance of winning.

"Get your hand off me, Terrible."

"This is none of your business, Mikey."

If only he had removed his hand before he called him that again. Every small town had a few people who deserved to have their asses kicked. Terrence was one of those people. It started in grade school when he'd made fun of Michael's hand-me-down clothes, then continued into middle school. It would have gone further had Terrible's parents not enrolled him in some swanky private boarding school in St. Louis. Private school exacerbated his arrogance. And made his ass more kickable.

Who was Michael to pass up the opportunity?

He turned so they were facing, his nose just inches from Terrible's.

"Take your hand off me."

"Stay out of my busin—"

It was just a shove, but delivered with enough force to deposit Terrible ass-first in the shrubs surrounding the Thompson's porch. With that done, he rang the doorbell. It was several moments before Kayla opened it. She was barefoot and wearing a skimpy robe.

"Terrence? Mr. Harper?"

Her eyes said it all. He might be Mikey to Terrence, but he had been Kayla's high school principal just a few months earlier. She was confused and more than a little scared.

"Do your parents know he's hanging around with you, Kayla?"

"Uh... They are... No, sir." Kayla was a lot of things, but she wasn't a liar.

"Please don't tell them, Mr. Harper. My Dad will... He'll be devastated."

"What you do with Terrible is your own business, Kayla, but I want you to look at that lady over there." He stepped out of the way so she could see Stella. Their eyes met, and something unspoken passed between them. Stella silently returned to her car. They watched her drive off. Michael grabbed Terrible by the legs and pulled him from the bushes, causing him to fall on his butt.

Michael spoke without raising his voice. There was no need. He had Terrible's full attention. "Hurt Stella again and Kayla's parents will hear all about you and their daughter."

Terrible appeared as if he might have something to say, but thought better of it. Michael left him lying on the dewy grass, hopeful it might leave stains on his rich-guy khakis.

The effects of the wine were long gone. Mallory was wide awake and very much on edge. It was as if Stella Duvall's life had converged with hers. It had to be a coincidence. There was no way Jake Springer had that kind of intuition. He wrote about sports for a living. He chased college girls and lived in the same house where he grew up. He was a fifteen-year-old in a grown-up's body. Nope, no intuition there.

But maybe…? Had he somehow known that—

Her phone jangled loud enough to startle her. *Jake Springer.* Returning her call. Probably wondering why she was bothering him when he was on a work trip. Or was it even a work trip at all? Men could be such liars. He was probably still in Kansas City, curled up with that cute little Kansas girl, talking about how difficult that straight-laced New York bitch of an editor was making his life.

She picked up the phone and snapped, "What? Why are you bothering me this late?"

"Uh…you called me."

"Well, it can wait. I don't want to take you away from… whoever you're spending the night with."

"I appreciate that, Mallory, but I'm alone. I just got back to the hotel. I'm here for work, remember?"

"So you said."

He was silent for a few beats. "What crawled up into your sphincter?"

"There's nothing in my…and that's a very crude thing to say."

"I'm not the one acting so snippy."

He had a point. But she wasn't done with him yet. "Answer one question. Did you know what was going to happen when I went to the office today?"

"I have no idea what you're talking about. What happened?"

"None of your business! Where did you get the ideas for the chapters you sent me?"

"Which ideas?"

"Stella losing her job, for starters."

"It just came to me while I was… Oh, no. Mallory, did you get fired?"

"No! And I told you it was none of your business."

"Then why are we having this conversation?"

"Because… And why did you have Terrence cheat on Stella?"

"I told you the other day. She's boring. They're boring. I'm trying to do as you suggested and bring emotion to the story. Do you like it?"

"I hate it. I mean, it's just…too real."

He chuckled. It made her want to reach through the phone and strangle him. "Then I guess I did okay, then, huh?"

Mallory took a deep breath. Did he not get it? Didn't he understand that he couldn't take Stella Duvall in such a different direction?

Obviously not.

"I'll see you this week. And plan on spending a lot of time learning how to write."

She disconnected before he could reply, tossed the phone aside, and went in search of another bottle of wine.

CHAPTER SIX

SUNDAY, DECEMBER 3

Her flight was thirty minutes late getting into Kansas City, but it wasn't like it mattered. Mallory should have scheduled a meeting to discuss Jake's latest chapter, but after her hissy fit and hanging up on him, she couldn't bring herself to get in touch. Oh well. It was just one more day. What was the worst that could happen? Being fired couldn't hurt much worse than sitting through Mr. Key's performance concerns. Did he think she could magically become a different person by holding Jake's hand while he finished the book?

Given the way the weekend had turned out, she wondered what her next move might be. A different job to go along with a different boyfriend? Did she even want a man in her life after the crappy way Hogan had treated her?

She exited the plane and was on her way to find a cab when someone called her name. She spun around and found Jake reclining across two seats. His Kansas City Royals sweatshirt was wrinkled, and he looked like he hadn't shaved in days.

"Are you catching a plane?" she asked.

"Nope." He sat up, yawned, and scratched his cheek. "I was hoping to catch you. I thought you might need a ride back to your hotel."

She looked him over as he got to his feet. "How did you know I would be on this flight?"

"I didn't. There are three nonstops from New York. The first arrived at four-thirty. You weren't on it, so I was hoping you would be on this one."

"You've been here for two hours?"

"Three."

"And if I hadn't been on this flight?"

He grinned. "I would have waited for the last one. It doesn't get in until ten-forty, though, so I might have ducked out for a cheeseburger."

"Jake, why? I can always take a cab."

"Yeah, but…you sounded pretty upset on the phone, and I thought this would give us time to talk." He paused before adding, "If you want to."

He was the last person she could envision unburdening herself to. But she'd already treated him pretty shabbily, so she kept that thought to herself. "I'm fine. Really. Just a few anxious moments. I'm sorry I hung up on you Friday night."

He waved her off. "Happens to me a lot."

"Really?"

He laughed. "No. Not really. As you saw with Gwyneth, women are attracted to my humor and good looks." He glanced at his sweatshirt, pointed to a spot that might be pasta sauce, and added, "Not to mention my cleanliness and hygiene."

Mallory laughed for the first time in days. It felt good. Refreshing. Maybe the world wasn't about to end after all.

"I'm parked in the short-term lot," he said as he grabbed her overnight bag and led the way out of the terminal. The weather was warmer than New York, but a heavy fog shrouded everything.

"Can you see to drive?"

"Are you forgetting I've lived here my entire life? I could find my way downtown blindfolded."

"Please don't. There's already been enough drama in my life this weekend. And if it's okay with you, can we not talk about the book? At least for tonight?"

"Fine with me. You hungry?"

While she had spent much of the weekend drowning her sorrows, she had barely eaten anything. "Yes. I am. Do you have a suggestion?"

He opened the passenger door of his pickup truck and placed her bag behind the seat. It was higher than a car, and when he offered his hand, she used it to hoist herself up.

"I've never known anyone who drove a pickup."

"Seriously?"

"Seriously."

He closed her door and went around the front. Getting in was second nature for him, but even in a sweatshirt, she could see the strength in his upper body. "We don't call them pickups here. It's just a truck. This one is pretty beat up. It belonged to my grandfather, and I can't make myself give it up."

"Sentimental value?" she asked.

"That and I'm cheap." He checked the time. "How about some Kansas City barbeque?"

"I'm not sure I like barbeque. Do they have salads?"

He rolled his eyes. "A salad at a barbeque joint would be like ordering a bologna sandwich at a steakhouse."

"You're taking me to a *joint*?"

"All the great ones are joints. That's the way we roll. No cloth napkins or fancy silverware. Just good food and plenty of it."

She thought about it for a moment. Then her stomach growled loud enough for him to hear.

He started the pickup...the *truck*, and said, "Barbeque it is."

Mallory looked beautiful. She was dressed in jeans, boots, and a flannel shirt with a puffy vest. But there was sadness in her eyes. Something had happened in New York. Jake had gathered from their brief phone conversation that it involved work, but she came back so there must be more. Was it something personal? Had someone hurt her? Could that be the source of her sorrow?

He pulled out of the airport parking lot and onto Interstate 29 toward downtown. Fortunately, traffic was light. Had it been a weeknight, the fog might have caused a few fender benders. If he kept his speed below forty-five, Jake was good to go.

The conversation was light, and there were numerous lulls as Mallory gazed out the window. He wanted to cheer her up—make her laugh as he had at the airport—but thought it would be better not to force it. It was a few minutes before nine when they entered the restaurant parking lot. The large sign and colorful building seemed to pull Mallory from her funk.

"Gates?"

"Named after the owner and founder. Been around since the forties."

He watched her survey the area. A few streetlights were burnt out, and the streets were empty. "Trust me. It's safe. And besides, I'm with you."

She smiled. "I'm from New York. I can handle myself."

"Yeah, but the big question is, can you handle a mess of Kansas City ribs?"

She shifted her gaze to the restaurant. "Bring it on."

She stuck close to him, because regardless of how much bravado she might claim, she wasn't in New York. She understood the ebb and flow of her hometown, where the sidewalks teemed with pedestrians regardless of the time of day. The area surrounding the restaurant was quiet and dimly lit. He opened the door for her, and her senses were overcome with indescribable aromas. There was a smoky quality in the air that was quite pleasing. They were barely inside before a counter worker shouted, "Hi, may I help you?"

"Oh, my gosh. I have no idea what I should get," Mallory said to Jake.

Again, the server called out. "Hi, may I help you?"

"Just a minute, please," Mallory replied as she scanned the menu board. Barely ten seconds passed before another worker blurted out the same question.

"Don't worry," Jake said. "It's what they do. Want me to order for you?"

The menu was immense, with cryptic selections like long and short ends, a four-bone, and something called burnt ends. Jake's offer seemed the best option. He spent a few moments studying the menu while the server again asked if they could help. "We'll have a half-slab, an order of burnt ends, a side of beans, a side of fries—"

"I don't eat fries."

Jake gave her a strange look. "You don't eat fries?"

"No."

He turned to the server. "She doesn't eat fries."

"Honey," the server said. "You ain't had our fries."

Jake pointed his finger at Mallory. "She's right. You haven't had their fries. And you said you wanted me to order."

She sighed. "Okay, but I'm not eating any fries."

He smiled, then continued the order. "Fries, extra crispy, two strawberry sodas—"

"I've never had strawberry soda. Isn't it for kids?"

"Ignore her," he said to the server. "Two strawberry sodas and two slices of yammer pie."

"Wait. What's yam—"

He raised his finger as a reminder that he was doing the ordering, then pulled out his wallet.

"Let me pay half," she said.

"Nope."

"Seriously. I'm on an expense account. Let me—"

"Can't a guy buy a lady dinner anymore without a lot of debate?"

The words, delivered good naturedly with a twinkle in his eyes, made Mallory smile.

"Suit yourself, Mr. Springer."

Jake watched her reaction as he placed the heaping tray of food in front of her. He saw interest, intrigue, and a bit of uncertainty. As he was moving the food around, a fry fell from one of the plates. Mallory grabbed it before it hit the table and shoved it into her mouth.

"There. Are you happy? I ate a… *Oh, my gosh.*" Pleasure was written all over her face as she grabbed another. Then another. "You can keep the other stuff. I'll just eat these," she said through a fry-filled grin.

"Slow down. There's plenty more." He placed a rib on her

plate, then playfully swatted her hand when she reached for a fork. "Ribs are finger food."

Mallory bit into it tentatively, chewed slowly, and smiled. "That's great." She took another bite, bigger than before, then turned her attention to the food still in front of her.

"Burnt ends," Jake said, placing several chunks of meat before her. "Try it with sauce and without." She did and the expression on her face looked as if she'd discovered heaven on earth.

"Why don't we have this in New York?"

"You folks are too sophisticated. And you worry about stuff like heart disease and obesity. None of that matters here. We have our cardiologists on speed dial."

She laughed good and hard, and Jake thought he saw some of the sadness slip away. "It actually might be worth the risk," she said as she sampled the beans.

Nearly an hour later, their dinner had been whittled down to a pile of bones and empty plates. Mallory sucked the last of her strawberry soda through the straw, licked the fork she'd used for her yammer pie, and belched.

"Wow!" Jake exclaimed.

Her face reddened. "I'm so sorry," she said as she brought a napkin to her mouth.

"Don't be. As my grandpa would say, it's not bad manners, just good food."

She seemed considerably more relaxed when they returned to the parking lot. Jake again helped her into the truck. "Where are you staying?"

"The Fountain Monarch. The one in Missouri."

"They're both in Missouri. That place is about as fancy as it gets."

"Only the best for an employee of Stratford and Key. At least for now."

Jake let the comment slide. They drove quietly for several

minutes before she turned to face him. "Jake, thank you for a nice evening. You don't know how much I needed it."

"My pleasure. Thanks for going. I get embarrassed when I order that much food by myself."

She smiled, and it was lovely. She was lovely. Oh, sure, that sharp-tongued editor was underneath some place, but for the moment, he just wanted to be close to her.

"You're probably wondering what happened in New York?"

He shrugged. "I'm not one to pry."

"I got passed over for a job I really wanted. Then I found out that my boyfriend has been screwing someone else."

With no idea what to say, Jake said nothing. The awkwardness was palpable. And then he remembered what he had written the previous week.

Stella losing her job.

And her boyfriend.

"Oh, gosh," he said. "Mallory, I'm so sorry that…what I wrote. And what you went through." Without thinking, he reached for her hand and squeezed it. She squeezed back. Even through the darkness, he saw tears in her eyes. She fought them away, then smiled.

"I guess that's what I get for going back unannounced, huh?"

He squeezed her hand again. She squeezed back again.

"No one deserves that. Is there anything I can do?"

She took a deep breath. "Well…yes. You can write the best damn book ever."

He watched the road ahead, avoiding eye contact. "Can I? I heard what you said on the phone. About having to learn to write. I've been wondering if I've taken on too much. I'm not a writer. At least not a romance writer. Maybe we should call Marcus Key and tell him that I—"

"Jake, no."

He looked at her curiously. What was going on? And why was he consoling someone who had criticized him so harshly? It had been obvious that she thought him under-qualified to finish Grandma Springer's book. And now that he was offering to back out, she was objecting?

She looked skyward, searching for thoughts that Jake wasn't sure he wanted to hear. She kept ahold of his hand, though.

"Look, Jake…about that…I was wrong to say some of what I said."

Jake again said nothing, but couldn't wait to hear what came next.

"About your writing… When you broke away from trying to write like your grandmother…it was…"

"It was what?"

"It was good! I mean, Terrence has always been so… vanilla. I found myself rooting for Michael to kick his ass." She grinned. "I actually hoped Michael would just kill him so I didn't have to read about him anymore."

Jake feigned shock. "Kill Grandma Springer's leading man?"

"He's so damned boring. Now Michael Harper? There's a guy I would go out with."

Jake grinned. "Maybe there's a little bit of me in him."

"I suspect there's more than a little bit, but it was good, nonetheless."

"Yeah, you say that, Mallory, but as I read through it this weekend I started to understand where you're coming from. Grandma wrote the first third of the book one way, now I jump in and start changing everything."

"Yes, you certainly are."

"And Marcus will hate it."

Mallory nodded. "Probably. You've certainly disrupted

the status quo. Publishers like things to remain the same. And like you said, the beginning and the end don't match."

"I guess the best solution is for me to throw out what I've written and try to copy Grandma's style. Boring as it is."

They were silent for a few moments as an ambulance and two fire trucks blasted by. After they'd passed, Mallory said, "Or you could rewrite your grandmother's section of the book to match yours."

"Rewrite the great Georgia Springer? Isn't there a law against that?"

"Jake, if I can be frank, Georgia Springer's prose is so 1950s. She writes about the present day as if it happened two generations ago."

"Yeah, but what about her audience? I met a lady on the flight coming back from New York who adored my grandmother. What about people like her?"

"Some adapt. Some find other authors to read. Look, Jake, it's your choice. You decide what book you want to write, and I'll help you write it."

He thought on it for a bit as he drove. What did he want to do? There was no doubt that Grandma's understanding of the world had stalled after she left Missouri for New York. She still envisioned the Midwest as a sepia-toned place where bad things never happened, vice and corruption were nonexistent, and everyone was a virgin until their wedding night.

And as they drove along city streets on their way to Mallory's hotel, the familiar surroundings seemed to jump out at Jake. It was as if he was seeing them for the first time. He knew that there was plenty of good there, but also a lot of conflict and pain.

Conflict and pain. Two things missing in Grandma's books.

Two things that, he felt, were necessary for great reading.

"You know," he finally said. "Marcus Key never said a thing about *how* I finish the book."

"He gave me that responsibility," Mallory said.

"So…if I decide to change Stella Duvall's world?"

"You'll still get paid. It will be my ass facing the firing squad."

"Bad?"

She nodded. "Yeah. Probably."

Jake pulled under the Fountain Monarch's canopy, shut off the motor, and turned so they were facing.

"Then I guess it's up to you what book we write."

Her smile was sweet. And sad. There was worry there, but also a flicker of excitement.

"Mr. Key told me Friday that I am close-minded and unfriendly."

Jake gave her hand a squeeze. "That's terrible. You're not like that."

"He also said that I focus more on things than people, and that I'm impatient."

"Yeah, he might be a right about those."

Mallory punched his arm. "Stop it. I guess my point is, he told me I needed to change my ways if I hope to move to the next level in the business. What better time than now?"

"Great point, but what if he doesn't want this much change?"

"Then I'll be waiting tables."

"And you're okay with that?"

She took a deep breath. It was obvious she had been considering the possibility. "Yeah, Jake, I think I am. On one account, Mr. Key was right. I've focused too much on climbing the ladder. Maybe now I just go with my gut."

"And what's your gut saying?"

"That you need to write this book your way. You showed

me a lot this weekend. Your writing is full of emotion. Your characters jump off the page. Very real."

Jake stroked the back of her hand. "Maybe too real?"

She groaned softly. "It was a hard weekend, but had I not experienced everything I did, I'm not sure I would have appreciated how much better you were doing."

It was a kind thing for her to say. And probably difficult, at least for the Mallory he had spent the previous week with.

She leaned in to catch his gaze. "So, are you up to it?"

"I'll try. As long as you're here to help me."

She squeezed his hand one last time, then pulled hers away for a second before sticking it out for him to shake.

"Partners?" she asked.

He shook as he answered, "Partners."

CHAPTER SEVEN

MONDAY, DECEMBER 4

Her kiss was soft and warm against Jake's cheek. He murmured with dreamy pleasure as he rolled over. Her breath was warm, and when she snuggled closer, he welcomed her. Her tongue found his lips. Now fully awake, Jake shuddered and pulled away.

"Corabelle, get out of my face!"

Corabelle barked and licked him on the cheek. She gave him her best goldie grin and looked toward the bedroom door. Her message was clear. *I gotta go!*

"Okay girl. Just let me take care of my own business first."

He pulled back the covers, sat on the edge of the bed, and stretched. Familiar with the signals that her potty break was moments away, Corabelle jumped down and headed out of the bedroom. She would be waiting for him next to the back door. Just like always.

Jake's thoughts returned to the previous evening. And Mallory. There had been a definite shift in their relationship. No doubt about that. But how much? Was she having some of the same feelings for him that he was for her? They had only held hands, but wow! It seemed to be much more than just one person consoling another. Had he misread the signals? He hoped not. They had held hands all the way back to her hotel. She'd confided in him about some hard stuff. She had to be feeling it.

Perhaps there would soon be time to explore all that. Maybe over lunch at that little French bistro in Brookside that he'd heard so much about or a day date at the zoo.

But no. He had to leave town. Work called. Kansas State was playing Iowa State 250 miles away. He had to leave by noon. Five hours in the car. Alone.

Or…maybe not. He reached for his cellphone.

It was a recurring dream. One she'd been having a couple times a month since she'd started dating Hogan. Springtime in Central Park. The weather, delightful. Sunny. Cool enough for a light jacket, but not so cold to worry that winter might return. The perfect New York City day.

Mallory and Hogan in a pedicab, one of those tricycle thingies with a covered seat in back for two people to get cozy while the driver pedaled. Thousands of them had passed her over the years, and she couldn't get over how happy the couples looked. Happy and so in love.

In her dream, Hogan always says yes to the pedicab. His arm is around her, keeping her warm against the breeze while their driver points out landmarks. It's just the two of them. Together. Close. No obligations, no worries. As they reach the head of the loop and begin the ride back, Mallory snuggles close and Hogan rests his cheek on top of her head. They are as close as two people can get, and she anticipates that moment when he tips her head and their lips meet. The expectation creates chills of excitement, and she's just about to reach up and pull him to her when he makes his move.

With more tenderness than he's ever shown before, he places his fingers on her chin and raises her head. Their lips are inches apart when she opens her eyes for one quick peek.

And finds that it isn't Hogan at all.

Because he isn't in her life anymore.

Instead, it's Jake Springer. Her breath catches as their lips are about to meet.

She wants very much to kiss him.

And then…

Mallory sat up, wide awake from the buzz of her phone. The room was dark thanks to the hotel's blackout curtains. The bedside clock showed seven-forty. She scrabbled about for her phone.

"Uh…hello."

"Hey, Mallory. It's Jake."

"Oh…hi Jake. I was…just thinking about you."

Yes!

She was actually thinking about him!

That would make what he had to ask a lot easier.

"I was thinking about you, too. I'm leaving for Iowa in a couple hours and wanted to see if you might want to go along."

"Where again?"

Her voice sounded heavy with sleep, but it was obvious she hadn't been. *Because she had been thinking of him!*

"Ames, Iowa. I'm covering a basketball game. And since you now like basketball so much, I figured you might want to go."

She chuckled. "Are the Kangaroos playing?"

"Not this time. It's the Wildcats and the Cyclones."

"Cyclones? Don't they kill people? It's sort of hard to cheer for that."

"They're friendly cyclones. So are the Wildcats. More like wild kitties. The game is tonight. I'll return home tomorrow."

There it was. Making sure she knew it was an overnight trip. We don't need any confusion on that little issue.

"I would love to go along and cheer for the friendly cyclones. And spend time with you."

Yes!

Yes! Yes! Yes!

"Okay! How about I pick you up at eleven?"

"I can't wait, Jake. I'll shower, pack, and be waiting for you."

She'll be waiting for me!

"Great! See you in a couple hours."

I wonder if they have pedicabs in Iowa?

If they do, is it too cold to ride in them?

Even if it is cold, Jake would keep her warm.

Just like in her dream.

Of all the things that crossed Mallory's mind while she showered, it was the pedicab that stuck. That and how the night might play out. Not the game. After the game. There would be that usual awkwardness about sleeping arrangements. It never went as smoothly as in the movies, where the guy swept the girl off her feet and carried her into the hotel room. Real life was a lot different. More tentative. And sometimes messy.

Was it too quick? Her brain might have some concerns, but they were being snuffed out by the excitement the rest of her was feeling.

Girl, you've known him for a week.

Shut up, brain.

You couldn't stand him a few days ago.

People change. They're different when you get to know them.

You're less than four days past a break-up you didn't see coming. Can you say rebound?

I'm not a teenager, stupid brain. I'm an adult. And the feeling of holding hands was... And the dream! Don't forget the dream. He was about to kiss me. In the pedicab. I want that! And brain, dreams come from you.

Not me, sweetheart. That was your raging hormones. They bypassed me.

Look, I'll be fine. We're two adults. If we want to...you know, we can. No harm, no foul, right?

Sure, until you have to be his editor again. Can you tell a guy you just slept with that his writing needs work?

Of course I can. It might be easier when he knows how I feel about him.

And what about Stratford and Key? Don't they have rules against this kind of thing?

Shut up, brain. Shut! Up!

You're already in enough hot water with Mr. Key. What if he finds out you slept with Jake Springer? What then?

It's Iowa, for crying out loud! How can he find out about something that happened in Iowa?

Maybe you're right.

Thank you.

And then again, there's always a chance that...

Jake was two blocks from the Fountain Monarch when Mallory's name popped up on his phone. Probably wondering why he was twenty minutes late.

"Hey, sorry I'm not there yet. I rented a car instead of taking the truck. It will be a lot more comfortable, and you'll —"

"Jake, I can't go."

"Oh, no, Mallory. Are you okay? Did something happen?"

"It's just… I have work to do. It'll be better if I stay here and get it done."

Her voice, so animated before, was flat. Almost unfriendly.

"Well…okay. I understand…I guess."

"Sorry for the short notice. If you have time, get some more writing done, and I'll review it when you return. Go back to the beginning and start revising what your grandmother wrote."

"I might have some time to work on it this evening."

Especially now that you're not going with me.

Yeah...don't say that.

"How about we get together tomorrow night? My place?"

The line was silent for a moment before she responded. "Maybe it would be a better idea if we meet somewhere… more conducive to work. The public library is open until seven. Could we meet there? Maybe five o'clock?"

"The public library?"

"Yes. It's nearby, and… You do know where it is, don't you?"

"Of course I know where it is. I grew up here, remember?"

He knew he sounded testy. Because darn it, he was. What was up with the change of plans? Why was she suddenly all business? Unless…

Had she reconciled with the guy in New York?

Jake wanted to ask, to confirm if his suspicions were correct. But she said she had to jump on a work call.

It would be a long drive to Iowa. And a long drive back. In a rental car he'd gotten so she would be more comfortable.

And a lonely night in a hotel he had hoped to share with someone he had feelings for. It was supposed to be an opportunity to talk. To really get to know her. To hear her life story and learn of her struggles and successes. To discover the things that made her happy. And the things that made her cry.

But it wouldn't be happening.

And not with Mallory Newell.

She was making it very clear that she was just his editor.

There wasn't any work to do.

No phone call either.

Mallory's day was wide open. Her night, too.

She had lied. A necessary lie, but a lie, nonetheless.

And she felt terrible about it. And as if that wasn't enough, her phone buzzed a couple minutes after noon with a call from the last person she wanted to speak to.

"Hello, Mr. Key."

It was hard to sound cheerful, but since she and Marcus Key weren't particularly close, Mallory thought she pulled it off.

"Mallory, I take it you made it back to Kansas City safe and sound?"

"Yes, sir. Sunday night." *After a hellacious weekend that you kicked off by being so damned critical of everything I do.*

"How is the writing going? Is Jake showing promise?"

"There is definitely improvement, sir. He was raw at first, but his more recent work is showing a lot more emotion."

"Is his style anything like his old bat of a grandmother?"

That certainly wasn't nice.

"That has been more difficult. His writing isn't as stilted as his grandmother's. In fact, we've been thinking about—"

"That's what you're there for, Mallory. You're familiar with the way she writes. I expect you to make it work."

"Sir, I understand. He… Jake… Mr. Springer has mentioned that he finds his grandmother's writing style boring."

"Incredibly boring," Key said. "But the show must go on, right Mallory? For one more book, at least."

"Yes, sir. The show must go on. And, Mr. Key, if I may circle back to our meeting last Friday, I have been considering what you said to me last week, and—"

"That will have to wait for another time. I have a partners' meeting in ten minutes. You do your best with Jake, and we'll talk after the holidays."

"Okay, sir. I'll call Charlotte and get on your calendar so we can…"

None of what she said at that point mattered.

Mr. Key was already gone.

And Mallory had nothing to do.

Oh, sure, there were always calls she could make. Job leads she could pursue.

But not today. What she really wanted was to get out of the hotel and do something. Anything that didn't involve writing, editing, or Stratford and Key.

Maybe lunch?

And not at the hotel restaurant. She was already tired of their uninspired takes on midwestern cuisine. Bland meatloaf. Pulled pork in a pasty sauce. Nothing close to the nectar they served at Gates. She wanted better.

She touched up her makeup, changed into a gray and black Dartmouth sweatshirt, and headed for the lobby. Patrick, the ever-present bellman, could recommend some good restaurants.

The bell stand was deserted, but all was not lost. The two guys she'd seen in the lobby several times since arriving were standing inside the hotel's front entrance. Though they had never chatted, they had developed a nodding acquaintance. One of them, a tall man with salt-and-pepper hair, came over.

"I hope this isn't being too forward, but we're headed out for lunch and thought we would see if you want to join us?" He held out his hand. "I'm Clay. My colleague's name is Brendan."

They looked safe enough, and it was Kansas City. Clay was probably in his late forties, maybe fifties. Handsome in that George Clooney way she'd always found attractive. Brendan was Mallory's age. Blonde, tan, receding hairline. The build of a guy who both worked out and worked outside. They were casually dressed. Their accents were northeast, possibly New York, but maybe Connecticut or Jersey. People from home.

Oh, what the heck. Why not?

"Hey, Clay, I'm Mallory. I would love to join you."

Clay and Brendan kept the conversation flowing on the walk to the Power and Light District, a beautiful ten-block square of office buildings, shops, and restaurants. They were in town as part of a team of architects, contractors, and construction workers renovating a former bank headquarters into loft apartments.

They picked out a sports-themed bar and restaurant across the street from a gleaming sports arena. The server led them to a booth near the back. Dozens of TV screens covered every wall, showing basketball, football, and a couple of sports Mallory hadn't seen before.

"Do you have a favorite?" Brendan, the younger guy, asked.

"Favorite what?"

"Team?"

"Not really. I sort of like the Kangaroos. I saw them play last week."

She could see from their blank expressions that they had no idea who the Kangaroos were. She considered telling them more, like how close her seat was to the action. And how she'd accidentally walked onto the court during warmups. She knew now it was called a court and not a field. Jake had gently corrected her. Not by calling her out, but by using the correct term several times while they'd chatted over the course of that evening at Municipal Auditorium. Hogan would have laughed at her.

Brendan was a fan of all sports, and through most of lunch his eyes were glued to a replay of a game he said had been played the night before. Rutgers and Temple. "I made sure not to check the score so I could watch the replay," he explained during a commercial break.

While interested, Clay wasn't consumed by the action on the screens. He lived in New Jersey, she learned. And from what he said, the project that brought them to town was his responsibility.

"My family and me run a consulting firm that makes sure the contractors stay on schedule." His fractured diction was a bit off-putting, but he made up for it with his attentiveness and conversation skill. He seemed enthralled that Mallory worked in publishing and, it turned out, he had done some work for one of their bestselling authors.

"Beautiful home out on Sagaponack. Are you familiar with that area of Long Island?"

"Only by name."

"Seven bedrooms, eleven bathrooms. I couldn't get over

how much house she was building. I mean, her kids are grown and have families of their own."

"She's planning for grandkids," Mallory said.

Clay looked at her curiously. Brendan's gaze remained glued to the game.

Mallory continued. "I know her a little. She was a stay-at-home mom who wrote while the kids were napping. Her first book surprised everyone. Tom Hanks made the movie. Sony bought it. She's never slowed down since. The only thing more important to her than her writing is her family. She built that house for them. A place big enough for everyone to be comfortable."

"She can certainly entertain them in comfort," Clay said with a laugh. He leaned in closer so he didn't have to speak as loud. "Mallory, you should see her writing space. Views of an unspoiled nature preserve on one side and a pond on the other... Wait a minute."

He pulled out his phone and scrolled through until he found the photo he was looking for. The writing space was as incredible as he'd described. And it was apparent that Clay loved his work.

They ate slowly so they could hold the table until Brendan's game was over. Cobb salad for Mallory. A turkey wrap for Clay. Brendan ordered nachos for the three of them but was the only one who ate more than a few chips. They mostly congealed in the center of the table while he watched the game.

"Have you discovered some good places to eat?" Clay asked.

"Mostly the hotel restaurant. I'm pretty busy."

Gosh, that sounded pathetic. These guys were experiencing all that Kansas City had to offer, while she chomped on generic hotel fare.

"I did go to a local barbeque restaurant…a joint, last week."

This got Clay's attention. "Which one?"

"Gates."

"Pretty greasy, I've heard. Not necessarily that place, but Kansas City barbeque in general."

Why was he dissing the food? The memories of the tray of deliciousness she'd shared with Jake made her want to defend it.

"You've heard wrong. It's amazing. You need to go. Try the burnt ends. And the ribs. And the fries. God, the fries are to die for. Ask for them extra crispy."

Clay laughed. "You sound like a local. Are you sure this is your first time in KC?"

Mallory shrugged. "I didn't even know that a lot of it is in Missouri."

"I keep wondering why everyone is so darned nice here," Clay said. "New York would chew them up and spit them out."

"I don't think they care about New York. And honestly, who can blame them?"

Clay asked what she meant.

"There is plenty to do here. At least from what I hear. The food is good. Everyone is friendly." She shook her head as thoughts of her previous weekend to New York poked through. "It's kind of sad how hardened we've become. Some stranger smiles at us, and we worry they're going to pull a gun on us. I'm starting to like things here."

The game ended. Brendan's team lost, but he wasn't beat up about it. He apologized for being an absentee lunch companion. They paid and headed back to the hotel. The afternoon was sunny and warm for December.

"What do you have going on the rest of the day?" Clay asked.

Brendan said he had to head to the construction site. "Our electrical crew is running into trouble with the thick walls the bank installed back in the day." He asked Clay if he wanted to go along.

"Yeah, I might. There are some things I need to check out, too. A little friction between your electrical guys and the crew doing the IT work." He turned to Mallory. "How about you, Mallory? Busy afternoon?"

There was no way she would tell the boring truth.

Nope, fellas. Nothing. Probably some TV. Maybe send out a few more resumes. Perhaps check out the fitness center.

They didn't need to know how far her career and personal life had tumbled over the past week.

She chose instead to keep it short. "Always busy. There should be some new chapters coming in from the author I'm working with."

"The sports guy?"

"Yes. He's doing some revising."

"What's he like, anyway? A good guy?"

Mallory wasn't about to share any of her real thoughts about Jake. He was a client. And those thoughts were incredibly complicated.

Kind-hearted.

Caring.

Handsome.

Single.

Intuitive.

"He's just…like any other client. He writes. I edit. Wash, rinse, repeat."

When they reached the hotel, Brendan stopped by the desk to check his account. Clay gently placed his hand on Mallory's elbow and steered her out of earshot.

"I'm going out for drinks tonight at a place I found a few blocks from here. Interested?"

"Oh, I'm sorry, Clay. Like I said, I have work."

He nodded and smiled, but she saw the disappointment. "I understand. I figured that, maybe later…after your work. The place has a band on Monday nights. Just a quartet, but they play a lot of slow standards. It's not real crowded or loud, which I like a lot."

"Thank you for asking, but…"

But what, Mallory?

Why not go? Why not listen to a band and have a few drinks? Clay seems harmless. And you're unattached now.

It wouldn't be right. I'm here to work with Jake, and he's...

He's out of town.

So, why not enjoy an evening out?

"Actually, yes, I would like to go. What time?"

"Is nine okay?"

It was.

Clay grinned. "We'll meet here."

It was a date. Her first as a newly single woman. Unless you counted barbeque with Jake. She decided not to count that. Because, after all, he was a client.

Nothing more. Just a client.

Clay was waiting when she stepped out of the elevator. He wore dress slacks and a dark sport coat over a pale blue oxford shirt. It was a good look. He wasn't one of those middle-aged guys who tried to look younger. He went with what worked, and it made him quite handsome.

"Wow!" he exclaimed as she came into view. She blushed but was glad she had taken her hair out of its usual ponytail and changed into the black slacks and creamy silk blouse. Clay seemed delighted with her choice. And that made her happy.

"You look pretty good yourself," she said. "Are we walking?"

"It's a bit too far. I had Patrick get a cab. I usually take my rental car, but not if I'm drinking."

He led her toward the exit where Patrick was waiting. He smiled at Clay. The smile disappeared when he spotted Mallory.

"Miss Newell?"

"Hi, Patrick."

"Are you going out tonight? With Mr. Markuson?"

"I sure am."

He held open the cab door. "Well, have a great time."

She stepped into the back seat and slid over. Clay followed. Patrick closed the door.

"Well, would you look who's back in my cab?"

Just hearing his voice made her smile from ear to ear.

"Tommy!" She leaned forward to pat him on the shoulder.

"Great to see you again, Miss Newell."

Clay watched with interest. "You guys know each other?"

"We met the day Miss Newell came to town." Tommy extended his hand to Clay. "I'm Tommy. Cab driver and part-time axe murderer."

Clay's eyes grew large. Mallory had a good laugh. "Tommy was very kind to me when I arrived. And being from New York I mistook his kindness for something sinister." She patted Tommy on the shoulder again. "I called him an axe murderer."

"But trust me, I'm not," Tommy interjected. "With my bum leg, getting away would be impossible."

The short drive was filled with conversation. Tommy wanted to know what Mallory and Clay thought of Kansas City. He delighted at hearing of her dinner at Gates, then recommended two other *joints* for them to try. Before they knew it they were in front of a dimly lit little place in a part of town called Westport.

"Good people here," Tommy said as Clay paid the fare. "The owner's name is Victor. Tell him you're friends of mine. That should get you a round of drinks on the house."

The name of the place was Padigan's, and as luck would have it, Victor was manning the host station. By mentioning Tommy, they were not only rewarded with a round of drinks, but also a table near the front. Not that it was necessary to be that close. Padigan's was intimate. Two dozen tables and a bar along the back wall. A small dance floor that might accommodate ten couples was located to the side. The band was warming up when they sat down, allowing a few minutes for conversation. Perfect for learning a bit more about Clay. They placed their drink orders, and Mallory dove right in.

"Tell me about your family."

What she really meant was, are you married? Attached? He didn't wear a ring, but that meant nothing anymore. There were other ways of finding out, though. And she intended to drill down until she knew the truth.

"Let's see," he said as a server dropped off their drinks. An old-fashioned for him, a pretty daiquiri for her. "Born and raised in New Jersey. High school in a town called Roxbury. Two years at community college, then three semesters at William Paterson University."

"Impressive. You graduated a semester early."

He smiled. "No. Actually, I dropped out."

Her surprise must've been evident. "It's not like you think. I was working summers for a construction company. The boss saw something in me, and by the time I was nineteen, I was supervising crews who had more years in construction than I had on earth."

"I imagine that was challenging."

"Yeah. At first. There were a few disagreements along the way, but we handled 'em."

His left hand clenched as he mentioned those disagreements. She suspected there was a story there, that Clay had probably had to use his fists to settle a score or two. He was very much a man's man. Sort of like a wild animal that tamed itself to fit into polite society. From where she sat, it was mission accomplished. He was handsome, well-dressed, and fun to talk to. Even if he didn't have a perfect grasp on the King's English.

"How about family?" she asked as the band members took up their positions.

He shrugged. "Like anybody, I guess. Mom stayed home and took care of me and my sister. Pop was a county cop. He retired on a pension ten years ago. They still live in the house where I grew up."

Mallory nodded but wanted to know more. It wasn't his parents she was wondering about.

"How about since then?"

"You mean wife and kids?"

Bingo! "Well, that and… Yes, that."

"Married at twenty. Divorced at thirty-six. Two kids. A son, Charlie, who lives with his family in Parsippany. My daughter's name is Hannah. She works for one of those think-tank places in Washington."

"Are you close to them?"

He shrugged and glanced away. "As close as we can be, I guess. They have their lives, and I'm on the road a lot."

Clay was about to say more when the band kicked off an old Frank Sinatra classic. Mallory reached for her drink. Her first sip nearly gave her a brain freeze. The daiquiri was icy cold and potent. No watered drinks for the owner's friends.

"Strong, huh?" he asked over the music.

"Whew." She laughed and took another drink.

The quartet proved perfect for the venue. Their song list, mostly older hits from the sixties and seventies, was purposefully muted. The slower, familiar melodies had couples on the dance floor from the start, and after a dozen songs and two drinks each, Clay asked Mallory if she wanted to join them. She had never been much of a dancer. Not that it mattered in the ear-splitting, overcrowded dance clubs she'd frequented with college friends. Hogan wasn't a dancer, and she missed the intimacy of two people moving together to a slow song.

Did Jake like to dance? Probably a question with an answer she would never learn.

Do your job and get out of town, Mallory. The sooner the book is done the sooner you can get on with your life. Whatever that might be.

But for now, a handsome man had asked her to dance. Hogan wasn't the only one with opportunities.

"I'd love to."

He stood and slid her chair out as the band began a Savage Garden tune from the nineties. Several other couples, mostly in their thirties and up, were also making their way to the dance floor. Clay took her hand and led the way, bringing to mind Jake's awkward description of Stella and Terrence's dance club date.

Spotlights swept back and forth as Terrence led the way onto the dance floor.

No ripped jeans in Padigan's, though. The Monday night crowd was dressy casual. Most of the men wore sport coats like Clay. The women were in dresses or dress slacks. Still, the memory of Jake's first few written words made her smile. Clay noticed.

"You seem happy to be here," he said, smiling back as they found their spot on the cozy dance floor. It was apparent that the surrounding couples were more familiar with one another. They danced close and their touches had a tenderness about them. Clay took her left hand in his right and pulled her close enough to slow dance without all of his parts touching all of hers. Nice. Conservative. She appreciated that.

And he knew how to dance. Not that it was necessary when they were doing little more than swaying to a slow melody, but he took the lead. His shoulder was just below eye level, allowing Mallory a view of the couples dancing nearby. A few danced silently. One couple, probably in their fifties, gazed into one another's eyes as they moved in perfect unison. The unspoken communication passing between them was obvious. Despite being well into middle age, they were still deeply in love.

And probably had a great time in bed.

Whoa! Slow down, Mallory. Get your mind off stuff like that.

Clay's timing couldn't have been worse when he asked, "What are you thinking about?"

If he only knew.

"Just about how…nice this is. It's been a while."

Some men might have made a joke of the unintended innuendo in her words. *It's been a while since...what?* Back in college, the frat guys she'd dated would have considered it an open invitation to take her upstairs. Even Hogan, in his thirties, could never pass up an opportunity to ply her for sex.

Clay was either very mature or very uninterested. And Mallory had just enough booze in her to hope it was the former. Even the most mature man would come around after enough slow dances and drinks.

And if he did come around? Was that what she wanted?

Yeah. Maybe. It would just depend on how the evening progressed. But so far, Clay checked all the boxes.

Handsome.

Mature.

Considerate.

Good dancer.

Unattached.

There was the age difference, but Mallory had always had a thing for guys in their forties and fifties. Especially the classically handsome ones. It probably came from the movies. Daniel Craig as James Bond. Gerard Butler. And older actors like Denzel and Brad Pitt, back when they were playing leading roles in the romantic films of her parents' generation. They knew how to take care of a woman. Not that she needed caring for. She had only dated sporadically after college and before Hogan. Her most consistent relationship was with her job.

Welp, kid, the job ain't what it used to be. And Hogan is gone. And Jake Springer is a client.

So why not get it on with the handsome stranger from New Jersey?

She moved in closer, so a few parts that hadn't been touching were. Savage Garden faded into a Chicago number from the seventies before the band jumped ahead to present day with a Sam Smith hit that was one of Mallory's favorites. Most couples returned to their tables, probably preferring the music of their youth to the music of the day. That left Mallory, Clay, and another couple with room to move. Not that they needed it. Mallory looked up and found Clay's eyes on her. The kindness was still there, but there was something else. He had probably noticed how she'd moved closer. His hand, which had rested on the small of her back, traced down a few inches. The effect was palpable. Mallory felt a flutter in her chest as she relaxed into his embrace. They remained there for the rest of the song and maybe longer. The next thing she knew, the band was playing an up tempo song she didn't recognize, and Clay was asking if she wanted to return to the table.

He helped her get seated, then slid his chair closer to hers. "Another daiquiri?"

She thought about it for a moment. She was feeling the effects of the first two, but they'd been at Padigan's for nearly ninety minutes. And she liked the way they made her feel.

"Yeah, why not?"

Clay placed the order, then returned his attention to her.

"How about you?" he asked as he slipped his hand over hers. "Anyone special in your life?"

"There was, but not anymore. I'm married to my work."

"Recent?"

"Yeah...pretty recent. But let's not talk about that. Why did you get divorced?"

Talk about nosy. Maybe the third drink was a bad idea, but it certainly would taste good.

Clay laughed off her question. "It's hard to remember sometimes. It's been fifteen years."

Their drinks arrived. Mallory wondered if he would use the interruption as an opportunity to change the subject. He didn't.

"Truth is, I never saw it coming."

Mallory sipped her drink, then asked, "Saw what coming?"

"Vanessa prefers women."

Mallory didn't know what to say. Her shocked silence caused Clay to laugh again. "My response exactly. Our romantic life had always seemed good. Things certainly slowed down after the kids, but that happens."

"How did you find out?"

"She told me when she asked for a divorce. We've been able to stay friends, but it wasn't easy. I'll be honest, Mallory, infidelity of any kind is hard to cope with, but when you find out your wife is leaving you for a woman? And you had no idea she even…liked that? It took me a few years to bounce back."

Clay's openness, and how he was able to express his feelings, made Mallory feel for him. As he shared more of that difficult period, she could see that he'd been very much in love with his former wife. And he'd been able to, with help, actually get through the pain and maintain a cordial relationship with her. It was a far cry from the way she felt about Hogan. They'd only been together a few months, yet she was still pissed enough to imagine burning down his apartment building. Sure, it was a stupid thought. There were ninety tenants in his building. It would be inconsiderate to penalize them just because Hogan was a low-life pile of poo.

Nothing like Clay.

She was halfway through the third drink when she pushed it away. "No more."

He nodded knowingly. "That's probably for the best." He leaned in and kissed her forehead. "How do you want this night to end?"

He remained close. Mallory felt his breath against her cheek. She lifted her face and met his lips. They kissed lightly. He pulled back a smidge and smiled before kissing her again. Whether it was the booze or that he was just the best kisser ever, Mallory couldn't be sure. Whatever it was, was pretty nice. And when he suggested they head back to the hotel, she thought it was a perfect plan.

They were barely out the front door before a cab wheeled to the curb.

"That's convenient," Clay remarked as he opened the door for her. The jolt she felt when his hand brushed against her backside made her gasp. He noticed and left it there.

"Fountain Monarch," he said as he crawled in next to her. The street around the bar seemed darker than before and the cab's dome light was burned out, so it was a moment before Mallory realized who was driving the cab.

"Hello again, Miss Newell."

"Tommy? Hi!"

He said nothing else as he pulled from the curb. Strange, but he probably didn't want to be obtrusive. Mallory hoped he hadn't noticed Clay's hand on her butt, and when he moved closer and nuzzled against her neck, she pulled away.

Later, she mouthed silently, motioning toward Tommy. Clay rolled his eyes and shifted a few inches away. She attempted to engage Tommy in conversation, but he remained uncharacteristically stoic.

And the cab ride seemed to take longer, too. They started along the same streets she remembered from before, and when they passed a few blocks west of the hotel, Clay said, "You missed your turn."

"Construction or something," Tommy snapped. They passed through the Power and Light District and several blocks further before coming to a stop at an underpass. Cars buzzed along the interstate above them, but the immediate area was dark and secluded.

"What are you doing, buddy?" Clay asked as he leaned closer to Tommy.

"Me and Miss Newell need to talk."

Clay said, "You should have thought of that on the drive to the hotel." He took Mallory's hand in his, a protective gesture that she appreciated.

"Nope. We need to talk now." There was a forcefulness in Tommy's tone that added to the scary feelings she was already having. He grabbed a folded newspaper from the seat and passed it back. When Clay reached for it, Tommy pulled it back. "It's for her."

"I don't know what your game is, but if you don't put the car in gear and drive us back to our hotel I'm going to—"

The cab was silent, other than Tommy's labored breathing. Mallory hoped the worst had passed.

Then she saw the gun.

In Tommy's hand it seemed huge. Mallory's first thought was that he really was an axe murderer.

"Here's what's gonna happen," Tommy said, his eyes on Clay. "You're going to get out and stand right over there under that lamp post."

"I'm not leaving Mallory in here with you."

"Miss Newell is safe. You, I'm not so sure about. Now get out."

Clay opened the door. Tommy said, "I'll leave the windows open so you can hear what is said, but if you make a move…" He waved the gun.

"You'll shoot her?" Clay's voice had risen, and Mallory was scared he might make a move that got both of them killed. "How could you?"

Tommy smiled, an expression completely out-of-place given the situation. "Miss Newell doesn't need to worry about me. But you do. Let's just say she and I need to have a chat about you and some stuff back in New Jersey."

Clay scrambled out of the cab and moved to the lamppost. Tommy handed her the newspaper. "Your bellman, Patrick, told me about this," he said. "We both felt you should know."

She was unfolding the paper when they heard footsteps outside the cab.

"Your friend just took off," Tommy said. "Probably for the best. Read the article at the top of the page, left side."

The paper was from Trenton, New Jersey. It was open to Page Four.

Roxbury Man Wanted for Bid Rigging.

The photo was a typical police station mug shot. The man's name was Phillip R. Bostock.

The face was Clay's.

"You can read through it, Miss Newell, but the gist is this. Bostock, or whatever name he's using, has a wife and family in New Jersey. He's been moving around the country using fake names to avoid detection."

"How did Patrick find this?"

"He grew up in Jersey. Whenever he tried to talk up Bostock about people and places back home, he always cut Patrick off." Tommy grimaced as he shifted in the seat. "Miss Newell, Patrick sees and hears a lot, and some of his family back home is engaged in… Let's just say, they know people who it's best to stay away from. Bostock crossed those people. They told the cops, and he's been running ever since."

"I can't believe that he's still married. He told me he was… Tommy, I think I need to find a new hotel."

"The Monarch will be fine. Bostock won't show his face there again. He'll disappear into the night, just like he did in Cincinnati a few months ago."

"How about the guy with him? Brendan?"

"That's his son."

"Flock of geese! Seriously?"

Tommy nodded.

"Why didn't you notify the police?"

"We did…and they were notifying the FBI, but who knows how long that might take? Look, Miss Newell, I got a daughter. She's a few years older than you, but if I knew she was out with a guy like him…"

"Do you think he would have hurt me?" Mallory's hands were trembling as she glanced out of the cab. Not another soul around. And no sign of Clay, or Bostock, or whoever he really was.

"He doesn't have a history of violence, but you never know. I think more than anything he just wanted some companionship."

Mallory took a few moments to pull herself together. Even after Tommy tucked away the gun, started the cab, and headed back to the hotel, her breathing remained ragged.

"Patrick alerted management, and they'll have extra security monitoring your floor, but like I said, Bostock won't be back."

"Tell Patrick I owe him a big thank you and a hug. And you..." She leaned forward and wrapped her arms around him. "You get your hug right now. Thank you so much, Tommy."

Tommy's grin made his entire face light up. "You're welcome. Not bad for an axe murderer, huh?"

There wouldn't be much sleep, so after locking and chaining the door, Mallory ran a hot bubble bath and slipped in. A security guy near the elevator of her floor had nodded and given a thumbs up. That made her feel better. The effects of the daiquiris were long gone. More than anything, she just wanted to tell someone about her evening.

But who?

It was nearly midnight in Kansas City, 1 a.m. back home. Her friends would be in bed. Jake would certainly find the story fascinating, but he was in Iowa, also probably asleep. And she didn't want to tell him *everything*. Dancing with a stranger was fine, but what would he think if he somehow learned she had plans for more? Especially since she'd put up walls around herself after they'd become so close.

And speaking of close, what had she been thinking? And how far would things have gone with Clay?

She knew the answer. They would have gone as far as things like that can go. She would have awakened the next morning next to a bid-rigging married guy on the run from some equally shady characters back in Jersey. Why was her life suddenly turning into an action-adventure movie?

She was an editor, for God's sake. A book-loving, slightly nerdy girl trying to find her way. Trying to keep her job. Trying to find love. And that last one. Love?

It might have been right next to her. No, not Clay. That wasn't love. The other one. The one who had held her hand while she spilled the details of her crappy weekend. The one who asked nothing of her in return.

The one in Iowa.

The one who would return to Kansas City tomorrow afternoon.

Yeah. That one.

CHAPTER EIGHT

TUESDAY, DECEMBER 5

The ping of an arriving email jerked Mallory from a deep sleep, one she hadn't expected after such a crazy night. She crawled out of bed and pushed open the curtains. Snow. A lot of it. At least a foot. It was drifting against storefronts and falling gently onto lamppost holiday ornaments. Other than a few tire tracks and a lone snowplow, the streets were deserted. A smattering of hearty souls trudged along the sidewalk, bundled against the elements as if it were Antarctica. Though it was three weeks until Christmas, Kansas City was ready.

She moved to the suite's living room and opened her laptop. Only three emails had come in overnight. One from the salon where she got her hair cut, another from her favorite bubble tea shop in Manhattan. The third was from Jake. Nothing from Stratford and Key. Nothing from any of the jobs she'd applied for. It was as if she'd fallen off the face of the earth. Kansas City was on the face of the earth, right?

She moved the first two messages to trash, then clicked open Jake's.

Mallory, here's the latest installment. Sorry not to get it to you last evening, but the game went to double-overtime, so I didn't get to my room until midnight. You'll probably notice that I didn't go back to the beginning like we discussed. We may not need to after all.

See you at the library at 5. Thanks, J.

There he was again, closing his email with his initial. 1998 all over again. Yet this time, it didn't bug her like before. It was who he was. A pretty nice guy.

Who also happened to be a Stratford and Key client.

And what had he meant about not having to change the beginning of the story? There was no way his story would jibe with Georgia's.

She opened the attachment and read the first few lines.

Stella was in bed but still wide awake when she heard someone at the cottage's front door. She pulled back the curtain just enough to see Terrence's car parked at the curb. She knew she shouldn't respond, but he'd been on her mind since arriving home. If it was the end of their relationship she at least needed to tell him. Face to face.

She threw on her robe and headed to the door, flipped on the porch light and peered out. He had changed clothes since his encounter with Michael, and even in the dim light she could see he was worried. But of what?

That he had lost her?

Or, perhaps, that Michael was with her? That she'd already moved on?

She opened the door and waited for him to speak. His lip quivered as if he might cry.

"Stella...it wasn't what you think." He took a deep breath. "If you've decided it's over between us, I will respect that. I'll get back in my car, and you'll never see me again."

"How can I not see you again? It's Adair. We're bound to run into each other."

He nodded. "Well, I guess so, but I'm begging you to let me tell you the whole story."

She held open the door and motioned for him to come in. She led him into the living room and took a seat in the wingback chair that used to be in her grandfather's den. When Terrence had been there before, they usually sat together on the sofa. He sat alone this time. Then, after pulling out a handkerchief and wiping his eyes, he told her everything.

"No!" Mallory's voice was louder than she'd intended for such an early hour. Her hands were balled into fists.

What was Jake doing? He had taken the story in such an interesting direction and now? He was pulling back? Like one of those silly dream sequences amateur writers used when nothing else worked.

Why, Jake?

Perhaps she was wrong. Maybe he was raising the stakes, making it harder for Stella to get together with Michael. Stella was too smart to fall for Terrence's lies. At least Michael's new and improved Stella was.

Throw him out, then call Michael and tell him you want to see him tomorrow! Yeah, it was late, but still…the two of you are perfect for one another.

She had to know if that was where the story was going, so she grabbed a bottle of water from the mini fridge, turned up the heat, and returned to the story.

And quickly learned her suspicions were correct.

Gullible Stella bought Terrible Terrence's story that he had gone by the Thompson place to see Kayla's parents about a parcel of land they owned outside of town.

"Kayla said they would be home anytime, and I should come in and wait. Then she excused herself to run upstairs. When she returned, she was wearing the robe you saw her in. She came on to me, Stella. Completely unexpected. I was able to hold her off, but not before she had crawled into my lap and..."

Just remembering the events of the evening caused his breathing to race. He took a moment to get it under control, then said, "Michael Harper has always had it out for me. He was a bully in elementary school and junior high. It got so bad that my parents enrolled me in a private school. It was the last thing I wanted, but I was scared to go to school, knowing he would be there waiting to beat me up."

He hung his head and gulped back a sob. Stella moved to sit next to him. She put her arm around him as he trembled.

How could she have been so wrong about dear Terrence? And about that deceitful Michael Harper?

A half-hour later, their relationship was mended, and Stella walked him out onto the porch. When he turned and took her in his arms, she didn't object. Earlier, she had hoped it might be the night of their first kiss.

She looked into his eyes and knew he was the man she would spend her life with. Maybe it wouldn't always be perfect, but somehow, she would make it work.

The first kiss was sweet and soft at first until Terrence pressed in. When she felt his tongue trying to find its way into her mouth, she pulled back.

"Not too fast, please," she whispered. He reluctantly agreed.

"May I see you tomorrow?"

She nodded. "I would like that."

Terrence kissed her hand, then stroked her cheek before stepping off the porch. She watched him go to his car and drive away. He was cresting the top of the hill at the end of the street when she lost sight of him. The night was silent, and the street was deserted except for one car parked across the street two houses away. She looked closer and saw the window was down. Someone was seated inside. Watching.

It was Michael.

She turned away, went back into the house, and shut off the porch light.

Why?

The sudden change hit like a gut punch, and the last thing Mallory needed after the events of the past few days was another gut punch.

She'd cheered for Stella as she coped with the problems life was throwing at her. She'd lost her job and her guy, but Mallory felt a strength emerging that she couldn't wait to watch blossom. She came away with a feeling that better things were ahead for former wallflower Stella Duvall.

And then Jake went and reversed course. It was such a typical guy thing. Just as a girl finds her voice, there's some man trying to take it away. Mr. Key and the bigwigs back in New York would certainly approve. They were happy to maintain a status quo that kept them at the top of the food chain while the profits rolled in. But from an editorial standpoint, Jake yanking Stella from that fifties mindset into today was a stroke of genius.

Why was he reversing course?

It wasn't the first time she'd seen authors regress in their writing. It usually happened between books, though. Once they'd experienced the success of a first book, they paid less attention to their craft and more attention to sales numbers and reviews. She couldn't count the number of authors who, after a breakout bestseller, suddenly thought of themselves as Harper Lee or Ernest Hemingway. Mallory had worked with a couple of them. Their newfound prominence brought with it an arrogance that, if not held in check, would guarantee fewer big paydays in the future.

But that wasn't Jake. There was no arrogance there. No feeling of sudden entitlement. He had readily admitted he needed her help. They'd even shaken on it two nights earlier.

Partners? Partners.

Was the stress of writing while holding down a full-time job too much? He didn't appear to have a problem with it, but some people were good at internalizing that stuff. And as a partner in a fledgling website, he constantly faced the pressure of keeping up a steady stream of content.

But the chapter he'd sent that morning? That didn't come from his heart. It was more like a Georgia Springer template.

And Mallory hated it.

And later that afternoon, when they met at the library, she would tell him.

And try to find out what caused the change.

Thoughts of that conversation were put on hold as an email arrived from Cheshire Publishing, one of the big New York houses. Word on the street was that they had an opening for an editor in their historical fiction division, and while that wasn't Mallory's favorite genre, it could serve as a steppingstone. With fingers crossed, she opened the message.

Dear Applicant,

Applicant? They hadn't even bothered to insert her name. She scanned the rest of the message. Boilerplate. Stratford and Key had one just like it. A way to blow off applicants with no one having to actually put any work into it. Some secretary, probably floors away from the decision makers, had pushed a button that generated an email response that kindly blew Mallory off. She moved it to the trash where it could slither off into oblivion while she took a hot shower and made a trip to the hotel coffee shop.

But while closing her computer, she caught sight of Jake's earlier email. Would he be able to get back to town? Was there snow in Iowa? How were the highways? She hit reply and typed out a message.

There is a lot of snow here. Be careful on your trip back.

And she signed it, *M.*

She spotted Jake as he entered through the library's ornate bronze doors. She had arrived twenty minutes early to scope out the place. It was lovely, both inside and out. Marble columns provided a feeling of safety and stability. The kind of place where a person wouldn't mind curling up with a good book and spending a few hours. A helpful librarian had offered the use of a private room for their work session, but Mallory preferred a table on an upper floor in the center of everything.

She stood as he entered. He saw her and waved. He looked haggard, and his eyes were red with fatigue. He approached tentatively. She stuck out her hand and sensed he had hoped for more. Thoughts of holding hands in his truck two nights ago gave her a warm feeling that she hoped didn't make her cheeks turn red.

"Hey," he said, glancing around. "It's been a long time since I was in here. I forget how nice it is."

"How was your trip?"

"The ride back was slow. It was snowing pretty hard. I counted eleven accidents." His shoulders slumped a bit. "The heat on the rental car gave out near the state line. Probably best you didn't come along. The last two hours were pretty cold."

"Yeah, Jake, about that. I'm sorry for the short notice. It's just that I—"

He cut her off. "I understand. This is work. We have a book to finish and all that." He glanced away. "It's okay. Really."

Poor guy. He'd just spent two days away from home. He had to drive through a snowstorm and nearly froze to death in a car he'd rented so she would be more comfortable. No wonder his writing had changed. He probably just wanted to get the book done. The sooner Stella and Terrence were out of his life, the better.

Did the same feelings extend to Mallory? Would he be happy when she was gone, too? Probably. And that was understandable.

"The least I can do is buy you a cup of coffee," she said, trying to brighten the mood. She led the way to a cute little coffee shop off to one side of the main floor. Offerings were limited, so it was hot chocolate for her, cappuccino for him. They moved to a table on the second floor. She pulled out her laptop. He did the same. Her opening line was cautious as she tried to feel him out.

"You took things in a direction I didn't expect."

He nodded. "I'm having second thoughts about the whole Stella–Michael thing."

"Why?"

"The more I thought about it, the more farfetched it seemed."

Why was he being so evasive?

"Couples break up all the time, Jake. I'm exhibit A of that." She grinned, happy that the pain wasn't as bad as before. But then, after everything she'd been through since, particularly her evening out with Clay the fugitive from justice, the pain of her breakup with Hogan was ebbing away.

Jake didn't smile, though. Whatever he was experiencing

was buried somewhere beneath that handsome exterior. "Grandma Springer wouldn't have liked it. A guy like Michael would never have a chance with Stella. I mean, look at him. He spends his entire life in Adair. Never really doing anything worthwhile." He shook his head. "It would never happen. Women like Stella wind up with guys like Terrence."

"That's not true, Jake. And I think you're missing the point about Michael."

"How can I miss the point? I created the guy."

"Then you should know more than anyone that Michael has so much to offer a woman like Stella." She leaned in so he would look up from his espresso cup and make eye contact. "He is handsome and kind."

"And smart," Jake said, smiling for the first time. "Don't forget smart."

Mallory laughed. "Very smart. And remember how willing he was to help Stella when Terrence dumped her? Michael was there for her. Just like..."

She paused. What had she been about to say?

Oh, my goodness.

Michael was there for Stella. Just like...*you were there for me*. Sunday night.

When I needed someone to help take my mind off a terrible weekend.

You fed me and made me laugh. You held my hand and listened.

And you expected nothing in return.

Jake was watching her, waiting for her to finish. His eyes didn't look tired anymore. There was a hint of expectation that wasn't there before—about what she was going to say. Unfortunately, she would say none of that. It wasn't right.

"I mean...Michael was there for her...because that's the kind of man he is."

Okay, so it wasn't what he was hoping to hear.

"And, Jake, I love Michael. And I have a feeling your readers will love him, too."

He nodded slowly. "You really love Michael?"

Mallory sighed. "Yeah, I think I'm starting to." She wagged her finger at him as she said, "But give it time, okay? They just met."

"What do you mean?"

"Real love needs time to grow."

He nodded, then pulled up a document on his laptop. "I have a confession to make."

"Okay."

"I wrote an alternative version."

Mallory slapped the table. "Well, what are you waiting for, sailor? Hit me with it."

Jake glanced around. There were people reading or working silently at the tables closest to them. An older guy in a shirt and tie was staring at them, a clear sign they were being too loud.

"I'll email it to you. Read it in the morning, and we'll talk tomorrow night."

"That sounds fair. Where and when?"

"Seven. The Cheesecake Factory on the Plaza."

She raised an eyebrow. "Cheesecake Factory? Really?"

"It's one of my favorite places. Have you been?"

She hadn't. "I don't think we have them in New York, but I've seen it on TV."

Jake chuckled. "You New Yorkers. You consider yourselves the experts on all things, but you have no barbeque and no Cheesecake Factory."

"Yeah, but we make up for it. When you come to New York, I'm taking you to the deli around the corner from my apartment. The Reuben will make your taste buds cry with delight. Then we'll get pizza at Henrico that…" She made a show of hugging herself.

Jake laughed again. "Is that a promise?"

"Absolutely. I promise you that Henrico is the best pizza you'll ever have."

"Not that. Your promise to show me New York. Is it…like a date?"

She held up both hands. "Not so fast, big boy. First you need to write a kick ass book, then we'll talk about New York."

She pointed to her laptop. "I'll read through your update, and we'll chat tomorrow night."

They left the library together. It was the best Jake had felt since she'd done the about-face on going to Iowa. She had even offered to show him around New York. A real date. Kinda. Sorta.

"Did you walk?" he asked.

"Yes. It's only eight blocks."

He pointed to a white sedan parked at an expired meter. "That's me, the rental car from hell. Want a ride back to your hotel?"

She giggled. "I hear the heat's broken. It might be warmer if I just walk."

"Good point. I'll walk with you."

"What about the rental car?"

He pulled on his gloves and waved at the car with one hand. "Screw 'em. I'll tell them it broke down. After what they put me through, they can come get it."

The snow had accumulated several more inches before ending late in the afternoon. A chillingly stiff breeze hit them as they turned the corner onto Main Street. Mallory moved closer so their arms were touching. Even through two thick coats, the feel of her arm against his short-circuited his brain.

He glanced at her as they approached the Power and Light District. She was beautiful. Incredibly so. Her winter hat accentuated her blue eyes, bringing to mind the first time they'd met, and his debate over their true color. He had decided then that they were azure, beautiful, but with the hint of an approaching storm.

And there had certainly been storms. It was impossible to believe that it had been barely a week since they met. So much had happened. So many storms. Her troubles at work, then the breakup. Those magical few hours on Sunday when they'd gotten to know each other. His disappointment when she pulled away.

Perhaps the storms were over. He hoped so. Thoughts of her inspired his writing. And if he had to live his romantic life vicariously through Michael Harper for a while, he would. There were many ways to let a woman know you're in love with her. Writing might be one more.

"So, how did you spend the time I was away?" he asked as they passed beneath the bright lights of the Power and Light District. Disney on Ice was in town, and despite the snow, the place was jumping.

"Funny you should ask," Mallory said. She pointed to a sports bar across the street. "Ever been there?"

"Many times. Great food. Have you tried it?"

She laughed. "Well, let me tell you about yesterday. It all started there when I went to lunch with a couple of guys I met in the hotel lobby..."

Back in her room, Mallory chucked her coat and boots, fell onto the soft comfy bed, and took a few moments for herself before jumping into Jake's writing. Everything seemed a little crazy at the moment. Her work life. Her personal life. That rejection email still stung. The anticipation she'd felt while dancing with Clay, then the shock of learning who he really was. Whose life was she living, anyway? Certainly not her quiet, orderly existence back in the city.

But amidst all of that, the evening with Jake had helped settle her jangled nerves. How did he do that? Even when he'd had a rough day, he made her feel better.

Could she do the same for him?

She hadn't yesterday. Bailing at the last minute was inconsiderate. She could defend her decision to remain in Kansas City by invoking Stratford and Key's no dating policy, but the way she'd done it was unfair to Jake.

And did she really care about those silly policies? Spending private time with Jake might be the least of her worries after Mr. Key got a look at what Jake was doing to Georgia Springer's book. If she was going to make one daring decision, why not two?

Still, it would help if one of the firms she'd applied to would at least contact her for an interview. She picked up her laptop and checked email, just in case.

Nothing.

But there was an email from Jake.

It was good spending time with you tonight, Mallory. I hope this version is preferable to what you read earlier. See you tomorrow evening. J.

"Well, let's just see, Mr. Springer," she murmured as she opened the attachment. It had been a while since she'd been excited about reading a manuscript, but she was now.

Michael found a comfortable spot near the arrivals area and took a seat. There was only one flight coming in that Stella might be on,

and while he had no idea if she was on her way back, he was willing to take the risk.

The fact was, Stella Duvall had been on his mind all weekend.

Discovering that Terrence had been cheating on her proved to be the knockout punch. First her job, then that. Michael had tried to console her, but sharing her feelings with a near stranger was too much, particularly after being hurt by two people she had trusted completely. Michael suspected that there had been little disappointment or heartache in her life, and in the end, she had retreated to the little house she rented from Herb Farquhar. When Michael went by the next morning, a neighbor said she had caught an early morning flight back to her parents' home.

Would she be on the incoming flight? It had been six days since she left, and she hadn't been on any of the previous day's return flights. Michael knew, because he had shown up each afternoon and waited. Just in case. A part of him worried she might never come back. What was there for her in Adair after losing her job and the man she trusted?

"There's one reason to come back," he whispered as he watched a plane descend. "I'm here. And I want very much to get to know you."

Mallory laid back and sighed with satisfaction. Jake was nailing it. And the fact that he was pulling on actual events as inspiration? That didn't bother her anymore. Jake Springer was writing a love story.

Her only question was—whose?

She finished the chapter, saved it, and started an email.

J

Sure, why not? It was becoming her favorite way to address him.

This is it! I feel something special growing between Michael and Stella.

She paused before adding, *and between us.*

Just seeing the words on the screen caused her breath to catch. She continued.

You've been so kind to me, and I'm sorry I cancelled going to Iowa with you. It would have been a fun trip, and a chance to get to know you better. I'm not sure what's happening here, but I like it. And I like you.

Thanks for a wonderful night, and for laughing at my crazy story about Clay the con man and Tommy the cabdriver. Maybe you can put it into a book sometime?

And if you do, I hope I'm there to help.

Good night,

M.

She read through it and was prepared to hit *send* when the same old doubts emerged.

Don't date clients.

You're on the rebound.

Last night, you were minutes from taking a criminal to bed.

He lives in Kansas City. And by the end of the month, you'll be back in New York.

It's not a smart decision, Mallory.

After reading the message a third time, she started deleting. The final message was simple.

Jake, this is good. I feel something special growing between Michael and Stella. I'll see you tomorrow evening at the Cheesecake Factory.

"Kinda gutted the emotion there, didn't you?" she mumbled.

One thing she didn't remove was her closing.

Not Mallory.

Just *M.*

CHAPTER NINE

WEDNESDAY, DECEMBER 6

Jake hustled into the Arrowhead Stadium media room and took a seat in the rear just as the Chiefs' representative announced that the coach and general manager would arrive in two minutes. The morning guy for one of the city's sports radio stations was seated directly in front of him. Jake leaned forward and tapped him on the shoulder. "Any idea what's up?"

The guy glanced at him dismissively, then sniped, "I guess you'll find out with the rest of us, pal."

Jake sat back, refusing to take the bait. A woman a couple seats away, a weekend sports anchor for one of the local TV stations, overheard the exchange. She caught Jake's eye and mouthed, *Asshole*.

All types of media were represented, from small-town newspapers to correspondents for national websites. TV and radio personalities typically sat in the front with beat reporters from the Kansas City Star. Most were friendly and willing to help a colleague. A few looked down on little guys. One or two, like the guy who had just blown Jake off, looked down on everybody.

Jake was definitely one of the little guys. That was okay, though. Three times over the last year he had broken important stories before the others. It helped to be local and a KC native. Jake had friends at Arrowhead and Kauffman Stadium, where the Royals played baseball. Some were well-placed in the organizations. Others worked security and, in one instance, as a janitor. If they saw or heard things, they let him know.

The Chiefs' general manager and coach arrived on schedule, their expressions all business. They took seats behind a bank of microphones, cellphones, and a couple of old school cassette players and announced that one of the team's key players, a lineman with a dubious reputation named Brian Mott, had been accused of trying to buy cocaine and beating up three men at a downtown bar earlier that day. The media was poised on the edge of their seats as the GM explained that an investigation was underway and that Mott would not play again until the issue was cleared up. The words were barely out of his mouth before nearly everyone in the room jumped up, each trying to be first with their questions.

One that didn't jump was Jake. He slipped out and sprinted for the exit.

Mallory leaned close to the window as the cab approached a blocks-wide spectacle of lights. "Oh, my goodness. What is this wonderful place?"

"The Country Club Plaza," the cab driver, not Tommy this time, replied. "They do this every year. Pretty nice, ain't it?"

Pretty nice was a huge understatement. White lights covered every building for blocks. A few of the taller ones added green and red accent lights high above the street. Christmas trees, brightly lit ornaments, and festive window displays gave everything a feel that didn't as much say Christmas as shout it.

"Here's Cheesecake Factory," the cabbie said as they came to a stop on the edge of the Plaza. "It's a good place and all, but being from out-of-town, you need to try some of the local spots while you're here."

He named several. Mallory committed them to memory as she paid the fare and headed toward the restaurant. Couples and families strolled along the busy sidewalks, window-shopped, and marveled at the decorations. It seemed, Mallory thought, the personification of Christmas, where love, family, and hope for the future reigned supreme. The restaurant was busy, but the hostess said the wait would only be twenty minutes. That was perfect. Jake would arrive at seven, just about the time a table would become available. Mallory took a seat near the door where she could observe what was happening outside.

Larry Rutledge and Jake had played little league baseball together. Later, attending different schools, they had lined up against one another on the gridiron. Both were regulars at Flip's Barbershop. Friends. Not tight but close enough to razz each other.

Which made Jake wonder if he'd done something to tick Larry off. They'd crossed paths in the Arrowhead Stadium parking lot when Jake was coming in for the press conference. He'd spotted Larry in his police cruiser and approached, intending to chat him up about the previous night's Kansas-Texas game. Larry acknowledged him but made it clear he was working and couldn't be bothered. Being on the clock had never stopped Larry from gabbing in the past, but Jake marked it up to his friend having a rough day, so he left him alone.

Was Larry acting that way for another reason? He recalled a pricy SUV parked in front of Larry's cruiser. Brian Mott, the subject of the press conference, owned an SUV much like that one.

Could it be?

Mallory asked the hostess to send Jake her way after she was seated. She scanned the drink menu. The lemon drop martini sounded yummy, but she didn't want to start without Jake. She called him, but it went straight to voicemail. Not wanting to drink alone, she opted for a diet soda and told the server her guest was running a few minutes late.

Jake approached Larry's cruiser and knocked on the passenger window, then opened the door and got in.

"What in the name of Kareem Abdul Jabbar do you think you're doing, Springer? You can't just crawl into an official vehicle."

"You know darn well why I'm here. That's Brian Mott in the SUV over there, isn't it?"

Larry considered him for a few seconds before nodding.

"Why is he just sitting here? Fifty reporters are going to be flooding this parking lot any minute now. They'll be on him like flies on French fries."

"We don't know what to do with him," Larry said. "They're already surrounding his condo. We take him to a hotel, and the press will be camped out in the lobby within the hour."

"He can't stay here, Larry. Tell you what…" Jake pulled out his truck keys and handed them over. "See if he wants to kick back at my place until things blow over."

Larry thought about it for a moment. "What's in it for you?"

"Before I answer, I want to ask you a question. And no cop B.S., Larry. Did he do it?"

Larry exhaled heavily. "Hell, naw, he didn't do it. The guys making the claim said that Mott was being a jerk to their friends. When they asked him to stop, he told them to come outside and settle it. According to the bartender, when they came back, one guy had a black eye, and the other had a busted nose."

"How do you know Mott didn't do it?"

"Look, Jake. I know the man. I do security detail for him off the clock. He says he got up and followed them out. The two guys went left into an alley that led out back. Brian went right, got into his SUV, and drove back to his place."

"Then why the big deal?"

"Mott's had problems before. You know that. Hell, Jake, you've reported on it. But the fact is, he's been a model citizen for over a year, and the dude has never used drugs in his life."

"Where's his agent? They're supposed to help with stuff like this."

"He fired the guy two weeks ago. He's still shopping for a new one."

Jake leaned his head against the back of the seat. There was a story needing to be told, but what was it? Part of him felt bad for Brian Mott. The guy had a reputation as a bad dude that had followed him through two cities before he signed with Kansas City, but he had always been fair with Jake.

"So, Larry, to answer your question about what's in it for

me, I get an hour of his time to get the whole story. Just the two of us. I'll report it as I see it."

Larry pursed his lips as he stared into the darkness. "That could possibly be arranged. You won't make me regret it?"

"Of course not. You know me better than that."

Larry grabbed his phone and made a quick call. Just a few softly-spoken words before turning to Jake and giving him a thumbs-up.

Mallory took another bite of the shepherd's pie she'd ordered, chewed slowly, and checked once more for any sign of Jake. She'd called three times and left messages. That was all he was getting from her. She flagged down the server, ordered one of those lemon drop martinis, then stabbed her fork in the shepherd's pie.

"Take that, Jake Springer," she mumbled. "Nobody makes me wait for ninety minutes."

The martini arrived in short order. She took a sip and found it quite pleasing, so she gulped it down and was ordering another when her phone buzzed.

Finally.

She expected Jake and felt a twinge of disappointment that it wasn't him. That passed quickly, though, because it was her friend Talia. That could be good.

"Mal, sorry for calling so late."

"No problem. I'm just finishing dinner. It's an hour earlier here in Missouri."

"Ugh, that's right. I forgot you were roughing it. How are things in flyover country?"

There was so much she could tell Talia about her short time in KC, but that wasn't the reason she'd called. "It's okay. The people are nice."

"That's good to know. Now, maybe I can get you the hell out of there and back here where you belong. I brought up your name to the people at Twisted Fishbowl."

Twisted Fishbowl? That didn't ring a bell. It sounded like a rock band or some seedy backstreet bar. When she didn't reply right away, Talia laughed.

"Weird name, huh? It's the publishing startup I told you about. The one working with indie authors."

Bingo! "Oh, yes, of course."

"Well," Talia continued. "They want to talk to you tomorrow."

Mallory squealed. A passing server stopped to ask if everything was okay. She pointed to the phone, then said, "Oh, my gosh, Talia! Thank you so much! This is the best news I've had in—"

"Don't get too excited. There's a catch. They don't do video calls."

Flock of geese! "What? Talia, everybody does video meetings. I thought you said they were innovative and progressive."

"They are. But they're adamant on meeting face-to-face."

Another server dropped off Mallory's martini. She considered it for a second before pushing it away. "I'm not sure I can get there. And if I can it would be in the afternoon at the earliest. I don't even know if there are flights leaving early enough to—"

"Mallory, listen," Talia said, cutting her off. "Tomorrow is interview day. I can get you on their schedule right after lunch, but that's all I can promise. These guys are moving fast, and from what I'm hearing, the applicant pool is quite deep."

Mallory rested her head in her hands. There was so much to think about. Just considering the logistics of making it to Manhattan from Kansas City within the next fifteen hours gave her a headache. But she didn't want to blow the opportunity.

She took a deep breath. "Tell them I'll be there."

Jake was pulling Brian Mott's Escalade into one of the Plaza parking garages when he spotted the sign warning drivers of the entrance height. He slammed on the brakes, not sure if the big SUV would fit. The last thing he needed was to peel off the top of Brian Mott's tricked out whip. A guy passing by with a very pretty woman on his arm stepped in front of the SUV, considered the garage entrance, and came to the driver's side window. Jake hit the button to lower it.

"You play sports?" he asked. "My girlfriend thinks you play for the Chiefs. Awful small for a football player, though."

"No, sorry. I run a website."

"I think he might be a kicker," the girlfriend said.

"Nope. Just a regular guy."

"No regular guy I ever saw drives a six-figure barge like this one. Anyway, you can get into the garage with no problem. This make is seventy-seven inches tall. The garage clearance is ninety-two."

Jake was impressed. "How do you know that?"

"He's a mechanic for GM," the girlfriend proudly proclaimed. "You're sure you're not a football player?"

"Positive. Thank you guys."

Jake found a spot on the first level and checked the time. Two hours late. Would Mallory still be there? He hoped so. With the craziness of the past three hours, he wanted nothing more than a bit of normalcy. And some time with Mallory.

He hustled up the street toward Cheesecake Factory, and was a few doors away when he spotted her dashing out. She made a quick left and slipped on the ice-glazed sidewalk. Within a few seconds, three people were helping her to her feet.

"Thank you," she said as she took a deep breath, her face red with embarrassment. "I appreciate your help. I have to go." She scurried up the street, making sure her feet stayed under her.

"Mallory!"

She slowed, but not much, and glanced back. "I have to get back to the hotel."

"I'm sorry I was late. I—"

"Jake, I don't have time right now. I'll talk to you in a couple of days."

She didn't break stride, so Jake sped up. By the end of the block, he was beside her. "Can I at least give you a ride?"

She slowed and nearly slipped again. "Can you get me there faster than a cab?"

"Absolutely." He reached out and placed his hand on her arm. "But we need to turn around. I'm parked back there."

He was driving an SUV. A very nice one. There was probably a story behind that, but Mallory didn't have time for details —or to hear his excuses for standing her up.

"I need to be in Manhattan tomorrow afternoon," she said as she pulled up a travel site on her phone. When Jake started to ask a question, she raised her hand. "I'll tell you later. First let me see if there are any flights."

"Try United. I remember when I booked my flight to meet your boss that they had a couple."

He was right. There was even a nonstop to Newark. Perfect. Almost.

"Ack! It leaves at six-thirty. That means I need to be at the airport by 5:45, which means I have to leave the hotel by—"

"I'll take you."

"I can't ask you to do that. It's early, and you—"

"It's the least I can do after standing you up, and... Mallory, would it be okay if I come along?"

"What? To New York?"

Jake nodded.

"Are you serious? Why would you...?"

He smiled. "You did promise to show me New York. Remember the Reuben sandwich? And pizza at that place you like so much?"

"Henrico's. But don't you have to work?"

"Not until Sunday. Things slow down as we get closer to Christmas."

She looked at the flight options again. "Because it's a last-minute booking, it will cost nearly six-hundred dollars."

He shrugged. "I'm a big-time romance author. I can afford it."

"Well, if you're sure. But what about your dog?"

"The neighbors will watch out for Corabelle." He merged into traffic and headed in the direction of the hotel. "And the timing is great. There's a very large man hiding out at my place until the police clear his name."

"Wait. What?"

"It's a long story. I'll tell you all about it on the flight. It's the reason I was so late getting to the Plaza."

"Yeah, that was pretty rude. I tried to call you."

"The large man I mentioned? He has my phone. Well, not really. He has my truck. My phone is in it."

"He stole your truck?"

Jake laughed. "We swapped for a few days until things get straightened out." He patted the steering wheel. "It's heated.

Who knew? Anyway, if you'll make my reservation with yours, I'll give you my credit card number."

"Do you give your credit card number out to just anyone?"

He shook his head. "Only people I'm dating, and as of this weekend, it sounds like that'll be you."

She opened her mouth to reply—probably to object—but seemed to reconsider and got busy making travel plans.

For both of them.

CHAPTER TEN

THURSDAY, DECEMBER 7

Mallory's TSA pre-check allowed her to scoot through security in seconds. When Jake finally made his way to the gate, she was dozing peacefully with her feet propped up on her carry-on and her arms wrapped around her purse. A guy seated nearby made no attempt to hide the fact that he was checking her out while she slept. Jake dropped his bag and took the seat beside her. He locked eyes with the guy doing the ogling, causing him to turn away for a second, before he did an about face, locking in on Jake.

"You're Jake Springer. I recognize you from the picture on your website."

Jake nodded. That happened sometimes, and it always surprised him.

"Great piece on Brian Mott. I never cared for the guy, but he didn't do what they're saying he did."

"Thanks, man." That had been the intention of the story, telling the truth about a guy whose pugnacious reputation followed him from the two teams he'd played for prior to Kansas City.

"How did you find those people willing to stand up for him?" the guy asked. It was a typical question from someone who didn't work in the field. As if Jake would spill his sources to someone on the street.

"Good old investigative journalism."

"Yeah, but you're not a journalist. I mean, you run a website."

That happened a lot, too. If your name wasn't attached to the byline of a traditional newspaper or on a TV screen below your face, you were just some hack who probably lived in his parents' basement. Jake used to fight that stereotype, but it didn't matter anymore. The guy asking the question hadn't seen the emails and texts he'd received overnight from the "real" journalists around Kansas City, including an invitation to come on the radio from the same guy who had blown him off at Arrowhead Stadium the evening before.

"Just lucky, I guess."

Mallory stirred when a gate agent announced preboarding for their flight. The nosy guy checked her out one more time as he stood up, nodded to Jake, and pushed through the crowd gathering at the gate.

"Someone you know?" Mallory asked as she stretched.

"Nope."

Their seats were in the back row, just in front of the restrooms. That wasn't so great, but at least the window seat was open, which made up for it. Jake was on the aisle. "Want to move over?" he asked.

Mallory glanced at the seat, then at him. "Not unless you want me to."

That was nice. "I'm fine with you staying right where you are."

"Besides," she added. "I saw that you sent another chapter overnight. I'll read it and give you my thoughts."

"Cool."

She elbowed him playfully. "When do you sleep? The email was sent at one-thirty. You picked me up at five. That's…not a lot of sleep."

"Whenever and wherever," he replied as he stretched his legs. "And if you don't mind, I'll snooze while you read."

The evening with Michael was already turning out nicer than any date Stella had with Terrence. She had some concerns when he'd recommended they drive ninety minutes to Kansas City. It was, after all, their first real date. She should never have worried. The Country Club Plaza was even more beautiful than she'd heard, and the restaurant he'd selected was amazing…

He was doing it again, using fiction to mimic real life. He wasn't even trying to camouflage it anymore, except to insert himself, via Michael, into an evening on the Plaza that he'd completely missed out on. She looked up from her laptop when she heard him grimace in his sleep. His head was turned toward her, and his eyes were pinched shut like an adorable little boy. It hadn't taken two minutes from announcing he was going to sleep to actually doing it. The plane's bumpy takeoff nor the crew announcements had caused him to stir. Fifteen minutes into the flight, and his head was starting to tilt. Mallory knew it was a matter of time before it came to rest on her shoulder.

She would be okay with that. He was obviously exhausted. Probably because of that football player crashing at his house. He had said little about it, and since she didn't know the first thing about football, or really care, she hadn't asked. To do so would only open her up to an embarrassing conversation she would be unable to follow. Football was like Greek to her, with terminology she could only guess at.

Pigskin.

Shotgun.

Quarterback.

It sounded like someone hunting little pig pelts for money. Not her cup of tea.

But the tea the flight attendant offered? Yes, she could handle that. She lowered the seatback tray of the empty window seat, accepted the hot water and tea bag, and went back to reading.

Bright lights gave everything a festive feel as they walked along the sidewalk. Michael offered his arm. Stella accepted, entwining her arm with his. That was where it remained. His touch was intoxicating, and she would be fine if they strolled for hours. They turned a corner and came upon a row of horse-drawn carriages.

"Which one would you like to ride in?" Michael asked.

Stella gasped. There was nothing like that in the tiny town where she'd grown up, and it had always been her dream to ride in a horse-drawn carriage. She considered each before choosing an egg-shaped one festooned with twinkling lights. Michael made the arrangements, then escorted her to the carriage. She reached for the rail to step up, but he placed a hand on her arm.

"May I help you?"

"Yes, please."

In his arms, if only for the moment it took for him to lift her into the carriage, she felt safe and protected. Not that she needed that. She'd made her way through life on her own terms, and under her own strength, but after the recent disappointments with Terrence and her job, having someone lift her up for a moment or two was blissful.

Once they were seated, the driver offered a plaid blanket for warmth. Michael placed it over them and took Stella's hand. Oh my, the way their hands fit together! The horse moved ahead slowly, and within a couple minutes, they were rolling past storefront windows decked out with all sorts of Christmas gifts and trinkets. Magical. Everything was magical.

Mallory's first thought was, *I didn't get a carriage ride. My prince didn't even show up for dinner.* And the place he'd selected? Cheesecake Factory. Fine. Very good, actually. But nothing like where Michael took Stella.

You're not Stella, dimwit. You're the editor. And Jake is the writer. And last night wasn't supposed to be a date. Get that through your thick head. But if that's the case, why did I allow him to accompany me to New York? To stay in my apartment? My tiny apartment? My tiny, one-bedroom apartment with the crappy foldout sofa bed that hasn't been slept on since my cousin Paul crashed there four years ago.

Mallory remembered his complaints about the lumpy mattress.

But then, Paul had always been a complainer. Even as kids, he would complain about how all her toys were girl toys.

Well, she would say, "It's because I'm a girl, you dipstick."

She couldn't make Jake sleep on that lumpy old mattress. Could she? They would just see how the day played out.

But first, she would finish the chapter, then start prepping for her interview with the team at Twisted Fishbowl. Geesh, that was a dumb name for a publisher. What would people think when they looked at her business card?

Twisted Fishbowl? What's that?

But then again, who used business cards anymore? Nobody. That's who. Nobody used...

Jake awakened to the pilot's announcement that they were on their final descent to Newark International Airport. Mallory was fast asleep. Her computer was still on the tray table. Her head was against his shoulder. He breathed in sweet-smelling scents. Shampoo or maybe perfume. They made him miss being close to a woman, so he left her to doze until the flight attendant announced it was time to prepare for landing.

"Mallory?" he whispered.

Nothing. She started snoring—man-sized snoring like Grandpa Springer after a hot day of yard work and beer.

"Mallory?"

Still nothing. Her mouth opened just enough to allow a dribble of drool to escape. Jake considered sneaking a picture to share later.

An embarrassing picture? And you wonder why you almost never have dates.

He nudged her arm. Her eyes flickered open.

"Hi," he said.

She shook her head and worked to focus. He wasn't sure for a moment if she recognized him, but that moment passed. She smiled and wiped the drool away with her sleeve.

"Was I snoring?"

"Nope."

"Good. Because I do sometimes. Not loud or anything."

Jake turned to hide his grin.

"Are we landing?"

"Yep."

She packed away her laptop. "I read your latest chapter. You've really got this story figured out."

"That's good to hear from an editor. No corrections?"

She laughed. "Lots of corrections, but the story itself? I love it."

"And Marcus? Will he love it, too?"

"Gosh, no," she said, rolling her eyes. "He'll hit the roof."

Jake shrugged. "I don't care."

Mallory didn't reply. Jake knew she cared very much. It was going to be a hard sell, but she'd encouraged him to go down that road. And she'd promised she would do everything she could to push the book along. Still, he didn't want her to lose her job over it.

But would it matter? He checked the time. In four hours, she would interview with another publisher. He'd checked the new guys out on the web. A start-up. Certainly something he knew a thing or two about. Twisted Fishbowl. Stupid name, but the credentials of the people involved looked decent. The leader had some experience in start-ups. He was probably shepherding a team of newbies who didn't yet realize they would put in eighty-hour weeks to get the new company off the ground.

Mallory would fit some place in between the newbies and the vet. And knowing her as he did, and knowing how New Yorkers were, he was certain she would ace the interview.

Then, if Marcus Key hit the roof, as she'd predicted, they could both tell him where to get off.

Their Lyft arrived in Manhattan with an hour to spare.

"I'm sorry to desert you for the afternoon, but you've got my home address and a key. You can go there anytime you want."

"I think I'll explore for a while. You'll be back this afternoon?"

"It depends on how long the interview lasts. Plan on dinner at seven-thirty."

"Pizza at Henrico?"

She smiled. "Absolutely."

She paid for the ride, and they stood for a few moments on the sidewalk. "My office is just down the street. I'm going to sneak in and hope nobody sees me."

"Why would you need to sneak in? You work there."

"They think I'm in Kansas City. I keep a change of clothes in my office. If I can make it in and out without being detected, maybe I can pull this interview off with no one finding out."

"Want me to sneak in ahead of you? Make sure the coast is clear?"

She laughed. "I'll be fine. I've got my strategy all planned out."

"Great. I'm going to Yankee Stadium."

"Really? Is there a game today?"

Jake grinned. "They don't play in winter. I'm hoping I can take a look around. So much history, you know?"

"You should have kept the Lyft. It's too far to walk."

Jake looked up and down the busy street. "I'm going to try the subway."

Mallory smiled brightly, then reached out and pulled up his coat collar. "You're not in Kansas, plowboy. This is the big city, so be careful."

His reply came in a wonderfully over-the-top country boy drawl. "If all else fails, ma'am, I'll just hitch up to one of them plow horses and git myself out of there."

Jake was trying to figure out how to pay for the subway when someone called his name. He turned and spotted Sam Cottner elbowing his way through the crowd.

"What are you doing here?" Sam asked as they bro-hugged.

"I came with a friend."

"Ahh," Sam said with a grin and a nod. "And might this friend be female?"

"How did you guess?"

"Because you never had that moony-ass expression when we drank beer and ate wings at the Peanut back in the day."

"That's because I knew you would stick me with the check."

Sam had a good chuckle at that. He'd always been good for a laugh. For seven months, they'd been colleagues at the Kansas City Star. Bottom-feeders assigned to high school football games and the occasional city council meeting when they didn't duck out of the office fast enough. Sam had parlayed the experience into a gig in Cleveland, then a much better gig with the New York Post. He covered college sports, mostly St. John's and Rutgers. But his star was rising.

"Hey," he said. "Great job scooping the big boys on the Brian Mott story. How did you do it?"

Unlike the guy at the airport, Jake was perfectly comfortable giving Sam the backstory. "He's probably sitting on my living room sofa at this very moment. Drinking my beer and eating my leftovers."

Sam's mouth flew open. "You hid him at your house?" He raised his arm for a high-five. "That's completely over the top awesome, man."

"I'm surprised you even heard about it."

"Any story about Mott gets national exposure. All the big boys were raking him over the coals yesterday, but since your piece came out, there's a lot of crow being consumed across America. I'm headed to the office now. I can't wait to tell everyone that I ran into you."

Sam pulled out his phone and took a selfie of the two of them, then asked, "Where are you headed?"

"I'm kinda hoping to see Yankee Stadium."

"It's hard to miss. Real big place."

"Inside."

"Oh, that might be harder. They do tours but only until noon." Sam leaned closer. "If I give you a tip, you have to promise not to share it with anybody, okay?"

Jake promised. Sam's plan was perfect, but first he had to get there. And before he could get to Yankee Stadium, he still had to figure out how to pay for the doggone subway.

The time Mallory had spent prepping could have been better spent exploring the city's burgeoning vodka bar scene or binging the latest Netflix series. Because it seemed that was all the nine people interviewing her wanted to talk about.

"What are you watching?"

"Which season of the Walking Dead was your favorite?"

"What's your go-to spot for winding down after work?"

Most appeared to be her age, more or less, but the questions made Mallory feel woefully out of touch with current culture.

She didn't watch much TV. Like most people employed in the literary world, she read voraciously. At least she *thought* literary people read. The people seated around her were the exception. There was no doubt they were smart. And they had no qualms with sharing their political views, then arguing amongst themselves despite the fact their views were the same.

The process was strange. Less an interview and more of a

sixties sit-in held in a big room with couches. Mallory sat in an old rocking chair with a dingy corduroy cover. She tried not to rock, but it was all so weird that a couple times she couldn't stop herself. Some of the Twisted Fishbowl team sat on the floor. One guy remained in the lotus position, facing away from the others and humming occasionally. Mallory couldn't believe his legs didn't cramp up.

The leader, if there was one, was Maya, a smiling, tatted girl with black fingernails. But she came and went throughout their time together. Maya had a degree in literature from City College and would be responsible for new author acquisitions, but when Mallory asked how she and her team planned to find those fledgling authors, she said they were still figuring that out. Had she asked Mallory her thoughts, she would have told Maya that her search should begin by determining what genres Twisted Fishbowl planned to pursue, then track sales figures to find who the most prominent indies in those genres were.

No one asked, though. And by the end of the interview, Mallory felt as if she'd been dropped into a weird alternate universe where book people didn't make plans or read books. They took a break a couple hours in. Maya pointed Mallory to the restroom. She considered doing her business and then ducking out. And she might have if her friend Talia hadn't set everything up. She didn't want to disappoint her, so she stayed.

And was it ever a good thing she did.

Sam's scheme for getting into Yankee Stadium was simple. Go to the main gate on East 161st. There would be three security guards there. Approach the smallest one, a guy with a tear tattoo under his left eye. His name would be Adrian.

Tell Adrian he was a friend of Sam's who needed to see Artie. Artie was Adrian's supervisor. He would go find Artie. Jake was to slip Artie a twenty, and bingo, an hour of private time in the cathedral of baseball.

But what if Adrian wasn't there? Or what if Artie wasn't there?

"They're always there," Sam assured him. "They work Monday through Friday from nine to five."

Yep. Except for that one day a year when stadium personnel attended sensitivity training. And that was the day Jake showed up. The security people were agency replacements who projected themselves as Vin Diesel wannabes. Even the female.

"You need to step back."

"This area ain't open to tourists."

The female was practically in Jake's face. "Move along. No congregating here," she barked.

"Doesn't it take more than one person to congregate?" Jake asked.

She blinked, then moved in even closer like a drill sergeant. She and Jake were eye to eye, and she was daring him to make the next move.

So he did.

"Congregate is a verb. It means to gather as a group."

The other two guards appeared over her left and right shoulders, forming a perfect V.

"Give us the word, Phoebe, and we'll haul him inside."

Inside was where Jake wanted to be, but probably not the way they were talking about. He tried to bring the tension down a notch. "I think what you meant was loitering. No loitering here."

Maybe that wasn't the best way to lessen the tension. Phoebe and the others weren't interested in a grammar lesson. And Jake certainly didn't want to be locked up in some dingy holding cell deep in the bowels of Yankee Stadium.

"Hey, look you guys," he said, holding his arms out in peaceful surrender. "I didn't mean anything. I was just hoping to see my friends Artie and Adrian. But they're not here, so I'll leave."

Jake turned and walked away. He heard snickering behind him, but that was okay. Nothing ventured, nothing gained. He strolled to the corner and took a left on River Avenue and walked under the raised tracks that bordered the stadium. Drawings and uniform numbers of famous Yankees adorned the exterior walls. If there was one thing Jake knew, it was stadiums and arenas. There was always a way to get inside. It was just a matter of finding it. And just as he reached the point where the stadium gave way to the 164th Street Garage, he found it.

When Mallory exited the restroom, a tall, slender man was waiting for her. Very tall, like the Kangaroos whose warmups she had interrupted earlier the previous week. Unlike the team of interviewers, who were dressed as if they were headed for a pickup basketball game or a slumber party, the tall man was tastefully dressed in dark slacks and a blue sweater.

"Mallory, I'm Price Ricketts. After hearing Talia speak of you, it's a pleasure to finally meet in person."

Funny, but Talia had never mentioned anyone named Price Ricketts. "Hello, Mr. Ricketts."

"Just Price. Nobody uses last names around here. The team meeting was a bit longer than planned. I hope you still have time to visit with me."

"Of course."

He led the way through the now empty rumpus room where her interview had taken place. They went up a set of stairs to a hallway with three offices. Two were empty. The third was his. It was plain in every way, from the carpet to the desk and chairs. Discount office supply store stuff. Just a few blocks from Stratford and Key, but a different world completely. There was a sofa against one wall, a threadbare thing that might have come from a secondhand furniture store. He invited Mallory to have a seat. He did the same, and despite it being a sofa, there was nothing weird about it. Price Ricketts was the epitome of decorum, and when Mallory glanced at the two framed photos on his desk, she understood why. One pic was Price with a beautiful woman, probably taken on vacation some place in the Caribbean. The other was of that same woman cuddling a newborn baby.

"That's Rosa. And the little guy is our son, Thomas. He'll be seven months old tomorrow."

"I'll bet he'll be tall," Mallory blurted out, happy for a bit of normalcy after the strangeness of the team interview.

Price laughed. "No doubt. Rosa is six-two. We played basketball at Boston College."

"On the same team?"

He laughed again. "You don't follow basketball, I take it."

"Well," she demurred. "I do like the Kangaroos. I went to their game last week."

"I see," he said in a tone that made it obvious he didn't. "Now, let me tell you about our little company."

There were at least twenty of them, guys and women, casually dressed, unloading stuff from a truck. It appeared to Jake as if they were hauling stuff into the ballpark for some special event. He'd seen it before in Kansas City. Corporations would rent out suites or meeting rooms on days when there was nothing going on at the facility. It was cool to tell employees they would spend the day at Yankee Stadium. What those excited employees usually discovered was it was just another day at work, albeit a nicer venue.

Jake sidled up beside the truck as if he belonged there. A queue of four workers were waiting for whatever the guys in the truck handed them. When Jake reached the front, he kept his head down and was handed a roll of artificial turf. He threw it over his shoulder and followed the others down a flight of stairs to a windowless conference room bearing the name of a Yankee great from the fifties. A guy with a Mets cap and a ticked-off expression looked him up and down, worrying Jake that he was busted. He shrugged, then told Jake to "put the fake grass by the boxes in the corner." Jake did, then stepped back into the hall. The others turned left toward the stairs and back to the truck. Jake turned right and was home free.

"Frankly, Mallory, I need help."

A few minutes into his account of what was going on with Twisted Fishbowl, Price Ricketts had gotten up and started pacing the room. His background was business, the same as many of the team he'd assembled.

"They're good people," he'd explained. "Smart people who know how to do what we hired them for." He stopped pacing and said, "What they don't know how to do is work."

"Then why hire them?"

Wow. Had she really asked that?

Goodbye, Twisted Fishbowl. It was good knowing you. *I might have stood a chance, but then I went and criticized the hiring practices of the guy in charge.*

He turned, so they were eye to eye. Given he was standing, and seven feet tall, his eyes were far, far away.

"Creativity comes at a price," he said. "All we need is someone to show them how to harness their ideas and get down to work." He crossed his arms and bent slightly at the waist. "I trust your friend Talia. If I could hire her, I would. Unfortunately, she's not interested. She mentioned that you've gotten sideways with Marcus Key and want out."

For crying out loud, Talia, can't you keep some things to yourself?

"I don't know about sideways, but sometimes I feel as if I'm…stagnating at Stratford and Key."

"Talia also said something else. She said you run circles around her and everyone else in the field. That you're willing to roll up your sleeves and get to work. She said you're driven to succeed and make no bones about it."

Forget what I said, Talia. You're okay with me.

"She also said you're too intense at times, but maybe at a place like this, you can learn to relax and let down a little."

Damn it, Talia. You never told me you thought I was intense.

"So, what exactly are you thinking, Price? What would my title be?"

He sat back down and rubbed his chin. "I don't have a title yet. Something like Chief of Work?"

"That sounds dreadful."

He smiled. "I guess it does. Let me think some more."

"What is your title?"

"Just Price. We haven't really considered titles and stuff like that."

"If I may be straightforward, that's a mistake. Without titles and the responsibilities that go with them, nothing gets done."

This got his attention. "Tell me what you mean."

"The minute things get tense, or deadlines loom, or

someone feels a job is getting too difficult, they jump to something else. It's human nature."

He considered this for a few moments. "So, how can we avoid that?"

Mallory opened her briefcase and pulled out a pad of paper and a pen. "Let me show you."

Miller James Huggins.

Manager of New York Yankees 1918-1929.

As a tribute to a splendid character who—

"How did you get in here?"

Jake looked up from the monument he'd been reading. The sun was shining in his face, so he had to squint to see her.

Phoebe.

The scary security guard from out front.

"I uh…"

"Get to your feet."

She didn't have a gun. The closest thing she had was a walkie-talkie. Still, Jake didn't think she was a person he wanted to mess with. Phoebe had the look of a woman who occasionally raised fists with the guys. And probably won.

"Look, Phoebe…"

She glared at him.

"I mean, ma'am…I'm here with…the crew that is setting up inside…and I just wanted to—"

"Come with me."

She motioned for him to follow. Like a new puppy tailing its master, he did. They returned to the conference room, where work was still in full swing. Two men and a woman, professionally dressed, had joined the grumpy guy who was barking out orders. They looked at Jake, then Phoebe. Their expressions were a mix of contempt, sympathy, and confusion.

Then the woman smiled. "Jake Springer? From Kansas City?"

Jake looked at her, trying to get a handle on who she might be. Then, a spark of recognition from the Chiefs game in New York a couple weeks before. She'd been seated next to him in the media dining area.

"Nan Spaulding. How are you?"

"Great… Better than you it appears."

The others in the room paused to watch. Nan, Jake remembered, was with one of the multitude of New York websites that covered the local teams. A giant compared to Total Sports KC. They'd swapped a few stories while waiting for the game to begin.

"You're the man of the hour, aren't you?" she said.

Jake glanced over his shoulder where Phoebe was sticking close. "Yeah, I guess I am. I came here to—"

Nan turned to the guys with her. "Jake broke the Brian Mott story."

She made introductions. Jake recognized their names. The younger of the two was a writer for the New York Times. The other, Roger Powell, was one of the most respected sports media executives in the world. Amazingly, both seemed as impressed to meet Jake as he was to meet them. They asked questions. Jake answered. Phoebe loomed behind him, waiting to lock him up or break his fingers. Fortunately, Nan picked up on his dilemma.

"He's with us," she said to Phoebe.

"It doesn't sound like it. You just met."

"He really is. My boss invited him and forgot to tell me."

"Yeah," Roger Powell said. "Jake is the keynote speaker at tonight's dinner. It'll be great."

"We're dying to know how the big boys in Kansas City do

things," the other guy said. They were pulling Jake's chain now, but he had it coming. And it worked. Phoebe left. Nan came over. The others followed.

"A word to the wise, Jake. Don't get caught sneaking into Yankee Stadium. We just saved you a seven-hundred dollar fine and a night in jail."

"I guess I owe you. How can I repay?"

"That's easy," the New York Times guy said with a laugh. "The first round's on you."

The stairs leading to Mallory's apartment were next to a pizzeria. Not the one she had been raving about, but did it matter? Was there such a thing as bad pizza? Even the stuff in the grocery store freezer tasted good to Jake. And the aromas wafting from inside made his mouth water. He considered grabbing a slice but didn't want to do anything to diminish Mallory's excitement about sharing her favorite place. He punched in the code and buzzed himself into a musty stairwell, then double-checked the apartment number before climbing to the third floor. Hers was the only apartment at that level. A dusty bicycle with deflated tires was chained to the stair rail, but a table of potted plants next to a window helped cheer up the dimly lit space. He pulled out the key she'd given him, reconsidered, and knocked. She opened the door and beamed at him.

"Welcome to Brooklyn!"

She was barefoot in jeans and a Christmas sweater. Her hair was pulled back in a loose ponytail.

Stunningly beautiful.

She held open the door, stepped back, and held out her arm. "Well, this is it," she said as he entered the apartment. "It's not much, but it's home."

Jake set his backpack on the floor and glanced around. The space was small, with a living room on one end and a tiny kitchen barely wide enough for two people on the other. It was decorated to perfection, though. At least for someone who loved books. A built-in shelf supporting a twenty-year-old television contained a variety of hardbacks.

"Those are first editions from some of my favorite authors," she said as she pulled one from the shelf and caressed the cover and spine. "Only a few have any real value, but they mean a lot to me."

Jake bent over and scanned the shelf, recognizing a couple of names and titles, but little else. Mallory's obvious affection for them made him want to know more, and he made a mental note to ask questions while they were together.

"Let me show you the rest of the place."

Most of the apartment could have been viewed from the door, but the few moments she took to give him a personal tour made it special. Pictures of relatives. A family trip to Yosemite National Park. Mallory's high school and college graduation photos.

"You look just the same," he noted as he studied her high school picture.

"Thank goodness the hairstyle is different," she said, looking over his shoulder. "Mother always insisted that I go to her stylist. Unfortunately, the only cut she knew was like Mother's. That's why I look like a middle-aged homemaker."

"Not at all. You were very beautiful." Jake returned the photo to the table and turned to face her. "You still are."

Her blush surprised him. She stepped back, glanced around, then said, "Let me show you the rest of the place. The bathroom is back here."

Unlike the rest of the apartment, which retained its early twentieth century charm, the bathroom had been updated with tile walls and flooring, a large mirror over a rectangular vessel sink, a roomy shower with two heads, and…

"A bidet?"

Mallory laughed. "Why so surprised? You don't have one at home?"

"Ha! It's all I can do to keep Corabelle from drinking out of the stool."

"Yuck. I think she kissed me a couple times that night when I was waiting for you to get back from your date."

"She probably did, and it wasn't a date. It was a—"

"Business meeting," she said, cutting him off.

"Speaking of which, how was your interview?"

She wagged her finger at him. "Don't get ahead of yourself. First the tour, then we talk."

"And eat, I hope."

"And eat." She led him into the tiny hallway and through a door into a good-sized bedroom with a cozy little alcove to the side. "I sleep here," she said, motioning to the queen bed that dominated the room. "And I work back there."

Jake touched the corner of the bed as he checked out the space. It was frillier than he expected from someone whose identity seemed wrapped up in her work. The work area contained a small wooden desk with just enough space for a laptop and lamp. He moved around the bed and peered out the window onto a trash-strewn alley with graffiti covering doors and blank walls.

"Not the best view," Mallory said as she came up beside him. "Views are gold in New York, and Stratford and Key doesn't pay gold-level salaries to editors."

"How about Twisted Fishbowl? Do they pay gold-level?"

"Funny you should mention that," she said, taking his arm and guiding him back to the living room. They sat on a worn but comfortable tan sofa. "Can I get you something to drink first?"

"I can wait until dinner. The suspense is killing me, Mallory. Tell me about the interview."

"Well…he asked me to come back tomorrow. He's going to make a formal job offer."

"Shut the door! Seriously?" As he spoke, Jake reached out and pulled her into a celebratory embrace that she accepted happily.

"Tell me everything," he said as they parted.

Mallory hoped he meant it when he said he wanted to hear the whole story, because she poured it out. The crazy interview, the strange questions about everything except publishing. And the meeting with Price Ricketts.

"That's really his name?" Jake asked. "It sounds like a name from a movie about a rich guy. Price Ricketts, millionaire."

"It's his real name. He's very nontraditional, and he needs someone who can get the company organized."

"Which means getting the people on task?"

"Exactly. We talked a lot about that."

Jake studied her for a few beats. "And you think you would like that?"

"Yeah, why not? I mean, it's different from editing, but if I want to move up, I need to lead people."

"And you believe these people are"—he searched for the right world—"leadable?"

"You don't think I can do it?"

"I'm sure that if anyone can, it's you. I was just wondering if this group will allow themselves to be led."

What was he getting at? Did he not think she could handle the responsibility?

Could she?

It had been a heady experience, talking leadership with someone who was exploring a new direction in publishing. Nearly two hours had passed in what seemed like minutes. And at the end, when he'd said she had the qualities and knowledge Twisted Fishbowl was looking for? Oh, wow. No one had ever said that to her before.

Did Jake see something she didn't?

How could he? He hadn't been there. He hadn't witnessed the dysfunction among the employees. Sure, they were smart and talented, but they needed someone to help them learn to operate as a team. Price knew it. And he saw those qualities in her.

And if the money was right. She would begin the new year at Twisted Fishbowl.

He'd said the wrong thing. He knew it as soon as the words were out of his mouth. But, darn it, there seemed to be more twisted about that fishbowl than just the name. Like the guy in charge, Price what's-his-name, who was incredibly tight with his employees, yet readily admitted he didn't know a thing about leading.

Employees were already in place, some for months, who had been allowed to plot their own courses. They hadn't even figured out how they would solicit and sign new writers.

Mallory would step into the middle of all that. And be expected to straighten up everyone, including the guy in charge. Sort of like a hired gun.

And if there was one thing Jake had learned about hired guns, it was that they were hired to be fired. Be it a few months or a couple years, when you were hired to bring order and vision to a group that had no desire for either, it could be a disaster.

But he couldn't tell Mallory that. Could he?

She was on cloud nine. Twisted Fishbowl was her ticket away from Stratford and Key. He got that. From what he could tell, Marcus Key had done a terrible job of laying out what he perceived as Mallory's shortcomings. What he forgot was that she'd been doing the job the same way for years. No negative feedback. No criticism.

And that was unfair.

And Jake understood why she wanted out.

Marcus owed Mallory an apology. An apology that would not be coming, because as a boss he had little experience with admitting he was wrong.

And come to think of it, Jake owed her one, too. For initially questioning her judgment about Twisted Fishbowl.

"Look, Mallory…I'm sorry."

She smiled, but her eyes didn't. "You don't owe me an apology."

"Yeah, I do. I wasn't there. I didn't see what you saw. Or hear the sincerity in Price Ricketts's voice when he bared his soul."

"Oh, Jake, that was exactly it. He wants so much for the company to succeed, and he wants me to work alongside him to make it happen."

"I appreciate that, but be aware that you can never truly work alongside him. He'll always be the boss."

She gave him a skeptical look. "And you know all of this, how? From running your website?"

"No, just from… I'm probably way off base. Like I said, I wasn't there. You saw it and liked it, and if you feel it's the job for you, you owe it to yourself to jump."

Mallory appeared to relax. "Thank you for saying that." She stood and held out her hand. He accepted and used it to get to his feet. "Now, are you ready for the best pizza you'll ever eat?"

He was. "But can I make a quick phone call first?"

"Sure. If you need privacy, go into my bedroom."

He shook his head. "It'll only take a minute. The guys at one of the local sports radio stations asked me to make an appearance on their morning show. I need to call them back."

"Jake, that's fantastic."

"Nah, I'm turning it down. It's work, and I came to New York for fun."

"Sure, it's work, but it would increase your visibility, right?"

Jake laughed. "Oh, yeah. We don't have much presence on the East Coast. Their morning show draws a million and a half listeners. But really, I would prefer bagels from that deli you like so much."

Mallory's laugh filled the tiny apartment. She smacked him on the arm. "That's the thing about New York. The delis are always open, but this..." She pointed to Jake's phone. "The New York media is big time. Call and tell them you'll be on. How did this come about, anyway?"

"It's a long story. Remember the guy at my house?"

"The one hiding from the cops?"

"He's actually hiding from the press. Anyway, I wrote a feature about him that helped clear some things up. They saw it, so they want to talk to me."

It was Mallory's turn to offer a celebratory hug. Jake thought he could get used to those. She was the most complex woman he'd ever met, but she also kept her feelings close to the surface. He liked not having to guess where she stood on things. The hug lasted a few moments beyond one of those *way to go, nice job* embraces. He didn't try to break it off, and she didn't either at first. But finally, she stepped back and said, "Make your call, but do it fast. The world's best pizza is waiting."

The four blocks between Mallory's apartment and Henrico's were a mix of brownstones, apartment buildings, restaurants, and shops. A smattering of Christmas decorations were interspersed with blue lights and other adornments associated with Hanukkah. The streets were alive with the aromas of food and the unfamiliar chattering of languages Jake didn't recognize. It was crowded and loud and a bit messy, but also exciting. So different from home.

Henrico's was small, like most restaurants Jake had seen in the city, with maybe fifteen tables. No traditional checkered tablecloths, but a warm feeling permeated the space thanks to an abundance of unfinished wood. Rough-hewn beams crisscrossed the ceiling, and the walls were richly paneled. The air carried the pleasing scents of tomatoes and basil. A harried server darting past to deliver a pizza and salad told them to grab a seat wherever. Mallory led the way to a corner spot near the kitchen.

"What's your favorite kind of pizza?" she asked as another server dropped off menus and water glasses.

"I like the basics. Pepperoni. Hamburger. Green peppers are good. I really like the supreme pizza you get at—"

Mallory was shaking her head before he was finished. "No, no, no. Those are great toppings, but the secret to Brooklyn pizza is the cheese mix and the crust. Provolone and mozzarella cheese. Thin crust. Keep the toppings simple and let the real taste come through."

"Fair enough. You choose, I'll eat. But no anchovies."

"Have you actually had anchovies?"

"No, and I don't want to."

Mallory laughed. "I ate the fries at Gates, remember?"

Jake took a deep breath, but she let him off the hook. "I'm just kidding. No anchovies, but how about olives?"

"I can do olives."

The server came up and inserted himself into the conversation. "So what I'm hearing so far is a large pie with olives."

"Now you pick a topping," Mallory said to Jake.

"Pepperoni."

"No, not pepperoni. Get meatballs."

"She's right," the server said. "We make our own meatballs. Get the basil leaves, too."

"Okay," Mallory said. "Meatballs, olives, and basil. Pick one more thing."

"Pepperoni."

"No!" the server and Mallory answered in unison.

The server said, "You need mushrooms."

"Yes," Mallory said. "That sounds perfect. Don't you think so?"

Jake knew when it was best to go along. "Perfect."

"Do you want wine? Beer?" the server asked as he punched their order into a tablet.

"Wine?" Mallory asked.

"Sure."

"Great. You pick."

Jake scanned the wine list and selected a chianti that was immediately shot down in favor of a house red.

"I hope you love it," Mallory said after the server left.

"I'm excited. And thanks for letting me help pick everything out."

They took in the surroundings for a few moments before Mallory asked how his day had gone.

"Not bad after I figured out the subway. Pretty interesting, really."

"Did you find Yankee Stadium?"

Jake laughed. "Well, I guess you could say that. I—"

"Hey, man, aren't you that Kansas City dude? Jake?"

The guy asking was huge with a gleaming bald head and arms like tree trunks. He was scowling, but not in that "I'm gonna kick your ass" way. His scowl was more of a "I think I know you" look.

"Yeah, I'm Jake."

The guy thrust out his hand. "I'm Lavaughn Lavery. I spent two years with the Jets. Brian Mott and I played on the line together."

Jake's hand disappeared into Lavaughn's. "I remember you, Lavaughn. Second-team All-American at Purdue. You went third round in the draft."

Lavaughn appeared delighted at Jake's recollection. "Yeah, sadly, that's where the story ended. Two years on the Jets, a back injury, then two long years of rehab only to get cut in preseason. That's all in the past now, though. I'm teaching fourth grade here in Brooklyn."

"Great for you, Lavaughn. And this is my friend, Mallory Newell."

Lavaughn's voice turned to butter as he took Mallory's hand in his. "A pleasure. Are you the reason Jake's in town?"

"Yes. I'm showing him the city."

"That means you…live here?"

It was obvious that Lavaughn had no issue with trying to move in on Mallory. She brought his advances to a screeching halt.

"I live wherever work takes me. Kansas City this month. Who knows where next."

Lavaughn nodded, then seemed to remember why he had come over. "Hey, Jake, I just wanted to say thanks for what you wrote about Brian. The dude will run through the fires of hell for his friends. He got in a couple of bad spots back in the day, and sometimes, the media won't let people forget."

Jake accepted the compliment, and Lavaughn took his leave as their wine arrived.

"You're a really big deal," Mallory said. "Radio. Strangers coming up to you in restaurants. Is there more to Jake Springer than I'm aware of?"

"There sure is," Jake said with a wink. "I'm an immensely complicated person, and it will take much time and effort to fully understand me."

Mallory raised her wine glass, smiled, and said, "Here's to understanding."

They clinked glasses and sipped their wine.

"That's exceptional," Jake declared. "If you pick pizza as well as you pick wine, I can't wait."

Watching Jake savor the pizza was a pleasure. By the last slice, he was folding it just like the native Brooklynites seated around them. Mallory kept up with him for the first two slices before giving up and leaving the rest for him.

"How about some cannoli's?" the server asked as he removed the empty pizza pan.

Mallory wondered if Jake had it in him. He'd just consumed a couple thousand calories of pizza, along with most of the wine and two glasses of water. There was no way he still had room.

"Two for me. How about you, Mallory?"

"Oh, gosh no. I'm stuffed."

The conversation had slowed while they ate, but as soon as the server stepped away, Jake leaned in and said, "You were right."

"About?"

"Everything. The pizza. The wine. New York. It's different when you experience it with a local."

"Born and raised," she said. "So, what do you want to do next?"

His eyes drifted skyward as he considered the possibilities. "What I would really like, and promise you won't laugh?"

"Promise."

"I would enjoy…going back to your apartment and hanging out."

"Really?"

"Yeah. We've spent a lot of time together the last couple weeks, but I still don't feel like I know you all that well."

"Oh, there's not really much to know."

Jake shook his head. "I don't believe that for a second."

As they gazed across the table at one another, Mallory noticed how comfortable he appeared. Being relaxed might not be a big deal back on his home turf, but in New York, he was an outsider in a town that could make things hard for outsiders. Yet here he was, completely at peace, his incredible gray eyes focused on her. She remembered that first meeting, when she'd been summoned to the tenth floor and encountered him in the waiting area eating snacks and looking more like a homeless person than the successful journalist he really was. He had been perfectly content playing the country bumpkin, not worrying in the least whether she or anyone else knew the real Jake Springer.

That was incredibly sexy and so different from the other guys she'd dated. They were more like Hogan. Buttoned-down career climbers who played whatever role necessary to get what they wanted.

But who was she to talk? She'd played that same game. In college, when she'd buttered up the professors to get the best grades and in her career.

And where had it gotten her? A job where the boss considered her close-minded and impatient? Where a friend like Talia considered her too intense? That sucked. And to think she'd had no idea because she was too busy trying to climb that ladder.

At the same time Jake was just…Jake. She wanted more of that in her life, and she was starting to think she wanted more of him in her life, too. She reached across with a napkin and wiped a bit of tomato sauce from the back of his hand.

"Yeah," she said, smiling. "I think hanging out is a great plan."

Jake couldn't get past the feeling that he should make his move. They were seated on her living room sofa, and he knew from an earlier conversation that it converted to the bed where he would likely be sleeping. He was turned slightly to face her. She was turned completely toward him, her legs curled up underneath her. Cuter than heck. The sofa had three cushions, and so far, they were his, hers, and the one between them. Somehow, he had to broach that middle cushion. He needed to make his move.

The problem was, he really didn't have a move to make.

There had been women in his life before, of course. But he knew his limits. And the better he got to know Mallory, the more he wondered if perhaps she was out of his league. She'd been to France and Brazil on family vacations. His parents took him to Silver Dollar City when he was ten. They'd dropped him off at the gate before going off to score weed from a grower in Arkansas who was a reputed dope legend. Mallory went to Dartmouth. The freaking Ivy League. He went to community college.

Yet she wanted to know everything.

About his upbringing: strange.

About his friends: pretty much just like him.

About his dreams: make a good living doing what he was doing.

Uncomplicated. Simple. Boring.

Fortunately, there was more wine. That took away some of the sting that went with being so boring.

"What's the craziest thing you've ever done?" she asked as she cradled her glass.

"Oh, my. That's tough… I mean, there are so many."

This got her attention. "Really? Like crazy teen stuff?"

Jake laughed. "Life actually became more normal later."

He could tell by the tilt of her head that she was intrigued. "Don't get the wrong idea. I was never beaten or abused. Not even close. My parents have always just been more about themselves than about other people."

"Were you neglected?"

He shook his head. "Grandpa Springer always had my back. And since we all lived together, at least when Mom and Dad weren't on one of their many discovery trips, I always had someone who loved and supported me."

"I can tell you loved him very much, too."

"He was a gruff old cuss, but there was never any doubt that he cared. Anyway, back to your question. I went with my parents to a"—he made air quotes—"*family nudist resort* for two weeks the summer before third grade."

"No way!"

"Yeah. It was in Kansas."

Mallory's eyes became huge. "A nudist camp…in Kansas? What did you do there?"

"Got really sunburned."

She gasped and her hands went to her mouth, causing Jake to burst into laughter. "That was a joke. It really wasn't terrible."

"Did you take your clothes off?"

"After a couple days, you felt more out of place if you didn't. And it wasn't like today where you have to always be on guard. It was all families, and they had rules and stuff. Actually, it was pretty fun. We swam and played softball. We had weenie roasts. Those are kind of interesting at a place like that. You need to always keep an eye on your weenie."

Her laughter was delightful to Jake's ears. She asked a few more questions, which he gladly answered.

"I've never told anyone about that," he said. "They would probably get the wrong idea."

She seemed touched by his admission.

And then he asked, "How about you?"

Mallory wracked her brain to come up with something. A family nudist camp? Now that was crazy. What did she have that might come close?

TP'ing the Feldman's yard on Halloween when she was thirteen? It would have been a better story had she not been overcome by guilt and cleaned it up before they saw it.

Claiming to be seventeen so she could see the R-rated movie, *Bridesmaids,* when she was fifteen?

Nope. But there was that one time… Gosh, she had tried to forget it.

"I gave a boy an apple tart to show me his thing."

That did it. She had Jake's full attention. Her face felt as if it was on fire, though.

"An apple tart?"

"Yes. Seventh grade. We had a cooking unit at school."

"I thought you went to a private school?"

"I did, but it was coed."

"So whose idea was it to make a deal like that?"

"Mine. Three of my friends had already seen his thing, and I didn't want to be left out."

"Wow. That guy got around. What was his name?"

"Kendall Throckmorton."

"That's incredible. I know Kendall. We met a few years ago."

Mallory's stomach dropped. "No."

"Yeah, and he told me about a time at school when all the girls wanted to see his thing, and how they would trade him stuff. One girl gave him an iPod."

Mallory crossed the middle cushion to slap him on the knee. "Now I know you're lying. Kendall Throckmorton lives in Hong Kong. He's an antiques trader."

"Do you keep up with every guy who showed you his—"

"Stop it," she said. When she reached across to give him another playful slap, he took her hand and kissed it.

"You crossed the line," he said, refusing to let go.

"What do you mean?"

He motioned to the sofa. "The middle cushion. We've both stayed on our cushions. Until now."

She looked at him, smiled, and asked, "Are you okay with it?"

"Yeah. Actually, I've been trying to figure out how to make the move myself."

"That should be easy for a guy who spent his childhood years at a nudist camp."

"Family nudist resort, and it was two weeks."

Mallory gazed at their entwined hands. "So, it looks like it's your move. There's still plenty of room on that center cushion."

His eyes met hers as he slid closer. She did the same. He raised his arm and put it on the back of the sofa, then onto her shoulders as their faces came to just inches from one another.

"Better?" she asked. She was close enough to discern the hint of cologne. His breathing deepened as he nodded in reply. They remained that way for several moments. "Are you going to kiss me, or do you have another crazy story to share?"

"Mmm," he said softly. "I'm done talking."

The first kiss was... *Oh, my.* Soft and warm and... *Oh, my.* He pulled her closer, a place she was happy to be. The stubble of his beard felt rough and masculine against her face and hand as she stroked his cheek. The kiss lingered. How it ended Mallory couldn't say, but if it didn't begin again, she was going to go crazy. And then it did. Deeper this time. More passion. More exploring. She raised up and pushed herself toward him, causing him to slide back against the arm of the sofa.

They were nearly horizontal, and the feel of his muscular arms encircling her waist made her want more. The kisses became more passionate, and from her position above him, she was in control of the moment. Jake seemed pleased with her being in charge, and when it became apparent that his pleasure had spread, she slowly and reluctantly pulled back. She used her arms to raise herself up, so she was looking down at him. Her breathing was ragged and brimming with desire. His, too.

Neither spoke for several moments, nor did their eyes stray from one another. It was her decision where things might go next, and as much as she desired them to go further, she was aware of the possible consequences. Most were of no concern, but there were a few that could best be addressed by time and conversation.

So, what to do?

Mallory wiped at the perspiration that had formed on her upper lip and considered how incredibly unsexy that must look. Her gaze came to rest on the vintage clock radio that had been her father's when he was in college forty years earlier. She remembered how, as a five-year-old, she'd retrieved it from the trash bin and placed it in her bedroom, and how she tuned it to an oldies station and danced with her pillow to the classic love ballads of decades past while pretending to be at a fancy ball where all the boys were in tuxedos and the girls wore gowns. And where she always wound up with the most handsome boy of all.

"Would you like to dance?" she asked quietly.

His voice was equally soft. "I never learned how. I always thought I looked dumb dancing."

"It would be impossible for you to look dumb." She pulled herself from the sofa and turned on the radio. After a few turns of the knob, she came upon one of the best slow dancing songs ever.

"Unchained Melody," she said, holding out her hand to him.

Jake got to his feet but appeared skeptical. "You're going to be disappointed."

"Take me in your arms and sway with the music."

He did as she said, and it was perfect. He was tall enough that her head came to rest against his chest. She heard the strong and steady beat of his heart, and it made her feel good, safe, fuzzy, and all the things a girl wants to feel when she's found the guy she's been hoping might come along. His strong arms held her while his hands caressed her back, causing shivers to launch themselves the length of her body. The song came to an end, but was followed by an old NYSNC tune that five-year-old Mallory had played repeatedly.

The dreams of those days were coming to life in real time. The most handsome guy at the dance was holding her. And for all she cared, the music could go on forever.

CHAPTER ELEVEN

FRIDAY, DECEMBER 8

Mallory ran a comb through her hair, applied a touch of lipstick, cinched her robe, and stepped out of the dark bedroom into the light-filled living room. Early morning sun gave everything an orange glow. She squinted as her eyes adjusted. Jake was seated at the tiny kitchen table with his back to her. His laptop was open, and he was hard at work, oblivious to her approach. She crept across the room and wrapped her arms around him from behind. He inhaled and laid his head against her chest.

"Good morning," she murmured.

"Yes, it certainly is."

She peered over his shoulder at the laptop screen. "Stella and Michael?"

"I'll have another chapter for you to read today."

"We haven't talked about the chapter I read on the plane yesterday, which I loved, by the way."

He looked up at her. "Are you sure? When I woke up, you were fast asleep. I figured it was my writing."

"More like an early start to the day. Speaking of which, how long have you been up?"

"A couple hours."

She groaned. "It's that sleeper sofa, isn't it? It's so uncomfortable."

"It wasn't that at all. This…" He pointed to the screen. "It woke me up. Stella wants her story told, and she won't let me sleep sometimes."

Mallory hugged him tightly. "That's what all the great writers say. The characters speak to them."

Jake snorted. "I'm a long way from being a great writer, but you're right. They definitely speak to me." He pushed the laptop away and pulled her into his lap. "Thank you for a great first day in New York."

"Between my interview and your trip to Yankee Stadium, we hardly spent any time together."

"True, but last evening was…" Another sigh.

"Are you disappointed that it ended with you on the sofa?"

He laughed. "You don't pull punches, do you? And to answer your question, if this"—he pointed at her, then back at himself—"is going to develop into something long-term, then we'll…sooner or later. I'm not going to push."

"You may not have to." She giggled. "With the way you kiss, I'll be the one doing the pushing."

He gently placed his hand on her chin and turned her so they were facing. "If that's the case, you know where to find me."

The kisses differed from the night before. Lighter and sweeter. Less hurried. Still, they caused Mallory's stomach to do silly little flip-flops. And she desired him even more.

It was a new day, though. He had a radio interview, and she had a follow-up with Price Ricketts at Twisted Fishbowl. All in all, a good and productive day.

And the evening? That would be anyone's guess.

❄

Jake had planned on making breakfast, but the only thing in Mallory's cupboards were a stale box of Cinnamon Toast Crunch and a can of soup. The fridge was mostly empty too, so he suggested they leave early and grab a bite. She was all in. At a deli around the corner from her apartment, they stepped into the queue of people jostling to place their orders on the way to work.

"People yell more than in Kansas City," Jake observed as they inched forward.

"Ha," she replied, gently elbowing him in the stomach. "Are you forgetting how they shouted for our order at Gates' Barbeque? They had me scared to death."

"It's all part of the show there." He looked at the surge of people around them. "With these folks, it's a way of life."

They reached the front of the line a few minutes later. The guy behind the counter didn't bother to look up. "Whattya have?"

Jake turned to Mallory. "What's good here?"

"No idea. I've never eaten here."

The guy finally looked up. He said nothing, but his scowl said plenty. A woman behind them barked at them to hurry up.

"What's popular here?" Mallory asked the guy behind the counter. He rolled his eyes.

"I ain't got time for this, lady."

Mallory raised up to her full height, which wasn't much over five-seven, but still caught the guy's attention. She pointed to Jake as she said, "Look, bud, he's visiting and you're being a total douche. How about a little New York hospitality?"

The guy continued glaring at them, but the woman who had shouted for them to hurry up apologized. "Get the two eggs on a roll with cheese and bacon," she said. Then, to the guy behind the counter, "And don't scrimp on the cheese."

When they were back outside with sandwiches in hand, Jake started laughing. "If you hadn't been with me, I might have run away when he gave us that stare."

"You have to be tougher, Jake." She lifted on her tiptoes and kissed his cheek. "Another day or so and you'll fit right in."

"I doubt it," he said as he unwrapped his sandwich. "I couldn't believe you called the guy a douche."

She giggled. "Did I really?"

"Um-hmm."

"Wow, I don't even remember." She held up her sandwich. "It worked, though."

She hailed a cab, and they jumped in and gave the cabbie the address of the radio station.

"No eating in the cab," the driver said brusquely.

Jake started to re-wrap his sandwich, but Mallory pushed a five-dollar bill toward the cabbie. He accepted.

"It's all good," she said as she took a bite. "And speaking of good, this sandwich is fantastic. I can't believe I haven't tried that place."

"And after calling the counter guy a douche, you probably won't be welcome back."

"He had it coming. And if that's the worst thing anyone calls him today, he'll be lucky."

They finished their sandwiches and leaned into one another while the cabbie continued toward Manhattan. Jake asked his name.

"Why do you want to know?" he asked, eyeing Jake in the mirror.

Mallory chimed in. "He's from Missouri. They talk to everybody out there."

The cabbie cracked a smile. "I'm Sahil. My cousin lives in Missouri. He tells me that people are very friendly there."

"He's right," Mallory said, squeezing Jake's arm. "Like this guy. He just got stared down by a counter guy at the deli and nearly peed his pants."

Sahil laughed. "Learn from your mistakes. Do you have business at the radio station?"

"Something like that," Jake answered, not wanting to come across as anyone special. Mallory filled in the rest of the story.

"He's going to be on Sports 107."

Sahil's eyes grew large. "Seriously? I listen to them all the time."

Jake gave Mallory a "why did you do that?" look. "I wrote a story about a football player in Kansas City that they want to talk about."

"No way!" Sahil's eyes were more focused on Jake than on the road ahead.

Jake nodded.

"Brian Mott?"

Jake nodded again.

"I read that. I'm glad he didn't do what they said he did."

"You're a Chiefs fan?"

"Not at all, but I have two-hundred dollars on them this weekend. If Mott hadn't played, I probably would have lost, but now..." Sahil smiled broadly.

"You're a real hero," Mallory said, laughing as Jake's face reddened. She kissed him, then added, "Now if we can just get you past your fear of delicatessens, everything will be good."

Sports 107 was housed on the ground floor of a Manhattan skyscraper. A receptionist alerted the on-air team of Jake's arrival, and he was escorted into the studio. Everything about the place screamed testosterone. The walls were plastered with posters of New York sports teams. The on-air hosts were male. Former athletes who, from what Mallory could gather, were a pretty big deal. One had played for the Yankees in the nineties. The other did something or other for the Giants. And while she wasn't sure what sport the Giants played, she could guess by the guy's enormity that it was probably football.

Mallory took a seat in a room outside the studio with a guy named Chris who said he was the producer. He operated a board that controlled everything from commercials to sound effects, all while keeping up a steady dialogue about whatever came to mind. His eyes occasionally drifted in Mallory's direction while he did his work. It was pretty obvious that he was checking her out but wasn't very good at it. And when he worked up the courage to ask if she and Jake were dating, she told him they were engaged. That cooled his jets.

She looked on silently through a window while Jake shined on the radio. His interaction with the hosts was funny and informative, and he seemed completely at ease. She especially liked the way he deflected their praise for his work.

"It's part of covering sports in the town where you grew up," he said at one point.

Gosh, he was good, and she was so proud of him. The segment lasted fifteen minutes, and when it was over, the on-air guys high-fived him and invited him back. When Jake came out of the studio, it was all Mallory could do not to jump into his arms and hug him.

"I'm sure glad that's over," he said as they headed for the door.

She smacked his butt. "Why? You were incredible. I had to pinch myself to make sure I wasn't dreaming."

He grinned and was opening the lobby door for her when a man in a suit and tie approached.

"Mr. Powell," Jake said, offering his hand.

"Great to see you again, Jake. You killed that interview." The man turned to Mallory. "Hi there, I'm Roger Powell."

"Mallory Newell."

"Mr. Powell and I met at Yankee Stadium yesterday," Jake said.

Powell laughed. "Jake was moments from being arrested when a mutual friend of ours stepped in and saved his skin."

Mallory looked at Jake. "Arrested?"

"Sort of," he conceded sheepishly. "I forgot to mention it."

"You certainly did." Then, to Powell, "Thank you for keeping him out of jail, Mr. Powell. It would have put a real damper on our weekend."

"You're welcome, and call me Roger. Both of you." He placed his hand on Jake's shoulder. "Have you got a couple minutes, Jake? There's something I want to run past you."

Jake checked the time, then turned to Mallory. "Unfortunately, I don't, Roger. Mallory has a meeting that—"

"It's fine, Jake. My meeting is only a few blocks away. I don't need to leave for an hour. Go ahead." She reached into her bag and removed her ever-present laptop. "I'll use the time to catch up on Stella and Michael."

The weekend getaway was Stella's idea, and after consulting the airlines, they'd decided upon New York City. She had never been there before, and Michael's experience in the Big Apple consisted of a single high school trip.

He wanted it to be a perfect weekend, so he'd started reading up on things to do. There was Central Park and the Empire State Building. Times Square. Broadway. So many possibilities.

He decided they should stay in Manhattan, but when he started checking hotels, he was shocked by the rates. "I could spend a month at the Adair Motel for what you charge for a single night," he told a reservation agent.

"It's New York," she snipped before hanging up.

And then, a stroke of luck. A hotel a few blocks off Broadway with a rate less than a third of the others. He called and inquired about two rooms, and was told that he could have adjoining rooms at a twenty percent discount if he was okay with one not having a window. That was fine. He would take the windowless room. The money they saved could be put toward a show or a special dinner.

Stella was even more excited than Michael. She had been without employment for three weeks, and the trip provided a welcome respite from the tension. Their afternoon flight arrived at JFK airport as the sun was setting. They caught a cab, gave the driver the name of their hotel, then sat back to take in the sights of Manhattan.

Except it wasn't Manhattan.

"Where is Times Square?" Michael asked the cabbie.

"Times Square's in Manhattan. This is Queens."

"But the hotel I booked. It's at—"

"It's right here," the cabbie said as he pulled up in front of a dingy five-story building.

"But I thought... The address is right off Broadway, so I..."

"Broadway is two blocks that way. But it's not the Broadway you thought it was."

"Oh, no."

Mallory looked up to see if anyone had heard her talking to herself. The small waiting room was empty, though, and

Jake's story of Stella and Michael's visit to New York was so gripping that she continued to read. She was still reading twenty minutes later when Jake returned.

"Ready?" he asked as he entered the waiting area with his coat in his arms.

She tucked her laptop away and reached for her coat, but he beat her to it. Many of the women she worked with would have insisted they were perfectly capable of putting on their own coat. That resulted in fewer offers from men concerned about outdated assumptions regarding women and old-fashioned chivalry. Independence was a good thing. An admirable thing. And Mallory had always considered herself a strong, independent woman. But there was something so… *nice* about a guy helping her with her coat. Hogan had done it a time or two, back when they'd first started dating. She suspected it was a habit with Jake.

"Thank you. Now, tell me how you were nearly arrested at Yankee Stadium."

He laughed. "You should have seen your face when Roger brought that up."

"You're the first guy I've dated who was in trouble with the law."

"A real desperado," he said. He pulled on his coat and reached for her hand. "The truth isn't nearly as dramatic."

By the time he'd finished his story of Phoebe the security guard busting him in Monument Park, they were back on the sidewalk.

"I don't think she would have arrested me," he said casually as they walked hand in hand.

"Above the law, are you?" Mallory teased.

"No, but I'm usually pretty lucky when I just apologize and own up to my mistakes. It always worked when I was a kid in elementary school, so I just rolled with it."

"You get in trouble a lot?"

"Sometimes you just have to take chances."

"Like with Brian Mott? I was reading up on him this morning. In fact," she squeezed his hand, "I read your article."

He paused in the middle of the sidewalk and was nearly knocked over by the surge of pedestrian traffic coming up behind them. A couple, typical New Yorkers, barked at him to watch out. And just like in grade school, Jake apologized.

"You read my article?"

Mallory nodded. "It made me cry."

Jake laughed, then started walking again. "That bad, huh?"

"He is so misunderstood. Why do people rush to judgment without knowing all the facts?"

Jake nodded thoughtfully. "He's far from perfect. Since you read the article, you know about his past. A couple teams gave up on him, and justifiably so, but people I know told me how hard he's working to put that behind him."

"It would have been easy to just pile on."

"Plenty of others did, and their stories were the first accounts the public had. I don't operate that way though."

He told her about seeing his cop friend, Larry, in the stadium parking lot, and how Larry had run interference for him that led to the big lineman holing up at his house on Kenwood Avenue.

"He really owes you a lot," she said as they waited for a light to change.

"He owes me nothing. We both benefitted from the arrangement. If he's like most players, he'll act like it never happened. We'll pass in the locker room or on the field, and he'll look right through me."

"That's terrible."

"It's journalism. A few guys pal around with the players and get their puff pieces. I want to be known as a guy who reports the truth." He glanced up the street. "How much further until we get to the Twisted Fishbowl?"

"Two blocks."

"Are you nervous?"

"A little. Price said he wanted to hammer out the details of my agreement. I've never negotiated a contract before."

Mallory watched his face for a sign that he couldn't believe she was that naïve. That was a Hogan thing. He would have rolled his eyes and told her how easy it was, and how he had negotiated hundreds of contracts.

Jake just nodded and kept walking. "You'll do fine."

It was Mallory who paused on the sidewalk the second time. "Is that all you have to say? I'll do fine?"

"What do you want me to say?"

"How about some advice?"

He tugged at her hand to get her moving again. "You know what you need. Make sure it's in the agreement."

"What if he offers me less than I'm making now?"

"You tell him it's not enough."

"And what if he says too bad?"

"You have to decide if you're willing to walk away. That might get you a better offer or it might not."

She pushed back a few strands of hair that had been blown by the breeze. "I think the offer will be for a lot more."

"That would be nice."

"Yeah… You really don't have a lot to say about stuff, do you?"

"Sure I do."

"Like what?"

Before she knew it, he had led her out of the flow of pedestrians toward a breezeway next to a department store. He kissed her. Deeply and passionately. Over his shoulder, she saw a woman about her age looking on. Their eyes met, and the woman winked and gave a thumbs up.

He pulled away and said, "I really like you, Mallory."

"That's a good start," she said with a giggle. "What else do you have to say?"

He kissed her again, probably smearing her lipstick. Screw the lipstick. The kisses were… *Oh, boy.*

"Dancing in your apartment was one of the most romantic things I've ever experienced."

"You mean one of the most romantic things you've experienced with your clothes on?" she teased, stroking his cheek.

He shook his head. "I mean it. The feelings were almost overwhelming."

His words moved her—the way he expressed them, with such emotion and sincerity. She'd never heard a guy bare his soul like that. It stirred something deep within her that a man was willing to express his thoughts without worrying if it was too…unmanly. She initiated the next kiss, eyes closed, so she wouldn't see the response of any onlookers. It was incredibly soft and warm and brought a shiver that had nothing to do with the near-freezing temperatures. Her legs went soft, but Jake was holding her so it didn't matter.

He stepped back and seemed to come to a realization of where they were and what had just happened. Mallory considered pulling him back toward her, but time was growing short. Her meeting was in fifteen minutes. Just enough time to reapply her lipstick, touch up her windblown hair, and prepare to make her mark in the publishing world.

They reached the Twisted Fishbowl offices with five minutes to spare.

"I'll be waiting in that coffee shop we passed on the last block," Jake said. "Text me when you're done, and I'll come running."

They hugged, then he held her at arm's length to get a good, long look at her.

"Do I look okay?" she asked.

"Stunning. Now go get 'em."

She started toward the door, then had a thought. "You never mentioned what that guy at the radio station wanted to talk to you about."

"Roger? He made me a job offer."

"Flock of geese! Really?"

Jake nodded.

"Did you take it?"

"There's a lot to consider, but we can talk later."

She was stepping inside when he called her name. She glanced back, a bit concerned about the time.

"I think I'm in love with you," he said, then turned and headed away.

Ninety minutes passed with no word from Mallory, and the baristas were making it obvious that Jake needed to move on. He checked GPS and saw there was a bookstore a few blocks away. Perhaps there would be a nook where he could begin the next chapter in the romantic saga of Stella and Michael. He wondered what Mallory thought of the personal similarities. He'd worried early on that she might tell him to cut it out—to stop idealizing their time together in the lives of his two leading characters. So far, though, nothing. And that was good because as he spent more time with her, Jake understood that his relationships before Mallory were nothing compared to what was developing between them. And that he really hadn't a clue about what true love looked like.

He couldn't wait to write the story of Stella and Michael's first dance. It would take place in Michael's hotel room, a place that, despite being a step or two above a fleabag, was where their forever love story would begin.

He grabbed his backpack, left a generous tip, and waved at a barista who glared at him in return.

"Sorry for taking up a table for so long," he said. She nodded. He was smiling as he exited the coffee shop. Mallory would have teased him about apologizing his way out of another tight spot. And they would both laugh.

He stepped out onto the sidewalk and nearly ran into her. Her eyes were cast downward onto the sidewalk. She looked up when she heard him call. She was crying.

He pulled her to him. She came into his arms and the dam burst. She tried to speak, but barely could. But somehow, through the tears and the moans, Jake was able to make out five words.

"I didn't get the job."

For a guy who considered himself clueless about women, Jake was an incredible listener. And consoler. And friend.

After that pig Price Ricketts told her she was being passed over, Mallory had spent forty-five minutes trying to pull herself together in a CVS Pharmacy restroom. Her plan was to act as if it wasn't a big deal, even though it was a huge fricking deal. It wasn't Jake's fault that Price wasn't as innovative and free-thinking as he'd claimed. Plus, he'd just been offered a job that could be career changing. And if there was one thing she'd learned from the months she'd spent with Hogan, it was that guys only had so much compassion before they wanted things to return to the way they were supposed to be, which meant having everything focused on them. So, she'd consoled herself, made herself look presentable, and pasted a smile on her face as she walked to the coffee shop where he was waiting. And then promptly fell apart as soon as she spotted him on the sidewalk.

After that, he'd taken care of everything. Hailing the cab. Holding her close and allowing her to cry it out on the thirty-minute ride to her apartment. Respectfully telling the well-meaning cabbie to mind his own business when he'd asked if everything was okay.

And the best? Whipping up a milkshake using ingredients he pulled together at her apartment, including a long-forgotten pint of Wegman's Cherry-Licious ice cream he found in the bottom of her tiny freezer. That made her smile for real. He brought it to her on the sofa where she'd collapsed as soon as they returned. She took a sip and savored the cool sweetness as it made its way to her aching tummy. She offered some to him, but he said no, then sat down next to her and kissed the hand not holding the shake.

"Want to talk about it?"

She did. Very much. The words tumbled out. The strange greeting she'd received from Maya, the girl who had led the group interview the previous afternoon.

"It was like she didn't remember me," Mallory explained. "But knowing what I know now, she acted that way because she was aware of what was going to happen. As soon as Price came out of his office I knew something was wrong. Yesterday he was so open and excited." She sipped the shake and smacked her lips. "Gosh, this is good." She gave him a milkshake kiss on the cheek. He smiled, but said nothing.

"But today, he was all business. He brought me into his office and said they needed more of an authoritarian for the position."

This was where Hogan would have tried to push her to the end of the story or tell her what he would have done in the situation. Jake did neither. He allowed her to share things at her own pace. She saw the flash of anger in his eyes as she poured out her frustration. She sensed his compassion, too. It felt as if he was shouldering some of the hurt and disappointment for her, and that helped.

That and the homemade milkshake. She noisily sucked

the last of it from the glass. He smiled, then took the glass and set it aside. He had barely said a word since she'd starting pouring out her pain, but she knew he was fully and completely there. Not judging. Not wondering what she might have done wrong. Just listening while she processed the hurt, anger, and disappointment. He just let her speak. And speak some more.

Until she started doubting herself.

"I'm not sure publishing is where I belong anymore."

His eyes grew large. "Publishing is your life, Mallory. It's what you do. It's who you are."

She snorted. "I thought so until a couple of weeks ago."

He scooped her hands into his, pulled them together, and caressed. "It seems you're at a crossroad."

"Yeah, it would seem so. Any chance you need a reporter for your website?"

He laughed softly. "Sure. What do you know about sports?"

"I like the Kangaroos."

Mallory felt some of the funk slipping away. Jake was right. She was at a crossroads. But what direction could she go other than straight ahead? She had a degree in English. There had been other offers after graduation. All in publishing. Everything had gone according to her master plan. Work hard, get noticed, move up.

What had she missed?

And what else was there? She could teach. She had her credentials. But really? Despite having had several wonderful teachers in her life, and a couple professors who'd taken an interest in her at Dartmouth, she couldn't see herself in a classroom.

"Jake, have you ever been at a crossroads?"

She liked how he gave the question a few moments of thought.

"Yes. When I worked for the newspaper, a couple of my buddies got advancement opportunities faster than me, and I started feeling sorry for myself."

"And now, looking back on it? Were you right to feel that way?" She squeezed his hand. "Because I'm feeling pretty sorry for myself right now, and I want to know if my feelings are real."

"They're real," he said. "I'm a witness to that. But to answer your question, had it not been for getting passed over, I might have never found the courage to strike out on my own."

"Are you saying I should take this as a sign to do something different?"

"Not at all. It's like what you told me soon after we met. When you didn't think my writing was very good. Remember?"

She laughed. "I was pretty hard on you."

"True, but you gave me one bit of advice that will stay with me forever."

He touched his chest with his fingertips, then gently placed the back of his hand above her heart. "Remember what you said?"

"Um-hm." She placed her hand over his. "Good writing comes from here." She giggled. "The heart, not the nipple like you said that night."

"I've thought a lot about that. It's not just good writing that comes from the heart, it's everything good." He lifted her hand to his lips and kissed it. "Be still for a bit. Allow your heart to stop hurting. Give it time to tell you what's next."

She liked everything that he said, especially his sincerity. There was at least one guy in the world who cared enough to listen. And he was listening to her.

She picked herself up and shifted onto his lap, so they were nose to nose. The kiss that followed was as perfect as the night before. So was the next one. She wrapped her arms around his neck and held on for dear life while she waited for the emotional ebb of the day's disappointment to wash away. He lifted his gaze to meet hers, and while she would have preferred to kiss more and talk less, it appeared he had something to say. And if he could be the world's best listener, she could at least be second best.

"I feel like your heart has already spoken to you about a couple things."

"Tell me."

"First is the direction you've allowed me to take on Grandma's book."

"Your writing led you there, Jake. That wasn't me."

"You could have stopped me. Knowing the resistance we're going to face, you probably should have."

She nodded and looked away. "I've never challenged the status quo. Mr. Key's head will explode."

"And what will your response be?"

"That it's good for the company and good for you."

He smiled. "Good answer. You sold me. Now all you have to do is sell Marcus Key."

"You said your heart has spoken to you about a couple things. What's the other one?"

He placed his hand on her chin and guided her gaze back to him. He kissed her again, then said, "I think you know."

She nuzzled against his neck and murmured contentedly. "How about your heart? Are you regretting what you said earlier? Before I left to go see Price? When you said—"

"That I thought I was falling in love with you?"

"Yeah, that."

He shook his head and made her stomach lurch. "That wasn't completely true." He wrapped his arms around her. "I don't think I'm falling for you. I *know* I am."

She saw his concern when her tears returned, but she

didn't want him to worry when there was nothing to worry about. So she smiled through the tears—the happy tears—and whispered, "I am falling deeply, madly, crazy in love with you, too."

Mallory was uncertain how much time passed. She was discovering that was the way it was when with Jake. The romance allowed her imagination to take flight. The quiet snippets of conversation served as an interlude that confirmed how special Jake Springer really was. They could have stayed that way forever as far as she was concerned, but her phone buzzed from across the room, and when she took a look around, Mallory saw only darkness.

"Where did the sun go?" she mused as she retrieved the phone. It was already six-fifteen. When she saw who was calling, her stomach clenched, and she considered not taking it. They would have to speak eventually, though.

She turned on the kitchen light as she answered. "Hi, Talia."

Talia jumped in with both feet.

"Price Ricketts doesn't deserve you, honey. I told him that myself just a few minutes ago. I also told him to never ask for my help again. It'll be a cold day in hell before he and his twisted, screwed-up fishbowl get any referrals from me."

"Thank you. And it's okay, really."

"No, it's not. He treated you horribly. I thought he was different, but it turns out he's just another misogynistic knucklehead. Screw him." The anger left from her voice as she continued. "And forgive me for dragging you back here for nothing."

"It's okay, Talia. I mean it. I've learned a lot about myself this weekend." She looked across the room at Jake, smiled, and said, "And it gave me the chance to show a very special guy around New York."

"Oh, Mallory, sweetheart, that's wonderful! Will I get to meet him sometime?"

"Not this trip, unfortunately, but perhaps next time he comes to town."

The call was over quickly. Mallory turned off the light and scampered back to Jake's lap.

"If you want me to meet your friend, we can go someplace and—"

Mallory placed an index finger over his lips. "I'm still pretty salty about her telling Price Ricketts that I'm too intense." She slid her finger from his lips and kissed him. "And I want you all to myself tonight."

"I like that. What would you like to do?"

"Nothing that takes us far from this sofa."

"Are you sure?" he asked with a grin. "I've got a cop friend who can get us Price Ricketts's address. We could go by and say hello. Maybe slash his tires. Or break a window or two at his house."

Mallory laughed, and it felt good and normal. Maybe her heart was figuring things out after all. "No, he's got a wife and an adorable little boy, so breaking his windows is out. But maybe we could run to the store and get some more ice cream."

"Are you serious?"

She was. The milkshake had been heavenly. And perfect for bruised feelings. And like every good thing, a little more was even better.

CHAPTER TWELVE

SATURDAY, DECEMBER 9

Mallory was awakened by a creaking sound from somewhere in the apartment. Despite two deadbolts and a couple of chains, there were still concerns about break-ins. But then it could also be someone moving around in a neighboring apartment. Ambient noise was a fact of life in New York.

Not this time, though. She listened closer and knew that the sound was inside her apartment. Then she remembered. Jake.

The bedroom was dark, thanks to the blackout shades she'd purchased a week after moving in. She reached out and patted the other side of the bed. Empty. The sheets were cool to the touch. He had been gone for a while.

Then another creak, closer. The door opened, and Jake stuck his head in and appeared to debate if he should stay or go.

"Mallory," he whispered.

She sat up and raked her fingers through her hair. "Hey, you."

"Sorry if I woke you." He was still whispering.

"Don't worry about that. Come in and open the shades. What time is it?"

"Eight-twenty." He stepped in and raised the shades, flooding the room with light. He was carrying two huge boxes.

"I got breakfast."

"For the entire building?"

"Well...remember how things went yesterday? At the deli?"

She laughed at the memory of the grouchy counter guy.

"The girl at the bagel shop was worse. And I didn't have you to rescue me. When I wasn't ready to order as soon as she called my number, she moved to the next person in line. Then, when I told her I was ready, she said she'd already called my number."

"But obviously you were able to order. And it looks like you ordered a lot."

He set the boxes on the bed. "Yeah, about that. I wasn't sure which ones to get, and I didn't want to have to go to the back of the line again."

She giggled. "So, you ordered everything?"

He opened a box. It contained at least two dozen bagels. "It's called the Celebration Box. A sample of the best of New York." He looked up sheepishly. "It was the first thing I saw on the menu, so I asked for it."

"How about the other box? More bagels?"

"They call it the Cream Cheese Sampler Box." He opened the second box and held up a plastic container. "Here's a pound of Walnut Raisin." And then another. "Jalapeno Cheddar. There's also plain, strawberry, and olive pimento." He picked up another. "And lox. Do you like lox?"

"Nope."

"I was worried about that. It wasn't included in the Cream Cheese Sampler Box, but the lady at the counter said I couldn't have bagels without lox, and I didn't want to make her mad." He set the lox spread back in the box. "She scared me a little."

"Well, come here and let me comfort you," Mallory said, patting the spot next to her. He slid under the covers and nearly knocked the Cream Cheese Sampler Box to the floor before saving the day with a heroic last second grab.

"Pretty smooth, huh?" he said as he cozied up next to her. "Can I fix you a bagel?"

"No, thanks. I'm not hungry."

The look on his face was priceless. Mallory dissolved into laughter that grew as he tickled her ribs. "You wouldn't say that if you knew how much all this stuff cost," he said as he pulled her close.

He smelled nice. Like bagels and outdoors. And sex. That was the part that drew her closer. She pressed her face against his neck and basked in his warmth. His physical response was immediate. The bagels would have to wait.

She was uncharacteristically quiet as they packed for their return to Kansas City. She said everything was fine, but Jake could tell her mind was on other things. And he suspected he knew what. Not the previous evening—that had been incredible. He knew it, and he knew she did, too. The way things had progressed seemed as natural as breathing. And the love they had made was…real love, some previously unknown—at least for Jake—level of intimacy that transcended the physical to touch his heart and mind. Afterwards, he'd struggled to describe it, wanting very much for Mallory to know how he'd been affected, but unable to find the words. It wasn't until that morning, after he'd returned with the bagels and they'd made love again, that he could articulate his feelings.

It was love. Total, complete, head-over-heels, mind-blowing, hang on for dear life kind of love that flooded every nook and cranny of his soul.

And he knew with more certainty than he'd ever known anything that he would spend the rest of his life with her.

He nearly said as much. When they were enjoying their bagels—poppy seed with strawberry cream cheese for her, plain with jalapeno cheddar for him—there was a moment when he almost asked if she could envision a future together. He hadn't, though. He didn't want her to think he was moving too fast. Or perhaps he feared she didn't share those feelings. She had just come out of a relationship, one that ended with heartache.

But when the time came, and Jake hoped it came soon, he would tell her how he felt. He would lay it out there and hope he didn't make a fool of himself.

And hope she felt the same.

"Would you mind if we leave an hour early?" Mallory asked as she folded a sweatshirt and stuffed it into her bag. "My laptop is acting up, and I want to run by the office and get my old one."

He didn't care. And he wondered if, somehow, a stop by Stratford and Key might make things clearer for her. Even though it was the weekend, and the place would be deserted, perhaps a few moments there might help reset her thoughts about her future.

Their flight left Newark at five, so after packing and another bagel, Mallory called for an Uber. Her pensiveness had passed by then, and their last moments in the apartment were happy ones. She finished her bagel, wiped her face with a napkin, and came around the table to sit in his lap.

"I'm so glad you came with me," she said sweetly. "I'm not sure how I would have handled yesterday if you hadn't been here for me."

Jake nodded but didn't speak. Words were unnecessary. It was a moment to be enjoyed quietly, as only two people could who were completely comfortable in one another's presence. A text alerted them that their ride was close, so they gathered their things and headed out. Jake took one last look around the apartment and tried to imagine living in such a place.

And for the first time, he could…as soon as he manned up and stopped letting the deli and bagel people push him around.

Mallory used her code to buzz them into the Stratford and Key building. The lobby was empty. It was possible that a few of her colleagues might be around on a Saturday afternoon, but she was willing to take the chance. Those who worked weekends usually left by noon, to at least give the appearance of having a social life. That stuff had never worried Mallory, though. She had happily showed up many Saturdays. And never shied from putting in a full day. What her third-floor colleagues thought of her was inconsequential. She used to love the work and was happy with the trajectory her career was taking.

The memories made her smile, but also caused her to feel melancholy. Would she ever love or care for anything about Stratford and Key again?

Of course, without the firm, she wouldn't have Jake in her life. Who would have thought it might turn out as it had? Just days earlier, she'd felt as if she'd been exiled to Kansas City.

Exiled? Hah!

"What are you smiling about?" Jake asked as they crossed the lobby.

"Just a thought. Are you ready to see my office?"

"I can't wait."

"Believe me, it's nothing like what you saw on the tenth floor. I barely have room to turn around."

"How much space does anyone really need? I mean, you're there to work, right? Anything beyond just enough is more for ego than getting stuff done."

She punched the elevator button, then took his hand. "Are you always so damned sensible?"

"It's a midwestern thing," he said, leaning over to kiss her. "Folks back home would say Marcus Key is all sizzle and no steak."

"That's a good one," she said with a laugh.

"All crown and no filling."

"That's not as good."

"All foam and no beer."

She rolled her eyes. "You can stop anytime."

She led him down the hallway to her office. As hoped, the place was deserted. She frowned as she passed Luis's dark office. He was probably cavorting on some beach in Bora Bora, laughing at the poor suckers back in Manhattan.

Funny, but the thought of Luis being assigned to Dawn Darby Endicott didn't sting like before. She was actually happy to be on her way back to Kansas City. There was still a lot of work to be done on the book, but that meant more time with Jake. Win-win.

"Here it is," she said as she opened the door and flipped on the lights. Jake stepped in and looked around.

"It smells nice," he said. "Like you."

She went to her desk and pulled a laptop from the bottom drawer. "This one is two years older, but I've always liked it better," she said as she removed the broken one from her bag and placed it in the drawer.

"They certainly provide you with nice equipment," Jake

said. "My laptop is six years old and holds a charge for about fifteen minutes."

"That's Stratford and Key for you," she mused as she zipped the bag and set it on her desk. "Anything you want to see before we head out?" She giggled. "There are snack machines at the end of the hall. I remember how much you enjoy Cheez-Its.

Jake smiled. "And I remember the death stare you gave me. Like I was a homeless person or something."

"Because I thought you were! Nobody shows up on the tenth floor in jeans and a hoodie."

"I wasn't trying to impress anyone. I didn't even know why I was there." He came to her and wrapped his arms around her waist. "But I'm sure glad it happened."

Mallory couldn't be sure if it was his kiss or where they were, but the sensation was electric. She squeezed her eyes shut and allowed the moment to go wherever it wanted. His lips moved to the side of her mouth, then came crashing back again. She moaned, hoping for more and wanting to make more happen.

And then everything stopped.

Mallory opened her eyes to see what had happened. Jake's were open as well, riveted on something just over her shoulder. She glanced back and saw Mr. Key standing in the door.

Panic. Embarrassment. Fear. She stepped back and forced a smile, nearly stumbling when her hip struck the edge of her desk. Jake reached out to steady her, his eyes never leaving Mr. Key's.

"Jake," Mr. Key said quietly. "Mallory. Why are you in New York?"

She couldn't find her voice. She pointed to the laptop. "I… Mine was…"

Mr. Key nodded. His eyes remained glued on them, taking in everything as if committing it all to memory.

Mallory's cheeks paled under his unwavering gaze. She knew she needed to speak—to extricate Jake from an awkward situation. But she didn't know what to say. The best she could hope for was that Mr. Key would step out. It was only a kiss. It wasn't like he'd caught them doing...other stuff.

But he remained in the door. Watching. Judging. He held his head high, the self-assuredness of knowing he was in charge allowing him to do as he wanted.

"Mallory, Jake, how is the book coming?"

The sudden shift in his tone left her momentarily off balance, which was probably just what Mr. Key wanted. She opened her mouth to speak, but Jake was faster.

"It's coming along fine, Marcus."

She'd forgotten that he addressed Mr. Key by his first name. Nobody she knew did that. He seemed completely unperturbed by it, though. He just stood there.

Jake continued. "Mallory has taught me a lot. My writing was stilted, and there wasn't much emotion. She's working with me to improve. I'm writing a chapter or two every day. We won't have any problem being done by Christmas."

Mr. Key flashed a quick smile. Then he turned to Mallory and asked, "Might I read a chapter?"

He didn't know Marcus Key well, but Jake knew his type. He'd seen them in locker rooms and front offices of professional sports teams. If there was one thing he'd learned from Grandpa Springer that continued to serve him well, it was that everyone had a tell. A slight change in their demeanor or countenance that let you know things weren't as they seemed. Marcus Key's tell was his face. The jutting of his chin. The squint that came from trying to maintain eye contact. And the coldness in his eyes that remained even when he smiled. Marcus Key might be a big deal at the board table, but he would suck at the poker table. He'd already read everything Jake had written. He was certain of it. And he wasn't happy.

"I'm not ready to share it yet," Jake said, tossing the ball back into Key's court. "At least not until Mallory takes another pass at it."

It wasn't the response Key expected. People like him weren't accustomed to being rebuffed. But Jake didn't work for him. He couldn't respond to Jake like he might to Mallory. He was motionless for a moment, working his jaw as if preparing to say something important. He reconsidered, though, and retreated to the door.

"Very well, then. I wish you both a pleasant afternoon."

Jake and Mallory remained where they were until they heard a ding announcing the elevator's arrival. When they were certain Key was gone, Jake said, "Well, that was pleasant."

He reached for her, but Mallory kept her distance. "Not here," she whispered as she grabbed her bag. "Let's go."

Ten minutes later, they were pulling away in a cab.

"Do you think he knew we were there?" Mallory asked.

Jake was certain of it. The bigger question was, why? There was no way he had shown up hoping to catch them in an intimate moment. It was something bigger, but he didn't know what. No need to ruin Mallory's day, though. At least not until he figured things out.

"He probably saw us enter the building," Jake said, giving her hand a squeeze. "Maybe he just happened to be coming in a moment or two after us."

Mallory twisted her mouth in an adorable display of deep thought.

"I've heard he works seven days a week. I guess we were guilty of bad timing, huh?" She kissed his cheek. The color that had drained from her face when Key made his appearance had returned. She was starting to relax. That's what Jake wanted. She'd done nothing wrong other than getting romantically involved with a client. And Jake was dubious that she was the first person at Stratford and Key to go down that road. It happened in many organizations.

But if it wasn't that, what was it? Why was Key acting so strangely? Time would tell. But until then, they would continue to work on the book. And growing their relationship.

CHAPTER THIRTEEN

SUNDAY, DECEMBER 10

It was a good day at Arrowhead Stadium. For Jake and the hometown Kansas City Chiefs.

The Chiefs buried one of their biggest rivals, the Denver Broncos, by three touchdowns in a game that was decided by the end of the first half.

And up in the press box, high above the action on the field, Jake was getting a lot of attention. He had been for most of the weekend, actually, but he'd been blissfully unaware. Who knew you could fly under the radar by going to New York? Few reporters had pulled punches in their rush to vilify Brian Mott. Then, when the truth came out, some refused to admit they were wrong. Only a few offered outright apologies. The rules of good journalism required that they all acknowledge that Jake broke the story. Most did. The few who didn't received terse calls from the local attorney who gave Jake a few hours of free legal advice each month in exchange for an ad-free subscription to the website.

Word hadn't gotten out until the day before that Mott

had holed up at Jake's house. By the time Jake was home, Mott was gone, and the house was spotless.

He left the stadium at four-thirty, an hour after the game concluded, and drove back into the city. Mallory was waiting for him at the Nelson Atkins Museum of Art. He'd dropped her off just as it opened that morning. Spending so many hours surrounded by art was hard to fathom, but she'd been so excited. She still was when she ran out to meet him.

"It's an amazing place," she exclaimed as she crawled into the truck and scooched over next to him. "And on Sundays, when there's a football game, there's hardly anyone there. It was like I had the entire museum to myself."

He was content to listen as she went into detail about the exhibits and other favorite things she'd encountered. She was so sophisticated, and as she described an exhibition of historical photography and another of Asian pottery, he felt a desire to spend time in her world of books and art and architecture. And to learn from her.

"How do you know all that stuff?" he asked when she finally ran out of steam.

"The same way you know so much about sports—by watching and reading and listening." She snuggled her head against his shoulder. "Speaking of which, did the Chiefs win the football game?"

He told her they did but didn't go into detail. Her football knowledge was about the same as his understanding of Asian pottery. They made a quick stop for burgers, then headed back to his house. Mallory was considering giving up her hotel room to be closer to him. Jake hoped she followed through.

Night was settling in as they turned onto Kenwood Avenue. Christmas lights flickered in windows along the street, bringing a festive luminance to the surroundings. Temperatures were unseasonably warm in the mid-fifties.

The heavy snow from the week before was mostly gone, and Jake spotted several kids' bicycles leaning against porches and stoops as he made his way down the street.

"There's a car in your driveway," Mallory said.

Indeed, there was. A late model sedan. As they got closer, he saw it was a Lexus with Alabama plates. Another unfamiliar car, a Tesla, was parked at the curb.

"Any idea who it is?"

He nodded. The Alabama plates gave it away. His parents lived in Alabama. But then again, perhaps it was a rental. He could always hope it was a rental.

Because the last thing he wanted was to find his parents waiting inside. Their presence meant one of two things. Either they were broke and moving back home, or there was something they needed to discuss. He'd experienced both, and neither was appealing.

"Do you want me to wait at the hotel?" Mallory asked as they pulled up in front.

"No. I may need you for moral support."

She laughed. "For someone who's supposed to be moral support, we've done some pretty immoral stuff the last couple days."

That made Jake laugh. "I still want you to come in. You might as well meet the parents." He shut off the truck and turned to her. "Just be warned. They're nothing like you've experienced."

"I'll go in with an open mind. Are you going to introduce me as your girlfriend or your editor?"

His eyes grew large. "Don't say anything about the book. They'll expect a cut of the advance. I'll just introduce you as Mallory and let them figure out the rest."

"What if they plan to stay for the night?"

"Then they'll definitely figure out the rest."

❄

Mallory walked with him to the back door. She considered keeping her distance, to give the look of propriety, but Jake grabbed her hand.

"Get ready for Corabelle. She comes in hard and fast."

"Nonsense. Corabelle loves me. We became good friends the night we waited for you to get back from your date."

It was becoming a favorite tease between them. Jake no longer responded verbally. He just rolled his eyes and pushed open the door. There was no Corabelle.

"That's strange," Jake said.

There were muted voices coming from the living room, but no barking.

Mallory replied, "Maybe you're not as popular as you thought."

The kitchen light was on, but no one was in there. Jake took off his coat, then took hers and hung them on a hook beside the door.

"It is my parents," he whispered.

"How do you know?"

He pointed to his nose. "The smell. Parliament cigarettes—that's their brand. At least when they're smoking cigarettes instead of something else." He took her hand again and led the way into the living room where three people were seated. The man and woman on the sofa, puffing away, were undoubtedly Mr. and Mrs. Springer. They stood when they saw Jake. Mr. Springer snuffed out his cigarette in a Diet Coke can while Mrs. Springer puffed away. No smiles. No kisses or hugs. Talk about strange.

"Son," his father said. "How are you?"

"Pop." There was no embrace. Not even a handshake. Jake hugged his mother, but it was stiff and formal. "Mom."

"Hi, dear."

Jake stepped back and glanced across the room to where a rotund, balding man was seated. He nodded, but said nothing. Jake blinked several times, as out of his element at that moment as he'd seemed at the deli in New York. He looked around the room, then asked, "Where's Corabelle?"

"That old mutt," his father said with a laugh. "I assumed she'd kicked the bucket by now."

The color drained from Jake's face as he dashed for the stairs. Mallory started to follow but didn't want to give the wrong impression, so she stayed. She was about to introduce herself to Mrs. Springer when they heard Jake's cries.

He'd found Corabelle.

"She's breathing, but she's not responding to my voice." The words tumbled from Jake's mouth as he lay on the bedroom floor next to Corabelle and spoke with his vet's answering service. His fear was palpable. He was sweating, crying, and shaking as he wrapped his arms around his long-time best friend. It was the first time Mallory had witnessed the depth of his feelings for Corabelle.

Corabelle's regular vet was closed on weekends. The answering service directed them to an emergency clinic in the suburban community of Overland Park. Jake ended the call and dropped the phone. He looked up and asked Mallory if she would go with him. She accepted immediately, though she was unsure how much help she could be. She had little experience helping others cope with illness and death. One grandparent had passed before her parents married. Two others were gone before Mallory was five years old. Grandma Newell, alive and well, spent more time on bus excursions and cruises than at her Queens apartment. There had been no pets. Her father considered them a waste of time and money. Not even a goldfish or hamster. Until that moment, seeing the impact Corabelle's condition was having on Jake, she'd never considered pets as anything special. How wrong she had been.

He gently took the old dog into his arms and carried her downstairs. When her head lolled to one side, Mallory stepped close and supported her while she stroked the dog's ear. Jake's parents and the stranger were still in the living room. Mrs. Springer came closer. She glanced at Corabelle before focusing on her son. She completely ignored Mallory.

"How long do you think you'll be gone?"

"Mom, I have no idea."

"Well, what should we do?"

"Mom, you didn't even let me know you were coming. I don't know why you're here, and I don't have time to find out now."

He didn't wait for her reply. They rushed out of the house to the truck. "If you'll get in, I'll lay her in your lap," he said to Mallory.

Corabelle was heavy and still as she lay across Mallory's legs. Her breathing was shallow, but Mallory continued to scratch her around the neck and ears as Jake sped through the city. A few minutes into the ride, they passed a sign welcoming them to Kansas. It was Mallory's first trip across the state line, and it made her think back to how little she'd known about the area when she'd arrived. And how arrogant she'd been to assume the Midwest was some backwoods cliché. Kansas City was, she realized now, the sum total of its people. Good people, like Tommy, the cab driver, and Patrick, the bellman, who had become her friends and protectors. And others like the lovely woman she'd met at the museum who'd struck up a conversation about dust bowl era photographers Walker Evans and Dorthea Lang, then invited Mallory to her house sometime to see her book collection.

And Anna Maria, a housekeeper at the hotel, who had left Mallory a plate of *orejas*, a delicious Mexican pastry.

And Quavon, the counter guy at the Fed Ex store next to the hotel, who remembered not only her name, but the name of her company.

Her little slice of Kansas City was growing because of people like them. And then, of course, there was Jake. Oh, my. How wrong she'd been about him. How short-sighted and misinformed. How quick to judge. How slow to reconsider.

How fast to fall in love.

It was after seven when they pulled under an awning with a large red *EMERGENCY VETERINARY CARE* sign over the top. Jake took Corabelle, cradling her like one might a newborn infant, albeit one that weighed as much as a ten-year-old. He whispered something in her ear, and she responded with a slight turn of her head. Mallory felt hope.

The waiting room was empty, and a man in scrubs quickly escorted them to an exam room. He asked a few questions, then said the vet would be in shortly. The room was similar to a physician's office, all fluorescent lighting and antiseptic smells. A poster described the benefits of spaying and neutering. Another warned of something called parvovirus. Jake's attention was on Corabelle, though. His head was close to hers as he whispered that everything would be okay. Mallory slid her chair close and put her arm around him. He leaned against her and looked up for a moment. The fear and despair in his eyes made him look incredibly vulnerable. She wanted to tell him that everything would be okay, to make him feel better.

But she didn't know if everything would be okay.

The vet was a young woman barely out of veterinary school. Her lab coat said her name was Dr. Cronauer, but she introduced herself as Jenny. Her eyes were expressive, and when she ran her hands over and around Corabelle, Mallory saw her worry.

Jake didn't, though. He was focused on his beloved Corabelle. Even when Jenny had him place her on the table, he stayed close, barely noticing the exam and tests. It didn't take long. She rubbed Corabelle's muzzle, then sat down across the exam table from them. Certain of what they were about to hear, Mallory stayed close to Jake's side.

"I'm sorry," Jenny said. She didn't get any further. Jake broke down and wept. He buried his face against Corabelle's neck and nuzzled against the side of her head. He kissed her ear, then her muzzle. Mallory started to cry as well. Jenny, with her heart of gold, stayed where she was, allowing them time to grieve, probably aware it wouldn't be enough, but knowing that no amount of time would ever be sufficient for saying goodbye. After a few minutes, Jake took several ragged breaths and lifted his head. His eyes were red and tearful, but he knew what needed to be done. Jenny explained the next steps, asked for Jake's consent, then said she would return in a few minutes.

Mallory felt helpless to do anything other than be there. Sensing her uncertainty, Jake reached for her, including her in those heart-wrenching last moments.

"Thank you for being with us," he mumbled, struggling to get the words out before another wave of grief struck. They were still there when Jenny returned carrying two syringes. With empathy far beyond her years, she explained what would happen and gave Jake the choice of being present as Corabelle took her final breath. He wasn't going anywhere, so that wonderful, sweet, understanding young woman made sure that the end came without further pain or suffering.

Jake said little as they returned home. Mallory remained by his side. The further they drove, the more he opened up.

"She was thirteen. That's pretty old for a goldie."

He told her about the day when Grandpa Springer brought Corabelle home. Jake had just turned sixteen. "He said he had a surprise for me." Jake laughed. "I was hoping for a car."

It wasn't a car, but it was the beginning of a friendship that spanned the length of Corabelle's life.

"She always liked me best," he said as they drove past the old Western Auto building. It's brightly lit sign high in the sky cast a golden brilliance along Grand Boulevard. "Even Grandpa knew I was her favorite."

"Did she mourn when he..." Mallory didn't want to use the words, *passed* or *died*.

"Definitely. She didn't eat much for a few weeks. I could see that she was hurt by him not being there. But Mom and Pop? They had barely bothered to learn her name." He looked at Mallory and smiled sadly. "What the heck are they doing here?"

Mallory had no idea. When they turned onto Kenwood Avenue, the Lexus was still in the driveway and the Tesla still parked at the curb.

Jake reached for her hand and asked, "Would it be okay if I stay with you tonight?"

Mallory understood. And she wanted to do anything she could for the man she loved so much. So, of course, she said yes.

CHAPTER FOURTEEN

MONDAY, DECEMBER 11

Jake woke up from a fitful sleep. Memories of backyard romps and other adventures with Corabelle kept him awake for hours. There were smiles and tears, and as he untangled himself from the sheets, he mostly felt drained. Cried out. Laughed out. Nothing left to give.

And then his phone rang. It was eight-thirty. Mallory was already up. He could hear the TV in the suite's adjoining room. The call was from his father.

Oh, yeah. Them. Probably still in Kansas City. Probably still in his house.

But then, technically, it wasn't *his* house. His parents had inherited it from Grandpa Springer's estate. Though they had spent most of their married life there, they never treated it as home. It was more of a stopping-off point to wherever they were headed next. For as long as Jake could remember, they were searching for the next big thing. Pop had worked the Alaskan Pipeline and the Texas oilfields. He'd sold cars, furniture, and timeshares. Mom had operated a bakery in Biloxi, a pet shop in Pecos, and a flower shop in Fairbanks.

Nothing lasted long. Pop's employers eventually learned that he was lazy and liked to smoke dope. Mom's creditors discovered she had the business savvy of a parakeet. They would show up back at the house on Kenwood Avenue to medicate or lubricate their wounded spirits before heading off again. Jake always stayed behind with Grandpa Springer. Right where he wanted to be.

And they were back again. If Jake wanted to know why, he would have to answer the damned phone.

"Hey, Pop."

"Jake. How's the dog?"

The dog? Didn't he even remember her name?

Jake did his best to maintain control. Getting mad never helped. Showing emotion of any kind was a waste of energy. Pop and Mom were tuned into each other. There was no room for Jake or anyone else.

"Corabelle is dead." Saying it hurt—really bad. He thought for a moment that he might become sick to his stomach. There wasn't time for that, though.

"That's too bad," Pop said. "She was pretty damned old, though, so I guess it was bound to happen, eventually. Hey, Son, when are you coming back? Mom and me need to talk to you."

"Who was that man with you last night?"

Jake's first guess was a creditor, possibly some high-interest loan shark, looking to recoup some cash. His second guess was an attorney looking for a retainer to keep one or both his parents out of jail for a controlled substance or public intoxication charge.

His final guess was a friend who tagged along because he had no place better to go. His parents attracted people like that. And while the guy looked okay and drove a Tesla, he could still be trouble.

"Oh...Clarence? He's a lawyer friend."

Hmm. A lawyer and a friend. That would likely change once he learned that they never paid their bills.

"So, Jake, will you be at the house this morning? We only have a little bit of time."

"I can be there in an hour."

He set the phone aside and tried to imagine why they needed to see him. Money was likely involved. Despite inheriting a substantial amount from Grandma Springer, including the advance that Stratford and Key had paid a few months before her death, Pop and Mom were probably broke. And he would do nothing to help.

Sorry, Pop. I'm barely getting by myself.

Screw you both. You barely had time for me as a kid. Now that you've blown through two inheritances, don't come here looking for help.

Of course, he would never mention the advance he'd received for completing the book. That was none of their business.

And why hadn't Pop asked about Mallory? He saw her at the house the previous night. Mom, too. Weren't they even interested?

And then, a thought. A foreboding one. Had they not asked about Mallory because they already knew who she was? And if they knew, how had they learned that bit of information? Did it involve the attorney friend, Clarence?

Was Jake about to walk into a financial ambush?

To believe that required an incredible break with reality. Mom and Pop would never have figured it out on their own. They were as familiar with the world wide web as they were with outer space.

But what if… Marcus Key?

Jake remembered the tells. Key knew more than he was letting on, and he had seen them kissing. But there was no way any of that could relate to Mom and Pop. Was there?

❄

Mallory looked up from her laptop when Jake came out of the bedroom. His eyes were still sad, but the smile playing across his lips was an indication that he was getting his head around Corabelle's passing.

"Hey," she said softly as she put the laptop aside and went to him. His kiss was sweet and needy. He was already dressed for whatever was on his plate that day, so those needs would have to wait.

"I'm going to the house. Mom and Pop said they won't be here long. I hope that's true." He paused before adding, "And I hope it's not about money."

It was hard for Mallory to fathom having to give money to parents. Her father would go without before asking her for a loan. Mom was equally resolute. That was how they'd raised her. Self-sufficient. Stand on your own two feet. Work hard. Make your way. She knew of at least five of her friends who were still living at home in their thirties. She was glad her parents had always made it clear that she was expected to strike out on her own after college. She'd resented it at first but was better for it.

"Do you want me to come along?"

"I don't want to expose you to that dysfunction."

She looked into his eyes and smiled. "If you plan to keep me around, it will be my dysfunction too. Everything fifty-fifty and all that jazz."

He laughed, and it made her feel good. "I appreciate that. And I do hope to keep you around for a while. But this..." He paused mid-sentence, as if struck by a thought. "You know, Mallory... What the heck? C'mon. You might as well experience the full depth of crazy that is my parents." He hugged her. "Just hang onto your purse."

Mallory hurriedly got ready, then they headed to the

lobby. The desk clerk, an auburn-haired beauty with the most appropriate name of Sunny, called out for them to have a great day. Patrick, at his usual position near the entrance, gave Jake a full-on appraisal. Mallory made introductions, and as soon as he and Jake started chatting, they discovered several common acquaintances. By the time they left the hotel, they were practically old friends.

"Does that happen a lot?" Mallory asked as they walked to his truck.

"What?"

"You know people who know people who…you know?"

He laughed again, a sure sign he was feeling better. "In Kansas City it does."

The morning was lovely. Sunny and slightly warmer than the previous day. It brought people out of the lofts and apartments that lined the downtown streets. It also seemed to lighten their loads, as several people waved and said hello when they passed. Jake had parked in a garage a block east of the hotel. They were on their way to Kenwood Avenue when Mallory received a text message.

Luis Dellarossa.

"Hmm."

Jake asked, "What is it?"

"A text from the guy who went to Bora Bora with Dawn Darby Endicott."

"My good friend, Dawn Darby?" he said with a grin.

"The same one who felt you up."

"She only patted my knee."

"Yeah, that one. Anyway…" She opened the message. "He wants to know if I have time to talk." She made a production of stuffing the phone into her pocket. "No thank you, Luis. I have no desire to hear how nice the beaches are."

"You wanted that assignment, didn't you?"

"I earned that assignment." She glanced out the window and sighed. "Apparently, I was never considered for it."

"Is Luis the kind to gloat?"

"I don't want to find out."

Mallory knew that he really wasn't, and he had left her that nice note on her door. The one about how much he had learned from her. That was sweet of him, even if it was done while basking in the adoration of others for getting the job with Dawn Darby. She would call him later. Or maybe tomorrow. Or maybe next month.

For now, there were things to do. Most notably, meet the parents. She mentally braced herself for the sideshow that Jake claimed were Mr. and Mrs. Springer.

It was Mallory's idea to take doughnuts. "They'll help ease the tension," she said. "Assuming there's going to be tension. Maybe they just came to see how you're doing. Or to drop off some Christmas gifts."

Since his parents had never taken the time to check on him in the past, and usually forgot Christmas, Jake doubted that was the purpose of their visit. But Mallory's optimism won him over, so they stopped by Lamar's for a dozen glazed.

When they arrived at the house, Jake felt as if he was the one visiting. Their Lexus was in the same spot, but the lawyer friend's Tesla was gone. Jake pulled into the backyard, his usual spot.

"Ready?" he asked.

Mallory raised the doughnut box. "Ready to spread sunshine and happiness to the entire Springer family."

He led the way into the kitchen. When he caught sight of Corabelle's leash, he turned away, but it was too late.

Fresh tears filled his eyes. He knew if he went further, he would encounter her water bowl on the floor by the sink and her favorite toys strewn about the kitchen. Just like always.

Except it wasn't like always.

Mallory, bless her heart, picked up on the situation immediately. "Stay here," she said, as she gave him a quick hug. She moved past him into the kitchen. He could hear her gathering the toys and placing them in the broom closet.

"Don't throw anything away," he said, trying to keep it together.

"I wouldn't dream of it."

It was only a couple minutes before she returned to his side, took his arm, and turned him so he could look around. It helped, though Corabelle's presence would be there for some time to come.

"Thank you," he said softly.

He could hear his parents talking in the living room, but fortunately, they hadn't come in while he was struggling with his emotions.

Then the doorbell rang.

"I'll get it, Jake," his mother called out.

"Let's go see who it is before they scare them off," Jake said, holding onto Mallory's arm as they left the kitchen. When they reached the living room, Clarence, the lawyer, was removing his coat. He nodded but didn't speak. Jake's mom avoided eye contact as she returned to her seat next to his father on the sofa.

"Jake," his father said, "with everything going on last night, I didn't get to introduce Clarence Townsend. He's representing us today."

"I'm sorry for your loss, Jake," Townsend said as he set his briefcase on the coffee table.

"I appreciate that," Jake said tersely. He made a point to

ignore his parents when he asked, "Why do they need representation?"

"We'll get into that." He turned his attention to Mallory. "Miss Newell, you—"

"How do you know who she is?"

"There is a lot I know, Jake. Besides representing your parents, I'm also representing Stratford and Key. They've retained me as local counsel to—"

Mallory stepped forward. "Jake, we should stop the meeting right now."

"It won't matter," Townsend replied. "This is only a courtesy meeting. You won't be asked to sign anything or make any decisions." The attorney glanced at Jake's parents. "All the decisions have been made."

"Still, Jake, I think we should have an attorney present," Mallory said.

Townsend shook his head. "I'll be here for fifteen minutes. No more, no less. If you choose to consult an attorney, you can have them contact me on your dime." He pulled out a card and laid it on the coffee table, then retrieved a legal folder from his briefcase.

"Perhaps the two of you should sit down." He motioned to the two living room chairs on each side of the sofa. His tone was one of control, as if they were in his office and he was calling the shots. Mallory and Jake responded at the same time.

"No."

Unruffled, Townsend opened the folder, glanced at the contents, then said, "Miss Newell, this is a notice of separation. Effective immediately, you are no longer employed by Stratford and Key."

He paused, either for effect or because he was a horse's ass. Mallory's mouth twitched, but she kept her thoughts to herself.

"The terms of the separation include salary and benefits for the rest of December and January." Townsend cracked a smile. "Quite generous, I must say. Stratford and Key would be justified for withholding all further compensation, but in the spirit of generosity at Christmas, they—"

The expletive that escaped from her mouth was one that Mallory had never used, even as a joke. She was a person who prided herself on selecting the perfect words for whatever situation she was in, but the two she used this time were both shocking and strangely therapeutic. They even caught Jake by surprise.

Not Townsend, though. That weasel had undoubtedly heard worse. He shrugged and returned his attention to the folder. "You can read the details after I leave," he said before turning to Jake.

"Jake, you have not fulfilled the terms of your agreement with Stratford and Key. Because of that—"

Jake took a step toward Townsend. "Says who?"

"Says the firm's executive committee."

"No one other than Mallory has read what I've written. How can they…"

"Email communications are available for the executive committee to review. Miss Newell signed a form agreeing to that when she started work."

"They've been reading my freaking emails?" Mallory's eyes were on fire.

"She might have signed an agreement, but I didn't," Jake said, color rising around his neck and cheeks.

"You have fifteen days to return the advance. If you cannot meet that deadline, the firm will take you to court for the funds plus interest."

Jake looked for a moment as if he might lash out. Again, probably something the attorney was used to. He stood his ground, ready to absorb a beating in exchange for a big payday when the personal injury suits started flying. Mallory placed her hand on Jake's shoulder and felt his tension begin to slip away.

Townsend snapped his briefcase shut. "That concludes our business." He nodded at Jake's parents. They stood and followed him to the door, stopping only to pick up their overnight bags. They were nearly out the door when the lawyer turned back to Jake.

"Just a reminder that this home belongs to your parents, Jake."

"Yeah? And?"

"They have the right to sell it whenever they want. And since you don't pay rent..."

Jake edged past Townsend to within a couple feet of his parents. "You'll sell the house out from under me?"

"We've never said that," Mrs. Springer said. At least she made eye contact. Jake's father stared at the floor.

Jake's laugh was harsh. "Man, I'm not sure what the two of you are getting from this, but it must be good if you're willing to toss me out of the only place I've ever called home."

Mrs. Springer flinched. His father still wouldn't meet his gaze.

"No one said the house would actually be sold," Townsend said, repositioning himself into the discussion. "Only that you need to be cognizant of—"

Jake pulled the door open. "Get out."

Nothing more was said. No farewell. No good wishes. It was the most screwed up family scene Mallory had ever witnessed. Didn't the Springers feel anything for their only son? Didn't they care at all?

Jake closed the door behind them and leaned against it, shaking his head in disbelief. Then he glanced at an old wall clock.

"Those lawyers sure know how to manage their time, don't they?" he said with a weary grin. Townsend had hit the mark almost perfectly. Fourteen minutes after opening his briefcase, they were gone, leaving behind a single folder and the stench of cigarettes. "And they didn't even say goodbye."

"Why do you think they were here?"

"There's money involved. I know that much. The problem is, I don't know how or why. Maybe if we go through the paperwork, we can figure it out."

The terms of Mallory's separation—*firing* was the more appropriate word—were as Townsend had described. The reasons were not a surprise, either.

Romantic involvement with a client. Insubordination...

"Mr. Key got me for refusing his request to see the manuscript."

"Which he'd obviously already seen by snooping through your email," Jake added. "And it was me who told him no. Not you."

"Yeah, but remember how he turned to me when he asked? That was intentional, wasn't it?"

Jake agreed it probably was. "Everything was intentional, including you being assigned to me."

"Mr. Key knows how I work. He sent me here to squeeze this book out of you as quickly as possible so he could appease your grandmother's loyal readers and be done with Georgia Springer. Luis would have been a more likely match, but he doesn't push authors the way I do."

"You're pretty tough," Jake said, grinning at her. "But I wore you down, didn't I?"

She smiled back. "You're definitely more charming than that guy in New York with crumbs on his shirt. But your version of the book is such a radical departure from the past. I was hopeful I could sell it to the executive team, but Mr. Key torpedoed that before I had the chance. That's so sad because the firm did almost nothing to promote your grandmother's books. I was looking at that account last week. They offered her no real editorial assistance. No suggestions for updating the characters. They just fixed the typos, slapped on the covers, and counted on Georgia Springer's small but loyal following to make them money."

"But now they won't even have that."

Mallory shoved her hands in the back pockets of her jeans. "Mr. Key is too smart to dump us without a backup plan. And I'll bet you a dozen more doughnuts that I know what it is."

Jake didn't have to ask. The entire screwed-up situation was suddenly as clear as day. His parents.

"No wonder Mom and Pop were in town. They're getting something from Key and his people. But what? And why? They can't write a book. I've never even seen them read one."

"It happens more than you might think. The firm hires a ghostwriter. The book is written exactly the way they want it, then they promote it as being cowritten by your parents. The son and daughter-in-law of the dearly departed Georgia Springer."

"Is that kosher?"

Mallory shrugged. "Who knows what's kosher anymore? There are books on the bestseller lists written by authors who have been dead for years. I guess that if someone wanted to dig deep enough, they could learn that your parents had nothing to do with the project, but how many people care that much?"

Mallory's phone buzzed. She checked caller ID and rolled her eyes. "Luis again."

"Maybe you should answer."

"And say what? Glad things are going so well for you Luis. Oh, by the way, I just got canned. Can I use you for a reference?"

"Good point." Jake raked his hand through his hair. "So, what happens next?"

"I suppose you need to get some work done. At least you still have the website." She glanced away, a beleaguered look on her face. "I guess that sooner or later I need to head back to New York."

Her words hit Jake with the impact of a kettlebell to the gut. Now that he had her, he wanted to keep her.

He opened his arms, and she came to him. The embrace communicated a mixture of fear and desperation. Two people who, having finally discovered one another, didn't want to be apart.

There was, of course, one option they'd not yet fully explored. It had to be on Mallory's mind, just as it was on his.

"Perhaps I need to give serious thought to Roger Powell's job offer."

Her eyes widened. "Seriously?"

"Why not?"

She motioned to the floor. "Because of this. It's your home."

"Are you forgetting that Mom and Pop can sell it out from under me?"

"I don't just mean the house. Kansas City is your home."

"Not if I move to New York."

Even as he was speaking the words, there was an undercurrent of uncertainty. Could New York be home? Could he ever feel as comfortable there as in Kansas City where he moved about as if he and the city were one? He'd celebrated the highs, like when the Royals and Chiefs were crowned champions of their sports. He had also endured the seasons of frustration in between.

But it was more than sports. Things he took for granted, like the good-natured insults he endured at Flip Murray's barbershop, or the Friday afternoon beers with his buddies. Kansas City wasn't just home; it was his way of life. It was always there, even when people he should have been able to count upon were not.

Could he leave?

Mallory never understood how someone could turn down the chance to live in New York. It was the center of everything. Los Angeles, London, and Paris might claim to be the most important cities in the world, but everyone knew that title belonged to New York. Not just in her career area, though New York's big publishing houses had a stranglehold on traditional publishing, but every field from fashion to finance. Okay, Los Angeles had Hollywood, but she would put a Broadway play up against anything she saw on TV or in some dark movie theater.

Nope. Turning down a chance to make your mark in New York was too good to pass up. Or so she had thought. But as she stood in that living room, wrapped in Jake's arms, she realized she had been mistaken. There was life outside New York. Quite a bit of it, actually.

He had doubts. She could see it in the furrow of his brow, and the way he tipped his head as he spoke. He wasn't feeling it. Maybe a little, but not completely.

And she understood. Kansas City had formed and nurtured him. It had kept him safe, while emboldening him to strive for more. It salved the wounds caused by neglectful parents.

And no place in the city was more important than where they stood. That modest old house was his oasis. Much more so than her tiny apartment. Much more even than the Manhattan apartment where she'd been raised. Kansas City was Jake's anchor, and Kenwood Avenue was his rock.

Damn his parents for threatening to take it.

"We need to fight this."

His eyes were on her. "Like, with a lawyer?"

She had no idea what she meant. She shook her head, flashed a devilish grin, and said, "I just want to kick somebody's ass."

"You cuss a lot, you know?"

Oh gosh, was he serious? Did she cuss too much? She'd never really thought about it, but... He laughed, and she knew he was teasing. But she made herself a promise to watch it. People didn't seem to cuss as much in Kansas City.

"If it helps," he said, "I would also like to kick some...butt."

That did it. The laughter came. Mallory felt the release, just as she had two days before when he'd helped her get past the feelings of rejection brought on by the people at Twisted Fishbowl. She saw how their shared laughter helped him, too. For the moment, it was just the two of them enjoying perfect love in an imperfect world. And thinking of how they could kick some butt.

"If it's okay with you, I'd like to stay here for a few days," she said, kissing him sweetly on the lips. "Can I tag along while you do your work?"

"It depends. Do you like rodeos?"

The look on her face caused him to start laughing again.

"Don't they kill bulls and stuff?"

"You're thinking of bullfighting. That's illegal in America. Rodeo is bronc riding, calf roping, and stuff like that."

She mulled it over for a few moments, happy to be in his arms. "Will I be a bother?"

"Not unless you stumble into the middle of the action like you did at the basketball game."

"Then count me in. Can I wear the boots I bought last week?"

"You bought boots?"

"Not cowboy boots. Nice leather ones. Red. They go with —"

Her phone buzzed again. She frowned, then pulled it out and checked the message.

"Luis?" Jake asked.

"Yeah…this is strange. He says he needs to talk to me ASAP."

"Call him."

"But I'll have to tell him what happened. He has no idea I was fired."

"It's a matter of time before everyone knows. Speaking to him allows you to control some of the narrative if Key and the others try to paint you as the villain."

He had a point.

"What time is it in Bora Bora?"

Jake consulted his phone. "Five in the morning."

"Wow, he must really need to talk."

Mallory texted, *Now? So early?*

Luis responded immediately. *Yes, please!*

She looked at Jake, shrugged, and placed the call. Luis answered on the first ring.

"Mallory, thank goodness you called. I need your wise counsel."

"Okay, Luis, but first you need to know that—"

"Whatever it is will have to wait. Sorry, but I need to talk to someone, and you're the most logical choice. Now I'm going to tell you something very important, but you need to promise not to judge, okay?"

"Believe me, Luis, I'm the last person who should judge anyone. In fact, some things have changed since you—"

"Mallory, I can't work with Dawn Darby anymore."

"I was in New York this past weekend and Mr. Key... Wait, what? Luis, did you say that you can't work with Dawn Darby?"

"Yes. It's impossible."

"Have you told Mr. Key?"

There was a deep sigh on the other end of the line. Jake was watching from across the room. Mallory pointed at the phone and mouthed, *What does he want from me?* Jake raised his hands in a *how the heck should I know* gesture.

"I haven't told him. I don't know how... Mallory there's more."

"Tell me first why you can't work with her, Luis. You're one of the best editors I know."

"Because I'm a pushover. You've always known that, Mal. I could see it in your eyes. You and some of the others think I try to be too buddy-buddy with the authors, and you're right. I've gotten by with it before, but not this time."

"Is Dawn Darby angry with you, Luis?"

"Well, not angry, but...are you sitting down?"

"Nope, and given the morning I've had, Luis, there's nothing you can tell me that will shock me."

"We're in love."

It was like one of those movie moments when the producers use the sound of a needle scratching across a record to signal a complete change in the story. Mallory plopped down on the sofa.

"What?" Jake whispered as he came closer.

Mallory was too stunned to reply. She couldn't even close her mouth. It was several moments before Luis spoke again.

"Mallory? Are you still there? Hello?"

"Uh...I'm here... Luis, did you say what I think you said?"

"It's crazy, I know, but you heard correctly."

"And you know that Dawn Darby is..." She did the math. "Twenty years older than you?"

"Twenty-six, but I don't care and neither does she. She wants to get married. Soon."

"And you, Luis?"

"She makes me happier than I've ever been in my life, but I'm afraid about what will happen to me at work. Did you know there's a stipulation in our employment agreement that prohibits relationships with clients?"

Funny you should mention that, Luis.

"I… Yeah, I know about that. What does Dawn Darby say about it?"

Luis laughed for the first time. "She says screw 'em. She brings in enough money for the firm that they'll do anything she wants."

"She's probably right."

"Yeah, maybe, but…I've never been one to break the rules. I'm a rule follower. What if Stratford and Key draw a line in the sand? What if they say rules are rules and fire me anyway?"

When Mallory didn't reply, Luis asked, "It's bad, isn't it? Do you think anyone has ever violated that policy?"

"Well, Luis…if you have a few minutes, I have a story to tell you."

CHAPTER FIFTEEN

MONDAY, DECEMBER 18

It was ten-forty when Charlotte came to the lobby and summoned Mallory to the tenth floor. Her appointment was at ten. Jake had bet her that they would keep her waiting at least an hour. She took the bet and won! Dinner at Henrico! Of course, had she lost, they would still enjoy dinner at Henrico. She had Jake convinced it was the best pizza this side of Kansas City.

Mallory's attempts to engage Charlotte in conversation were mostly met with stony silence. "I've been instructed to keep my mouth shut," she finally admitted as she made eye contact for the first time. Mallory saw it pained the longtime executive assistant to behave in such a manner.

When they stepped out of the elevator, Charlotte directed her to the same waiting area where she had first encountered Jake three weeks earlier. How could it have been that short a time? So much had happened. So much had changed. Mallory had changed. Her eyes had been opened to what a merciless place Stratford and Key could be. In the past, when employees were terminated, she had assumed they had it coming. Either they hadn't worked hard enough or weren't willing to put in the extra hours. Perhaps they'd taken for granted the fact that they worked for one of New York's preeminent publishing houses.

Boy, had her views changed.

Another twenty minutes passed before Bruce, Charlotte's counterpart, made an appearance.

"Hey, dear," he said somberly, holding open his arms for a hug.

Mallory flashed an uncertain smile. "Aren't you worried about getting too cozy with me?"

He rolled his eyes. "I'm a gay black man who's unafraid to play those cards in a discrimination suit. And I'm damned good at my job. They ain't laying a finger on me, sweetheart. Now give me a hug."

"Thanks for not treating me like a pariah."

Bruce glanced over his shoulder to make sure the coast was clear. "Don't be hard on Charlotte. She's two years from retirement and her 401k still needs to grow. She's only protecting herself. I know she thinks the world of you. Now, if you'll come with me, I'll take you to your meeting." He leaned in closer and whispered, "Don't expect as warm a greeting as this, though."

Mallory chuckled. She knew she should feel nervous. Mr. Key had always intimidated her. Prior to Kansas City, she'd felt that she'd earned his respect, but obviously not. Now, knowing where she stood, she felt remarkably at ease.

Her comfort level was immediately put to the test when she was shown into his office rather than the adjoining conference room where he typically conducted meetings. Rarely did anyone from her floor gain access to his inner sanctum. Bruce announced her arrival, then stepped out and closed the door. Mallory caught the wink he gave her before taking his leave. Mr. Key had his back to her, appearing to be immersed in a spreadsheet. Two minutes became five. Then seven. The silence would have unsettled her before, but she wasn't that person anymore, so she waited and studied him as he studied his numbers. She noticed how the back of his shirt collar was slightly askew and his tie was twisted. Whoever made sure he was impeccably dressed had missed those minor details. Would they be fired, too?

He coughed but said nothing. It was a power game, and he assumed he had all the power. Mallory waited patiently, knowing that there would come a time when everything shifted in her direction. Because she knew things that Mr. Key didn't.

And exactly eleven minutes after she'd been shown in, Mr. Key turned in his chair and stared at her. His eyes bore deep into hers, but she didn't flinch. She didn't need to. Not anymore.

"You're intelligent enough to know that this meeting is a waste of time," he stated.

Mallory had rehearsed, so she was ready. "The employee contract I signed entitles me to a termination hearing."

Mr. Key was ready, too. "And we offered you one."

"With someone in the legal department. They weren't my immediate supervisor. That's you, Mr. Key."

She had considered dropping the *mister* crap and just calling him by his first name, before deciding that a lack of respect on his part didn't warrant the same from her. Her parents had raised her better than that.

"Don't you think I'm aware of that?" he snapped. "You got your way, Mallory. You're here. You have five minutes to state your case." He checked his watch. "Your time starts now."

"No, sir, that is incorrect."

It didn't take Jake long to appreciate how nobody put together a media event like New Yorkers. And when that event involved one of the city's largest communication companies, well, that only added to the spectacle. Crystal bowls full of peel-and-eat shrimp, fancy plates of hors d'oeuvres circulated by servers in jackets and ties. And, as a show of respect to Jake's hometown, ribs shipped in from Arthur Bryant's, one of Kansas City's oldest and more revered barbeque joints.

And judging by the way the media tore into them, they were a hit. True Kansas City comfort food, but Jake was too nervous to enjoy them for fear that he would drip sauce onto his new dress shirt or suffer a gastric rebellion.

Roger Powell sidled up, a tiny dollop of Bryant's sauce clinging to the corner of his mouth. "You doing okay, Jake?"

"Yeah… Yeah I'm good. I never expected it to be like this." He nodded across the room to where a man and woman were chatting. "Are they who I think they are?"

He didn't have to say their names. Roger responded right away. "Yeah. They do some stuff for us in between their network duties. Want to meet them?"

"Yeah…no, not yet." Jake laughed. "I'm afraid I'll be too star-struck to speak."

"You get used to it," Roger said, patting him on the shoulder. A late arrival caught Roger's attention, and he excused himself to say hello. Jake made a stop by the bar for a diet soda, then moved to a corner where he could observe the comings and goings on an A-list of sports media stars and athletes he'd watched on TV. New York royalty, there to welcome him into their fold.

Was he ready?

"There is nothing in the agreement I signed that limits how much time is provided for my termination hearing."

"Fine, but after five minutes, you'll be talking to yourself because I have another commitment."

There was plenty Mallory could say. If Mr. Key had another commitment, he shouldn't have kept her waiting so long. Or that by getting up and leaving, he would violate her right to a hearing. None of that mattered. She only needed two minutes. She cleared her throat, sat forward, and let rip.

"Mr. Key, during my time here, you were pleased with my work. I—"

"Who said I was pleased?"

She reached into her bag and pulled out a thick file. "I have years of employee reviews with no concerns."

"Those are boilerplate. They mean nothing. Everyone knows that."

"Mr. Key, other than the occasional compliments I received from you and the one meeting two weeks ago when you shared your concerns about my work, these are all I have to go on."

He snorted. "You're even more naïve than we thought."

We? Who the hell was *we*? She had barely interacted with the other partners, and doubted if they would recognize her if they passed on the street. Less certain, but still determined, Mallory soldiered on.

"These reviews led me to believe that you were happy with the way I did my job. You liked how I pushed clients to complete their manuscripts. In fact, back in March, you said I reminded you of yourself when you started in the business."

"Nonsense... No, not even nonsense. That's fabricated bullshit."

Mallory held up a printout. "It's in this email from March 15."

He rolled his eyes. "Let's get this over with. I don't know

how you expect to continue in publishing after this little tantrum."

"I definitely plan to remain in publishing. In fact, I interviewed with a startup recently. A place called Twisted Fishbowl. Are you familiar with them?"

She wondered if Mr. Key would lie. He glanced away for a split second, but his eyes returned to hers. He knew that she knew.

"I had a confidential meeting with someone there, yes."

"And if what you said about me became public? How would you feel about that, Mr. Key?"

The color drained from his face. He remembered what he had told Price Ricketts. Especially the part where he called Mallory a "bitch on wheels." Talia felt terrible about how Price had treated her, and she had a history with him that allowed her to get to the bottom of things. Price had called Mr. Key for a reference the evening following her interview. Mr. Key, probably a few drinks into his night, had spoken off the cuff. Off the cuff remarks are the stuff successful lawsuits are based on. *Score one for the good guys.*

Common sense would dictate he own up, make amends, and live to fight another day. Apologizing to a lowly former employee wasn't a page in Mr. Key's playbook, though.

"You had a promising career, Mallory. It's sad that you allowed your ambition to get the best of you."

"It's ironic you say that, Mr. Key, because I never considered myself to be overly ambitious until I came to work here. The culture of this firm pushed me to become that way. The way you pit us against one another. How you openly compare us? Those rah-rah meetings where you hand out the plum assignments. It's toxic. I only wish I had understood that sooner."

"Is there anything else, Mallory? Because all I've heard so far are the ramblings of a disgruntled former employee unwilling to take responsibility for her lackluster performance."

Mallory smiled. He was really good, and he was putting on an Oscar-worthy performance.

But she wasn't done. And when she heard the commotion outside the office, she knew things were just getting started. The door opened, and Dawn Darby Endicott breezed in, followed closely by Luis and a very frazzled Charlotte.

"Mr. Key," Charlotte stammered, "I tried to convince them to wait, but they just—"

"It's fine, Charlotte," Mr. Key said coolly. "Dawn Darby, if you'll give me just a moment to finish up here, I'll be happy to—"

"Mallory can stay, Marcus." Dawn Darby took Luis's hand in hers. "I just wanted to let you know that Luis and I are getting married."

Time seemed to stand still. Mr. Key's mouth was frozen mid-word. Luis, typically a person who preferred to remain out of the limelight, appeared bewildered. Charlotte scurried for the door as if the office were on fire. Dawn Darby was as poised and confident as ever.

Mallory remained in her seat and watched.

Mr. Key recovered first.

"Well...Dawn Darby, that's...wonderful...I guess."

Bless her heart, Dawn Darby didn't miss a beat. "If it's wonderful for us, Marcus, why isn't it wonderful for Mallory and Jake?"

She rested her hand on Mallory's shoulder in a show of support. Her message was clear. Mallory might have been just another employee—a person on the organizational chart, who could be treated as a replaceable commodity—but Dawn Darby was no commodity. She was a goose who laid golden eggs. Every eighteen months, her golden eggs hit the bookstore shelves, buoyed by movie deals and national tours. She was part of the reason that Mr. Key and his tenth floor associates lived in luxury apartments and vacationed at their rustic but pricy beachfront cottages on Long Island.

But then again, Dawn Darby was actually not a goose at all. She was more of a lion. And the lion was about to roar.

"Marcus," she said, her voice barely above a whisper, "it's time to call in the people who really run this place."

Mr. Key's manicured fingers balled into fists. "Dawn Darby, you can't—"

"Darling, I can do whatever I want. Now pick up the phone and call Josiah. Tell him to grab Bernie and get in here. Now."

Jake remained off to the side while Roger introduced some of the people behind the scenes at his sports media empire. He was good that way, Jake had learned. Never using the spotlight to boost his ego, but to add luster to the powerhouse that was Liberty Sports Entertainment.

Though Jake would be a small, practically miniscule part of the organization, Roger made him feel integral to the organization's future success. As he made his introductions, Jake's mind drifted to the Stratford and Key headquarters where a very different type of meeting was taking place, involving a man who was used to getting his way at the expense of those who worked for him.

Would the tables be turned, or would it be status quo? Was Dawn Darby Endicott enough of a force, or would their little foursome—and that was what Dawn Darby, Luis, Mallory, and Jake had become over the past week—have to resort to Plan B? Jake hoped it wouldn't come to that because he had no idea what Plan B looked like. No one did. When

Luis had asked about it, Dawn Darby patted him on the butt and told him not to worry.

Roger's words brought him back to the moment.

"We're here today to make a very special announcement. Many of you have met Jake Springer. All of you are aware of his work, including his recent feature about football player Brian Mott."

Applause rained down from every direction. Jake glanced around nervously. His long-ago Kansas City friend, Sam Cottner, gave him a thumbs-up from across the room. Without Sam's ill-fated advice for getting into Yankee Stadium, Jake would have never met Roger. He flashed a smile that he hoped communicated a message of, "thanks, but this is kind of embarrassing and I would rather be covering the debut of a high school phenom in Iola, Kansas." Sam shook his head. He knew the truth. The days of high school basketball games on the Kansas prairie were behind him.

He had bigger fish to fry.

After a ten-minute recess, the meeting shifted to Mr. Key's conference room. Then, when more people were summoned, to a larger room on the ninth floor. Dawn Darby laughed at Mr. Key's attempts to exclude Mallory. He hadn't understood at first that she was part of the grand scheme. It became clear when Dawn Darby's attorney, a brunette who looked like a movie star, showed up. Mr. Key hurriedly summoned the firm's attorneys along with the two primary partners, Josiah Stratford and Bernard Mulvihill. They brought their number twos. There were eleven people gathered at the table. Four on Dawn Darby's side, and seven on the side of Stratford and Key. It wasn't a fair fight. Dawn Darby had them on the ropes from the start.

"How dare you fire this young lady. She's been an exemplary employee for years. She's also young, beautiful, and single. How can she help it if she falls for a handsome guy like Jake Springer? Why, the first time I saw him I fell for him too."

Josiah Stratford rarely appeared at meetings and was thought to be a bit of a recluse. It was apparent that in the partners' pecking order, the older, more genteel Stratford was top dog.

"Miss Newell will be rehired immediately," he proclaimed. Then he paused and turned to Mallory. "Provided, of course, you wish to return after the way you've been treated."

Mr. Mulvihill, the junior of the three partners, nodded in agreement. Mr. Key moved to speak, but Stratford's withering glare shut him up. Mallory was speechless, which was fine because Dawn Darby wasn't finished.

"If she chooses to return, it will be as my editorial assistant."

"But what about Mr. Dellarossa?" Stratford asked.

"Oh, I have other plans for him," Dawn Darby said. "But there is one other thing." She turned and levelled Mr. Key with an icy stare. "We want to know what kind of deal you made with Jake's parents?"

Stratford and Mulvihill appeared surprised by this revelation. "Yes, Marcus," Mulhivill said, speaking for the first time. "Tell us about this deal we've heard nothing about."

Roger Powell had the media eating from his hand as he shared the story of Jake's near arrest at Yankee Stadium.

"Had it not been for his midwestern charm, and an assist

from Nan Spaulding, he might have spent the night at the 44th Precinct."

Those gathered laughed good naturedly at Jake's dilemma. It might have been embarrassing had Roger not said what he said next.

"That day pretty much sums up the career Jake Springer has carved out for himself in the dog-eat-dog world of sports journalism. He wanted to experience Yankee Stadium, but when it appeared there was no way for that to happen, he made it happen. Take the story he wrote on Brian Mott. While others speculated about what happened, Jake called on trusted sources he had developed over the years. No one in Kansas City had any idea where Brian Mott was. They couldn't corroborate or refute that he had fallen back to his old ways. Many took the easy way out and assumed he had."

Roger let the truth soak in. The few people not focused on Roger were watching Jake. As members of the media, they were enthralled with what he had done, and even though they had heard the story before, they hung on every word.

"Jake broke the real story, and he did it the old-fashioned way. By working his sources and building trust with the central figure." Roger chuckled as he said, "Including giving Mr. Mott a quiet place to stay for a few days."

The laughter was louder. They got it. And they respected that Jake protected Brian Mott while scoring an exclusive interview.

Roger continued. "Instead of a rush to judgment, Jake reported the facts. No spin, no deception. Just plain old investigative journalism."

When Roger paused again, the room erupted in applause. And while he hadn't been embarrassed by Roger's recollection of the day at Yankee Stadium, the outpouring of respect from those around him made his face burn. He kept his head down and wished Roger would hurry up.

And he wished that Mallory's text would arrive soon. He was becoming worried that things on her end weren't progressing as planned.

$20,000.

That's how much it had taken to get Jake's parents to sell the rights to Georgia Springer's books to Stratford and Key.

Mr. Key seemed pleased with himself when he shared that morsel with his partners. They didn't share his pleasure, though—at least in front of Dawn Darby and the others. Josiah Stratford asked for a few moments to meet privately with his associates. Dawn Darby, who was turning out to be a real badass, said that if she left the room before everything was hammered out, she would take her writing empire to a firm up the street. Still seemingly oblivious to the magnitude of the dustup he had caused, Mr. Key reminded Dawn Darby that their contract extended for one more book.

"True," she said sweetly. "I'm thinking it will be a children's coloring book."

Josiah Stratford appeared stricken. He understood the clout Dawn Darby wielded, and the impact of losing one of the biggest authors in the world.

"Dawn Darby," he said kindly. "Tell us what we can do to maintain our relationship."

Dawn Darby flashed a megawatt smile. "You've always been such a darling, Josiah. It's quite simple, really. Sign those book rights over to Georgia Springer's handsome grandson, Jake. He has nearly completed the book his grandmother started before her death. And from what I hear, it will introduce her works to a new generation of readers."

"Done."

"Thank you, dear. Jake plans to author one new book a

year in the Stella Duvall series. Under his own name of course."

Stratford didn't bat an eye. "That sounds fine. Now, Dawn Darby, you know that series isn't anywhere near as lucrative as your books. It might be difficult for Mr. Springer to make a living from the series."

"Oh, darling. You just wait until I infuse a little Dawn Darby magic into the mix. The new Stella Duvall series will fly from the shelves. And I would venture that many readers will want to go back to the beginning, which means you sell more books, too."

"But, Dawn Darby, you've always been adamant about not promoting other writers' works."

"I've never had a stake in their work. Until now." She reached for Luis's hand. "Dear Luis and I will publish the new books under our own imprint." She winked at Luis and said, "Tell them what we're calling our little enterprise, darling."

"Blissful Publications."

"For the bliss this wonderful man has brought into my life," Dawn Darby gushed.

Stratford wasn't smiling. "So, you're going to start your own publishing company? Am I to assume you want to publish your own books as well? If you plan to leave Stratford and Key, Dawn Darby, why should we agree to any of this?"

"Exactly," Mr. Key said, his face a mottled red. "You're using us, and we won't have it."

Dawn Darby pointed her finger at him. "Be quiet, Marcus." She turned in her chair so she was looking squarely at Stratford. "Josiah, you've been more than fair to me. In fact, back when I was just getting started, you were not only fair, you were...*much more* to me."

Flock of geese!

Was Dawn Darby suggesting that she? *And Stratford?*

Mallory nearly gasped when she saw the way Dawn Darby waggled her eyebrows at the septuagenarian. She wasn't the only one. Even Mr. Key appeared astonished.

The only people who took the revelation in stride were Luis and Stratford himself. Dawn Darby must have confided in her new love about whatever went on with the old man.

"You've never mentioned that publicly, Dawn Darby," Stratford said calmly.

"I figured it was okay now with Helena's passing last year. You received my condolence card, didn't you, dear?"

"Yes, and I appreciated it very much. Losing Helena was difficult for the entire family."

Holy cow! Had they just stepped into the middle of a soap opera scene? Dawn Darby and Stratford had been involved with each other? While he was married? The hits never stopped coming. Everyone appeared shell-shocked about what had been disclosed. And worried about what might follow. The first to recover?

Mr. Key.

"Josiah, you were aware of the firm's policy on client relationships. Hell, man, you wrote it."

"You're certainly right, Marcus. It was thirty years ago. Do you want to fire me? Oh, and by the way, don't think we aren't aware of a few of your personal transgressions. Would you like us to review them?"

One of the firm's attorney's cleared his throat. "Perhaps it would be better if we had this discussion privately, Mr. Stratford."

"There will not be any discussion. It happened. It ended. No one was hurt, and as long as each of you remember your obligation to keep these discussions confidential, it will remain right here."

"Unless Jake includes it in one of his books," Dawn Darby quipped.

"Speaking of Mr. Springer," Stratford said. "Where is he?"

"So without further ado, I introduce Kansas City's own, Jake Springer."

Jake hadn't expected the nerves to hit like they did. His legs were shaky, and he knew that the same members of the media who had applauded his work fifteen minutes earlier could turn on him at any moment.

After all, it was New York.

How hard could it be? Roger had explained the partnership. His company had bought out Jake's partners and now owned seventy-five percent of Total Sports KC. The plan was for Jake to oversee things for the time being while developing other projects with the people in New York. His first task was to hire a small team of local writers who cared as much for Kansas City as he did. He was comfortable with the agreement because he was comfortable with Roger. There was also the safety net of knowing that he could step away if personal projects demanded more of his time. Truth was, there was only one outside project, and her name was Stella Duvall.

And as he approached the podium, he received the text he'd been waiting for.

Everything is a go. You're an author now.

Love you!

M.

Back at Mallory's apartment that afternoon, Jake scanned the agreement, looked up, and shook his head.

"Just twenty-thousand? Really? That's all?"

Mallory wasn't sure what she could say to assuage his feelings. She knew things between Jake and his parents had always been tenuous, but he was cut deeply that it took a paltry $20,000 to sell him out.

"They would have earned a lot more than that from the royalties," he said glumly.

"Mr. Key probably didn't make that clear to them. He showed up with a check and a promise, and they accepted it."

"Of course, they did," Jake muttered. "They're probably broke and don't have time to wait for royalty checks."

It was hard to believe that Jake's parents could put a dollar amount on their relationship. While they didn't appear to be savvy about matters of contracts and royalties, they had to realize that $20,000 was not a lot of money. It would get them by for three or four months, tops. The damage to the relationship with their son, though, would last much longer. That made her incredibly sad.

"Mallory, don't be down about it. It's been like this for as long as I can remember."

That was one more thing she loved about him. He was consoling her for the crappy way his parents treated him. How had two such screwed up people produced such an incredibly caring and loving son? And why couldn't they see how special he was?

Mallory certainly did. And she had no plans to let him get away.

They were seated on her couch. She watched for several moments as he perused the hastily prepared documents she'd brought back to the apartment.

"So Dawn Darby still writes for Stratford and Key?"

"Yes, she signed a five-book deal."

"How does she feel about that?"

Mallory grabbed an old blanket she always kept close by, then snuggled against him and pulled it over them. "They know what they have with her, and they treat her like royalty. Plus, she doesn't have to worry about all the stuff that goes into publishing books. She just writes."

"But what about you? You still have to answer to Key and the others."

"Look at Item Fourteen. Next page."

She waited while Jake read. "Am I understanding this right? You *don't* work for Stratford and Key?"

"Nope. That was Dawn Darby's attorney's idea. Stratford and Key provides her with a generous editing stipend that she spends as she wishes." She looked up at him and smiled. "And what she wishes is for me to be her editor. I'll edit the next three books. After that, we'll see where it goes." She flipped to the next page. "Don't miss Item Nineteen."

He read it twice. She could see when the light came on.

"Is this real?" he asked.

She smiled. "Did I mention how amazing a negotiator Dawn Darby is?"

"You did, but..." He looked up and blinked several times. "I keep the advance?"

"Every penny. Mr. Stratford didn't question it at all." She giggled. "He was too busy being pissed at Mr. Key."

He spent a few more minutes reading the agreement. It was an incredibly sweet deal, even for Stratford and Key. They kept their golden goose. Jake kept his advance. Luis would oversee publication of Jake's future books. Dawn Darby had an editor who would keep her on schedule and a new man in her life, and though they were separated by over twenty years, she and Luis were over the moon about each other.

And the icing on the cake? Mallory had a great job with

one of the top authors in the world. And the opportunity to spend as much time in Bora Bora as she wished. She'd worked hard to get there. It was funny, though, that now that the promise of warm sand and sun-drenched beaches was within her grasp, she felt strangely ambivalent. It probably had a lot to do with the guy next to her.

He would spend the next few months in Kansas City, New York, and wherever else he needed to be. He would also be writing—putting the finishing touches on his first Stella Duvall book, and starting another.

Dawn Darby was already promising the first would be a best seller. She would see to it. How well things progressed beyond that would depend upon Jake's skill as a storyteller.

"I can bring readers to your doorstep," Dawn Darby had said. "But it will be your responsibility to get them into the house."

Mallory knew Jake could do it. His writing was showing great promise. There was already a depth to his prose that she knew would touch readers' hearts and minds. Not just silly love stories, but stories of people overcoming obstacles to find love.

And if there was anything Mallory knew about readers, it was that they love an overcomer.

So much change.

So.

Much.

Change.

His little website was now part of a conglomeration of similar sites and media outlets. That was both exciting and daunting. And it might have been scary as heck, had it not been for two very important things.

One was Stella Duvall. Jake craved the time he got to spend in her world, crafting and recrafting—making her into a strong modern woman far removed from his grandmother's storybook world. It was as if Stella gave her life to him and asked him to do with it as he pleased. Sometimes his laptop pulled at him like a magnet.

Write, it would say.

And he would. Because he had learned that he loved writing. He loved creating something from nothing, bending and shaping words and characters until they became part of his soul.

Stella would help him deal with the changes in his world.

But even more important was Mallory. His heart melted to mush when they were together. He wanted to put her on a pedestal and spend his days showing her and the world how much he loved and adored her. She was his inspiration and muse. With each chapter he wrote, Stella became more and more like Mallory. Strong, decisive, and certain of where she was headed.

"So, what's next with Stella?" Mallory asked as she lounged against him. He stroked her hair and heard her sighs of pleasure.

"I have several chapters that you haven't read yet."

She turned to face him. "When did you find time?"

Jake shrugged. "Whenever and wherever. The ideas almost write themselves."

"Let me see," she said.

"Not yet. There are things in there that I would prefer you see…later."

She laughed. "Are you writing about us again?"

"I never write about us," he said, his tone full of mock indignation that his smile betrayed.

"Ha. What about the date on the plaza?"

"There were no horse-drawn carriages on that date."

She reached up and squeezed his nose. "Only because you didn't show up in time. And what about Stella losing her job? And breaking up with Terrence? You can't tell me that those weren't based on my life."

"I didn't even know about those things when I wrote Stella's story. If I had, I would have made it different."

"Don't change a thing," she blurted. "But about those new chapters? When can I read them?"

Jake laughed. "As soon as I…try them out in real life."

"With me?"

"Always with you."

CHAPTER SIXTEEN

SATURDAY, DECEMBER 23

Mallory's first football game proved interesting enough. The Kansas City Chiefs defeated the Seattle Seahawks, and while Mallory still wasn't sure what was going on much of the time, she had picked up a few of the nuances. One team tried to get the ball past the other team, then they did it again in reverse. The atmosphere was charged, though, and she counted forty-three Santas among the 70,000 fans in attendance.

Even better than the game was the reception Jake received from his colleagues in the press box. Mallory was so proud to watch as person after person stopped to offer their congratulations. Everyone seemed genuinely excited that one of their own had made good.

As the game progressed, Mallory's interest waned. The Chiefs had a big lead and while the outside temperatures were in the twenties, the press box was warm and cozy. Perfect for reading.

So, she pulled out her laptop and placed it on the table where she and Jake watched the game. He glanced at her and smiled, then returned his attention to the action on the field.

He understood that sports would never be the all-consuming passion for her it was for him, and he seemed fine with that and unbothered that she was the only person in the crowded press box reading a book instead of watching the game.

That was who she was.

And more than anything, she wanted to find out what Stella and Michael were up to.

Jake rose early each morning to write. By the time Mallory appeared, usually around eight or eight-thirty, he had already completed a couple of chapters that he couldn't wait to share. Without the constraints of worrying about what the partners at Stratford and Key might think, his creativity had taken off. Stella and Michael were experiencing life to the fullest, as two young lovers should.

And each chapter, in its own way, mirrored things Jake and Mallory were experiencing. Lunch at a French bistro. An evening of jazz at a downtown club. They rode the city's delightful streetcar from end to end, reveled in the beauty of Christmas at Hallmark's Crown Center, and took early morning runs past stately Union Station. And while Mallory still didn't understand what first and ten meant in football, she was learning the names of the charming out-of-the way neighborhoods that made Kansas City unique, places such as Brookside, Westport, and the West End.

She was not only falling in love with Jake; she was developing an affinity for where he grew up. Even the neighborhood he called home delighted her, a place as diverse as any in New York City. A place where neighbors looked out for one another.

Now, if only it could stay that way. If only that adorable house on Kenwood Avenue could remain his forever home.

That question would be answered in short order. Mallory knew that was the reason he was unusually reserved as they left the stadium. A conversation loomed. And hopefully, some mending of fences. Those broken fences weren't Jake's fault, but he felt it was time to make things right. She sensed his concern as he drove. She reached for his hand, something that had become second nature in a very short time.

What was it about her touch that helped ease his worries? She didn't have to say anything, but he knew she was there for him.

The next few hours might be the most important of his life. He had initially mentioned his plan to Mallory on their return flight from New York. She had listened intently, asked a few questions, then encouraged him by saying, "I think you'll be glad you did it."

It was time to find out if she was right. He turned onto Kenwood Avenue and spotted his parents' Lexus in the driveway. It would be just the four of them. No lawyer. No outside meddling from the likes of Marcus Key. He parked and shut off the truck.

"Can I do this?"

She nodded and squeezed his hand.

"After all the hurt? After all the times they let me down?"

Her smile was beautiful. The tears brimming her eyes attested to her love and concern. She didn't speak. She didn't need to. He knew it was time. As they approached the back door, Jake instinctively prepared for Corabelle's happy greeting. His mind still hadn't fully accepted her not being there anymore. Her absence poked at his soul. But, as Mallory had reminded him, he carried her in his heart. Her devotion and unconditional love were part of him.

They stepped into the kitchen and were met by the smells of fresh coffee and cigarettes.

"Hello," he called out.

"We're in here," his mother answered from the living room. "Coffee's on if you want some."

Mallory poured cups for the two of them, then they joined his parents. His mother gave him a hug, then pointed to the Christmas tree in the corner.

"Those are our old ornaments, aren't they?"

Actually, they were Grandpa Springer's ornaments. Like everything else, Christmas had been an afterthought for his parents. Had Grandpa and Jake not purchased and decorated the tree each year, there probably would have never been one.

But dredging up old memories wasn't the purpose of the visit. It was time to move past stuff like that. And to let his parents know that, despite all that had happened and all the times they had fallen short, Jake loved them.

And there was also the matter of the house.

They were different from before. Mallory wasn't sure if Jake had picked up on it yet, but she had. From the way his mother hugged him to his father's warm smile. Something had changed.

Perhaps it was the spirit of Christmas. Mallory had always scoffed at the idea that there was such a thing, writing it off as nothing more than people being nice to one another because nice was expected at Christmastime.

Whatever caused the change, it was good. Cal and Janine Springer were engaged and attentive. They appeared overjoyed when Jake told them how important Mallory had become to him. She felt hopeful that things would work out, but then again, it was just small talk so far. Jake had more he needed to say. And when there was a lull in the conversation, he charged ahead.

"It's time for us to be a family."

He was trembling as he spoke. Mallory scooted close and rubbed his back to remind him that she was there for him. His parents appeared stunned. His father blinked several times. There were tears in his mother's eyes. Mallory glanced at Jake to see how he was holding up. He was watching them as closely as she was, but had nothing more to say. The ball was in their court.

Several moments passed before his father got to his feet. Mallory was worried for a moment that he might leave. He approached Jake, then kneeled down in front of him, close enough so that their heads were nearly touching.

"We don't deserve you, Son."

Janine, still on the sofa, began to sob. Mallory considered going to her side but remained with Jake instead, just in case. He seemed at a loss for words. His father was fighting his emotions as well.

"Taking the money from Marcus Key was wrong. We know that now."

"We knew it then!" Jake's mother said sharply.

"We did know it then," Jake's father agreed. "But we got in trouble with some credit cards, and..."

They were broken and ashamed. Mallory could see it in their stooped posture and the grim looks on their faces. Two people in midlife used to putting themselves ahead of everything else were on the verge of reaping what they had sown. Perhaps they had arrived thinking that Jake planned to shut them out of his life. And perhaps the fear of that had led them to give serious thought to their lives. Or maybe it wasn't any of that. Mallory wanted to hope for the best, though.

"Dad," Jake said, regaining his composure. "Perhaps I can help with your problems, but you and Mom will have to allow me into your lives first."

Jake's mother wrapped her arms around her husband and her son, and for a moment Mallory felt herself left out of their intimate circle. Then Jake reached out and pulled her in.

Then she knew she'd found home.

It was a special moment—a quiet moment. Three people trying to put a difficult past behind them. Another hopeful of helping them heal and becoming at least a little like the family she'd grown up in. Their road to reconciliation wouldn't be without its bumps, of that Mallory was certain. Too many bad habits ingrained for too many years. Time, space, and distance had worked at pushing them apart. Indifference and life itself had kept them apart. They would have to work at growing together. One step and one day at a time.

Jake's father cleared his throat. "Jake… Son…your mother and I want you to know that we will never make you move out of here."

Mallory saw Jake's reaction. Surprise? Perhaps something stronger?

"The lawyer came up with that on his own," his mother said. "We told him later that we wanted nothing to do with you leaving this house."

"You're the one constant here," Jake's father said. "We came and went as we wanted. We chased dreams and escaped from life, but you were always here. You and Dad."

Dad, Mallory knew, was Jake's grandfather. He was the person most responsible for making Jake into the man she loved.

It gave her joy that his parents desired reconciliation. And it would make what Jake had to say that much easier. He cleared his throat as he spoke and sounded much like his father had moments before. It was the first resemblance Mallory had detected between parent and child.

"Dad, about the house. I want to buy it from you and Mom."

His mother spoke first. "No, Jake, that's not necessary. You've kept the place up. It's yours for as long as you want. Your father and I insist."

"I believe you, but please understand that I want something of my own. And since this house has been in our family for so long, I think it's only right that I take over ownership."

Jake's father started to object, but Jake cut him off. "Can we at least sit down and discuss it? I believe you'll find what I'm proposing to be fair to all of us."

"And stay for Christmas," Mallory blurted.

That was unplanned, but she saw in Jake's expression that he agreed. And, as it turned out, so did his parents.

CHAPTER SEVENTEEN

CHRISTMAS DAY

The flight from Kansas City to Los Angeles was four hours. That would be followed by a nine-hour flight to Tahiti and a five-hour layover before an island hopper to Bora Bora. It would be a long Christmas day, but the best ever, and Mallory was too keyed up to sleep.

Jake, not so much. He was out before the plane lifted from the runway. How did he do that? How could he remain so calm after everything that had transpired over the past week?

Gaining a big-name investor for his website.

The opportunity to carry on his grandmother's writing legacy.

Reconciliation with his parents.

The purchase of his beloved family home.

And the prospect of two weeks on the island paradise of Bora Bora.

Everything in the man's life was changing, yet he slept like a baby.

Simply amazing.

There was something uniquely special about Jake that kept him grounded. That helped him remain centered on what was important, even when everything else was kind of crazy. Watching him doze in the aisle seat, his head lolled to one side, his mouth twitching adorably, Mallory couldn't imagine being anywhere else—or with anyone else. When people talked about having that one special person who was their rock, well, she'd never understood that. Until Jake. The man was a rock of stability and kindness and decency. And he was there for her.

If only she could grab onto enough of his inner peace to catch a few hours of sleep, so she could arrive in Bora Bora refreshed and ready to surprise him with the skimpy red swimsuit she'd bought back in November. She'd nearly returned it to Macy's after the crushing disappointment of initially being passed over. She was glad now that she hadn't, and she couldn't wait to see Jake's reaction when he saw her wearing it.

Dawn Darby's invitation was quite precise. "We'll get some work done, but mainly, I want you to enjoy your time here." She also wanted to get a look at Jake's manuscript. If he was nervous about sharing his writing with one of the world's most celebrated authors, he didn't show it. He'd reluctantly admitted to Mallory that he still hadn't read any of her books. To him, she was just the attractive older woman who flirted with him that first day at Stratford and Key, then, later, fought for his chance at a writing career.

Dawn Darby's flirting days were over. She was enthralled by Luis's eternally chipper disposition, and how he didn't mind letting her decide what they did and where they went. The same qualities that had been an occasional stumbling block as an editor served him well as the paramour to a famous writer.

Two weeks of beach, sun, and time with Jake. Away from the daily stresses of work and life. Mallory felt herself begin to relax at the thought of it.

But sleep?

It wasn't happening.

She could always read for a while. Jake had a couple chapters for her to review. His laptop was in the seatback pocket, so she eased it out and turned it on. The password, she knew, was *jakeslaptop*. She'd teased him about being an easy target for thieves, but he didn't care.

There was a file on the desktop containing each chapter of the manuscript. He'd separated them into sub files labeled *edited* and *unedited*. She moved to the unedited chapters and found two completed and one in progress.

She opened the first and started to read.

Jake came out of his deep slumber when the pilot announced they were beginning their descent into LAX. Afternoon sun slanting through the window caused him to squint. When his eyes adjusted, he saw that Mallory was had been crying.

"Mallory? What?"

She wiped her eyes with a tissue, then leaned against his shoulder. "Why couldn't you have slept a few more minutes?"

He put his arm around her. "What's wrong?"

"This." She pointed to the open laptop. "The reconciliation between Michael and his parents. It's incredibly lovely and…" She held his gaze. "You bring so much feeling to your writing."

He felt a surge of relief that her tears weren't for something serious. Laughing, he said, "Yeah, but what happens when I run out of real-life inspiration?"

"I have no doubt that you'll be able to create great things in that active imagination of yours."

He hoped she was right. There were already ideas floating around his head about where Stella and Michael might go next. Perhaps life would take them away from Adair. Maybe to New York, or even Bora Bora. He hadn't mentioned it to Mallory, but he was looking forward to the trip as much for research as fun. Would Stella and Michael become world travelers? Perhaps. If it could happen to Jake Springer, it could happen to them. The kid from Kenwood Avenue was on his way to a tiny island in the Pacific to hang out with a famous writer. And he was accompanied by the most beautiful woman he'd ever known. A woman who fed his mind and soul and made him a better person. Just look at the changes. Jake Springer an author? Seriously? Writing romance? Would anyone have guessed it was possible?

Yep. One person. And she was seated next to him. Crying over his prose without realizing that she was the muse behind it all.

She was right about his ability to create new stories. All he had to do was think of the possibilities ahead of them. The love they would share, the adventures they would have. The inspiration would always be there, and her name was Mallory.

He couldn't wait to share the next chapter with her.

"Hey," he said, suddenly remembering an earlier conversation. "Didn't you say that we would be staying at a place of our own?"

"Dawn Darby has a guest house near the pool. She said we would have our own kitchen and everything. Why?"

He yawned and checked his watch. "I was just thinking that I've never cooked a meal for you. Maybe while we're there, I'll whip something up."

She laughed. "I would love that. What's your specialty?"

He considered the question for a moment. "Do you like pasta primavera?"

"It's one of my favorites. Do you know how to make it?"

"Hmm, maybe. I'll let you be the judge of that, though."

She kissed his cheek then rested her head on his shoulder. "I'm sure it will be the best pasta primavera I'll ever eat."

Mallory woke up without any idea of what time it might be. She lifted the window shade and gazed into an abyss of darkness. A TV screen tracking their flight showed them someplace in the middle of the Pacific. She checked her watch, then realized it was pointless. The watch had no idea what time zone they were in or how far they still had to go.

She stretched the best she could in the confined space, then rolled her shoulders to work out the kinks. The cabin was silent and, except for a few reading lights and TV screens in rows ahead of them, dark. The engines provided a steady drone that some passengers, including Jake, found conducive to sleep. It had worked for Mallory for a while, but she was wide awake again and in need of mental stimulation. She reached for Jake's laptop and fired it up.

There was nothing left to read.

She was completely caught up.

The only thing that remained was a single unfinished chapter.

She searched his laptop for something to help pass the time. He had a few word games, but they required internet connection, and they'd both been too cheap to spring for that. There were also two movies, but they were those dreadful action adventures that would scare her too much to fall asleep again later. There was nothing left.

So, she clicked on the unfinished chapter and found she was reading the future.

Stella Duvall's. And her own.

"Firestone Realty, how may I direct your call?"

Though several months had passed since he'd tossed Terrence Firestone into the bushes in front of Kayla Thompson's house, Michael still shook his head in disbelief when he called the Firestone family business and received a friendly greeting. How much things had changed.

Who would have thought that Stella would wind up working there?

Fortunately, Terrence's father and sister were quite charming—and tired of his antics. The issues became especially problematic after Mr. Firestone's decision to step away from the business at the end of the year. Maryann, Terrence's sister, couldn't handle things on her own. They needed help. One thing led to another and after receiving a heartfelt recommendation from Mr. Patterson at the paper factory, the Firestones had made two important decisions.

Terrence was sent packing. His father had shown more backbone than anyone could remember. Terrence was now in Columbia, Missouri, and word was, he was struggling to find his way as a full-time realtor. Full-time work just didn't agree with him.

And with Terrence out, and his father nearing retirement, Stella had been hired.

Not as a secretary or administrative assistant. Mr. Patterson had stressed how overqualified she was for that. Stella was a full-fledged realtor. And not just any realtor, she was the realtor of choice for people looking to buy or sell their homes in Adair and Saxon County. At least once a week, Michael checked the reviews clients left on Google.

Stella is incredibly kind and hard working.

We not only gained a realtor, we gained a best friend.

I'll never buy a house from anyone else.

The voice of the receptionist on the other end of the line brought Michael back to the moment.

"Firestone Realty...may I help you?" Then a pause. "Michael? Is that you?"

Busted. Undoubtedly because he had done the same thing twice before. Allowing his mind to take flight as he thought about how perfectly Stella fit into life in Adair. And into his life.

"Oh...hi, Addison. Yeah, it's me. Is she in?"

Addison giggled. "She's walking some clients out. Can you hold for a moment?"

He would hold for as long as it took. He would battle snow-storms, grizzly bears, and anything life could throw at him as long as he knew when he made it through, Stella would be on the other side. Waiting for him.

"Hi, Michael!" She sounded so strong, so self-assured. She'd arrived in Adair less than a year before. Back then, from afar, she'd seemed fragile. Someone who could easily be manipulated. Terrence had tried, and succeeded, for a short while.

But the Stella on the other end of the line was a survivor, yet still as kind and caring as anyone Michael had ever known.

And so in love with him. As he was with her.

"Hi, Stel." That was what he called her. Stel. She loved it.

"Hey." Her voice was lower, more intimate. There was also a hint of excitement. He knew how much she cherished their time together, particularly when they went out. She called them excur-sions. She would often ask what he had planned for their next one.

Oh, boy would she be surprised at what he had planned this time.

"I made special plans for the holidays."

"Oh, yeah? Can you tell me, or are you going to keep me in suspense?"

"Would you believe...my place? I'm preparing my famous pasta primavera."

Hold on! Pasta Primavera? Jake was at it again. Mallory felt a twinge of guilt for jumping ahead, but she had to know where this was going. Obviously he planned to cook for her while on vacation, but what other tricks did her man have up his sleeve?

She continued reading to find out.

"Umm, that sounds delicious. But if it's famous, why is this the first time I've heard about it?"

"I only make it for very special occasions. And I mean, very special."

He heard the rustling of paper on her end. She was probably checking her calendar to see what relationship milestone she might have missed. There weren't many. They'd only been dating for a few months. But when you were newly in love, you could create memories from almost anything.

"I'm not sure what we're celebrating, but if it means I get to try your famous pasta primavera, I can't wait."

He liked the way she emphasized the word "famous." As if it was really something incredible rather than a recipe he'd plucked from the internet and spent the past several days perfecting.

"Trust me, darling, it's a special occasion." He pulled a small box from his pocket, opened it, and gazed at the ring. He had debated long and hard about which ring would be the perfect match for her beautiful, delicate hands. Everything about Stella was understated, from the way she dressed to the accessories she wore. A large showy ring might assuage his ego, but he suspected she would prefer something simple, so he'd settled on a small crystal clear diamond.

And that evening, he would get to see it on her finger. Provided she said yes.

Yes to spending the rest of her life with him.

Yes to small-town life in the only place he'd ever wanted to live.

Yes to a home with a white picket fence.

And children.

And a dog.

And sunsets on the back porch. Holding hands and thanking God for bringing them together.

It was incredibly uncomplicated. Incredibly simple.

Incredibly perfect.

"So..." he said, trying to keep the emotion at bay. Trying to create the ruse that the night ahead would be much like any other. "Can I pick you up at six-thirty?"

"You can," she said happily. "I can't wait to be with you."

Michael disconnected and took another look at the ring before tucking it into his pocket.

"I hope you love it, darling," he whispered to himself. "And I hope you'll say yes."

Mallory closed the laptop, relaxed her head against the seatback, and sighed. Then she glanced to her left to see if Jake was still asleep. Of course, he was. She caressed the back of his hand and considered the future. Stella's. And her own.

"Ask her," she whispered. "And she will say yes. There's nothing she wants more than to spend forever with you."

BONUS EPILOGUE

The best love stories don't end on the final page. Join us for one last visit with Jake and Mallory as we see where life takes them after the story ends.

You'll also be signing up to receive updates and information about future Robin Paul books, short stories, and other fun things.

Click below or copy the link to be taken to the bonus epilogue.
https://BookHip.com/HGNQSAM

AUTHOR'S NOTE

People sometimes ask if there is any truth behind specific events and places in our books. In a word, yes! Plenty of the places and lesser events are real. And since Kansas City is Robin's hometown, there's even more than usual.

Jake lives at **3737 Kenwood Avenue**. We've always loved KC's Hyde Park area and even considered buying a home there at one time. The residences are a delightful mix of early 20th century bungalows, apartment buildings, and Kansas City shirtwaist homes. There is, however, no Kenwood Avenue between 36th and 39th Streets.

Didn't you love Mallory's delight as she tore into that half-slab and burnt ends at **Gates Bar-B-Que**? Folks, that's real. And if you haven't tried Kansas City BBQ, you're missing out on one of God's finest creations. Locals will argue all day about which is best. Even the two of us, who agree on almost everything, differ on this important topic. Robin is all about Jack Stack. Paul will die on the hill that is Arthur Bryant's. You try them and let us know your favorite. And if you wind up at Gates, remember this secret insider tip: order the fries extra crispy.

Other Kansas City locales, including **Municipal Auditorium**, the **Power and Light District**, and the beautiful **Kansas City Public Library** are real. Paul wrote a book in the library one summer when we were renting a loft after our house sold.

And the **Country Club Plaza**... you need to experience it during the Christmas season. Until then, Google it and take a look at the magnificence that is the Plaza at Christmas. And if you visit, take a carriage ride.

Can you tell that we LOVE Kansas City? Especially the people. Kansas Citians are NICE. Just like Tommy the cabdriver. They are proud of where they live, and love sharing it with visitors.

Oh, yes. Write Christmas also takes place in New York City. We don't know as much about NYC despite having a daughter who lives in the area. **Yankee Stadium** is real, but you already knew that. Paul worked for the Kansas City Royals for a few years and firmly believes he can sneak into any ballpark in America. He called on that skill to get Jake into Yankee Stadium.

We've spent time in Brooklyn and love it. Hopefully our images of the area around Mallory's apartment caught the vibe that is that fun community in the Big Apple.

Oh yes, one more thing. Remember Charlotte, the executive assistant at Stratford and Key? She confided to Mallory that when she's about to cuss or swear, she substitutes the word 'sharks' instead. Our friend and audio producer Matt is the source of this little gem. When he makes a mistake he exclaims, "Oh, sharks!"

As for everything else, we just made it up.

So, there you go.

ALSO BY ROBIN PAUL

Christmas Presence - A Garland Grove Holiday Romance

Christmas Carl - A Garland Grove Holiday Romance

Blues Christmas - A Garland Grove Holiday Romance

Christmas Class Reunion - Inspired the Hallmark Channel Original Movie

Clear Christmas - A Later in Life Second Chance Holiday Romance

Write Christmas - A Kansas City Christmas Romance

Drifting Together - A Bethany Beach Summer Romance

Go to www.robinpaulromance.com or scan the code below to learn more.

Made in the USA
Monee, IL
25 October 2023

45215958R00162